BAD SHEPHERD:
A CADE TAYLOR NOVEL

MICHAEL HEARNS

BEATI BELLICOSI
BEATI BELLICOSI PUBLISHING A DIVISION OF BEATI BELLICOSI MEDIA

ISBN: 979-8-9897279-2-6 Hardback

ISBN: 979-8-9897279-3-3 Paperback

ISBN: 979-8-9897279-4-0 Electronic Book Text

Library of Congress Cataloging-in-Publication Data

Name: Hearns, Michael, author

Title: Bad Shepherd: A Cade Taylor Novel/Michael Hearns Description: First edition. Miami: Beati Bellicosi (2025) Identifiers: LCCN ISBN

First Edition: November 2025

Editor: Julie Hutchings

Cover Photography by Glen Thuncher

Cover Design by Dillon Hearns

Author Photo by Ricki Witt Braswell

For additional information and speaking engagements visit Michael Hearns on the worldwide web: http://www.MichaelHearns.com

Beati Bellicosi Publishing a division of Beati Bellicosi multimedia. Copyright 2025 by Beati Bellicosi

Printed in the U.S.A

Also by author Michael Hearns:

"Trust No One"
2020 Beati Bellicosi

"Grasping Smoke: A Cade Taylor Novel"
2021 Beati Bellicosi

"One More Move: A Cade Taylor Novel"
2022 Beati Bellicosi

"Choices and Chances: A Cade Taylor Novel"
2024 Beati Bellicosi

Acknowledgments

"Bad Shepherd," the fifth novel in the Cade Taylor series, is a milestone I could hardly have imagined a scant five years ago when I put pen to paper on the debut Cade Taylor novel "Trust No One." What began as a tentative foray into storytelling has evolved into a transformative experience, one that has touched my soul and resonated deeply with the growing legion of Cade Taylor fans. I am profoundly grateful for the passion this series has ignited and deeply honored by every reader who has joined me on this path.

My deepest thanks go to my editor, Julie Hutchings, whose discerning eye has helped to shape the Cade Taylor saga through all five novels. With professional brilliance, Julie has navigated the pulsing energy of each novel, helping to refine my stories into their finest form. Her skill and vibrant spirit are a gift beyond measure.

To my remarkable son, Dillon Hearns, words fall short of capturing the full extent of my gratitude and love. I am endlessly blessed to call you my son and continually inspired by the wisdom and insight you share in every conversation. Your guidance has enriched my life in ways I never imagined, and I am honored to share these moments with you. My heart swells with pride for the incredible man you are.

To my beloved wife, Ricki Witt Braswell, you are the heart of my story. Your boundless love and steadfast support have illuminated every step of our shared journey. Through life's twists, shadows, and surprises, your faith in me has been my anchor, transforming my fleeting dreams into the pages of these novels and enriching every facet of my life. My gratitude for you is eternal, my love infinite—this work, and my heart, are yours always. I love you.

Now back to you the reader I simply say, let's get into the story!

To Ricki and Dillon. I love you both.

Chapter One

THEY SAID I had a real problem.

My "real problem" was how I came to be sitting in this office with fake plants.

The drive to the psychologist's office at 1450 Brickell Avenue was uneventful by Miami traffic standards. I parked under the elevated metro rail tracks, which ran behind the thirty-five story building. Being a city block west of Biscayne Bay, the upper floors have an uninterrupted view of the crystalline water. Salt tinged warm bay breezes swirled around me, tousling my hair as I walked through the open mezzanine lobby. I took the elevator upstairs to the 12th floor where I found the doctor's name stenciled on the door.

Dr. Beatrice Rangela, Psy.D, L.M.H.C

When I entered the office, I did not feel the inviting, cozy atmosphere the psychologist was trying to create with her decor. The waiting room was adorned in fake plants and poorly chosen framed art, more than likely straight from one of those pretentious catalogs with a name like *Bedford Farms Selection* or some other marketing agency-created abomination. I was having a perplexing time trying to understand why a board-certified psychologist in sunny Miami would have fake plants in her office. I was on time for the appointment I was ordered to attend.

I didn't want to be here. But when you work for a police department and they decide to send you for a psychological evaluation, well, you go.

I approached the small, frosted window which had three post-it notes imploring guests to *not* push the button. It would be easier to disconnect or remove the ring button than leave it to chance that patients who may or may not be psychologically struggling would follow simple directions. I considered myself in the 'may not follow' category.

I rang the bell.

The receptionist slid the glass back, trying to conceal her exasperation. At that moment, to tell you the truth, I was sorry I pushed the button. She didn't warrant my poor attitude.

"May I help you?" she asked through a forced smile. "Yes. I'm Cade Taylor. I have an appointment."

She looked down at a list propped below the window, glanced at a computer screen off to her right, then looked back at me with a confused look on her face.

"You're the detective from the Coral Gables Police Department?"

She could only see me from my torso up. My dark, shoulder-length hair was pushed back, contained by a dark blue Hartford Whalers baseball hat. With my goatee and earrings, I surmised I wasn't like most detectives she'd seen come into this office. I'd been an undercover detective in the Coral Gables Police Department's Vice Intelligence and Narcotics (VIN) Unit for nearly nine years. For the past seven of those years, I'd been detached to the Drug Enforcement Agency (DEA). Defense attorneys, legal attachés to our drug task force, even judges gave me a surprised look upon meeting me. I could see no reason why it would be any different with the receptionist.

"Yes. I am Cade Taylor a police detective with the Gables."

"I like your hat," she said as she fumbled to attach a sheet of paper to a clipboard.

She informed me the doctor would be late and asked me to fill out a sign in sheet. On the little sill between us was a cup crammed to the brim with ballpoint pens. I didn't really see the need for thirty or more pens for a waiting room that only had seven chairs.

Seven chairs.

Uneven number.

There were two sets of chairs with tables between them, placed side by side—a professional nod to a caregiver with a patient. Three more chairs were on the other side of the room evenly spaced apart. Five *Psychology Today* magazines were conveniently placed on a corner table, either a testament to the profession or a subtle hint for patients to engage in self-help. It wasn't the strategically placed chairs that gnawed at my thoughts. It was the absurd number of fake plants. I mean if you can't depend on the psychologist to care for plants how could she possibly care for her patients? Did I really need to be here? Why did the police department send me to a psychologist?

Nine years is a long time. A long time indeed, especially to be undercover in Miami. Seven of those years I'd been cross-designated and assigned to the DEA in Miami—the busiest field office in the DEA's network of worldwide stations. I'd been engaged in large cocaine and high-volume money laundering cases for longer than the good doctor I was waiting on spent in undergrad and grad school. I wondered if time was truthfully a barometer, could it determine which of the two of us had a better grasp of their profession? Me or the tardy doctor? Regardless of the specialty I have yet to meet a doctor who'd ever been on time. Unlike the psychologist, I couldn't suggest calming exercises, mindfulness, and exploratory conversations about my past. In the VIN lifestyle there's no room for error or timidity. The drug trade, especially in Miami, is a nefarious world. An unforgiving world where mistakes are not correctable. It's like tightrope walking over a vat of hydrochloric acid. Tragedy comes quickly with one misstep. This I knew all too well to be true. Maybe that's why I was here.

I passed the time thumbing through one of the *Psychology Today* issues. I'd just settled in to read, *"Cognitive Effects of Focal Neuromodulation in Neurological and Psychiatric Disorders,"* when the door to the inner office opened. The doctor stood in the doorway and called to me.

"Detective Taylor?"

I closed the magazine and rose up from the chair.

"Anything worth reading?" she asked as she held the door open for me.

"I was hoping for the swimsuit edition," I said as I drew closer to her.

"I hardly think that will happen. Besides, hope is not a strategy," she said.

"I guess you never asked the most popular girl in high school to the dance, because I can assure you that aside from a half-empty bottle of Pierre Cardin cologne steaming in your glove compartment plus a stick of stale Wrigley's gum, there wasn't much strategy other than hope," I said.

We were now walking down a bland uninspiring hallway with drab durable industrial carpet and beige taupe painted walls. Neutral non-confrontational colors. Tactile minimalism and nothing to potentially trigger fearful and wavering minds. Her office was the second door on the left.

"Welcome, Detective. Please make yourself comfortable." She motioned to an overstuffed loveseat, and I settled into it with an ungraceful plop. A smattering of diplomas hung on the wall. Some had the word "Diplomate" in the title. They were all designed to face the loveseat I was sitting on—a nod to establishing credibility, and dare I say, dominance.

She sat in the padded chair opposite me. Dr. Rangela was on the threshold of what many would consider to be middle-aged, dressed conservatively in a crimson blouse with black slacks. Her makeup had the appearance of repetitive daily application. It was nothing adventuresome. More than likely a morning ritual she had fostered day in and day out to a self-satisfying perfection. To be candid, her hairstyle was a bit hard to explain— brown with blonde highlights. It was a conglomeration of a poorly tied-back bun with loose strands of hair curling and dropping around her ears. To describe the way it looked would be similar to trying to describe and determine the outer tendrils of a tumbleweed.

"I'm so glad you kept our appointment. I'm Dr. Rangela," she said as she clicked a Bic pen. The pen had garish purple glitter on the end cap. She opened a steno pad and placed it demurely on her lap.

"Do I get one of those?" I asked her.

"No. Only I do the writing. If it concerns you, I can limit my notations," she said with a barely contained chuckle.

I stayed quiet.

"Let me start. As I said, I'm, Doctor Rangela, and aside from the counseling services I offer my private patients, Miami Dade County has contracted my services to spend time with first responders who may be experiencing ongoing, latent, or even delayed cumulative post-traumatic stress anxieties, or are challenged by the experiences of their occupation."

I stayed quiet.

She cleared her throat.

"I did not request to see you. The Coral Gables Police Department requested that you be here today to meet with me. I've had the opportunity to peruse your file that the Coral Gables PD forwarded to me. A cursory review shows an aggregate sum of very violent encounters you've had. Some of them resulted in fatal endings from police shootings, involving you. Have you experienced any depression, feelings of regret, doubts of judgement, malaise, or sadness that you think may be attributed to these fatal events?"

"No."

"Nothing?" she pressed.

"I feel like I was acting in the scope of my employment using the tools and training that were afforded me."

"Well, that's rather textbook wouldn't you say?"

"I didn't say. You just said that" I answered.

"A rather robotic response. Do you feel the detachment in your words equally detaches you from your emotions?"

"I don't see myself as detached. On the contrary, I am full-on in the moment. Those instances you referred to were all 'in the moment.' Actions and reactions," I replied.

"I understand that, but the police department has asked me to talk with you and determine if the past events of your life are potentially shaping your future events."

"So, if I'm hearing you correctly, you're trying to evaluate if what happened in my past will manifest in my future. As if killing people in the line of duty is some sort of harbinger for me to do it again."

"Manifest? Harbinger? Maybe you should be the psychologist," she said.

"We have only one thing in common: We're both being paid to be here. Other than that, I don't think we have anything in common. Psychology is a Voodoo science."

"Insulting my chosen profession won't get us anywhere—"

"We aren't *going* anywhere. Just because you ask the questions doesn't mean you get the answers. One misspoken word from me, one facial grimace, one 'I crossed my legs too often,' and the mere interpretation can upend my career. No thank you, Doctor. I'd be just as happy to sit this one out."

"Options are negotiated with car dealers. This is not an option. The Coral Gables Police Department has determined that it's incumbent upon me to evaluate your suitability for duty, given the fact that you've had a number—in quick succession, I might add—firearm discharges. Many of which have led to the demise of those you were shooting at," she said.

Inwardly, I was fuming. Externally, I maintained my composure and decided to use the clock to my advantage. I stayed in my chair and attempted to project a relaxed demeanor. The seconds trudged along, feeling like minutes. The silence felt louder than most conversations I'd had.

She won. I spoke next.

"What constitutes 'quick successions'?" I asked her.

She glanced at the papers on her lap. "Within the last year."

"So, within the last year I've been involved in on-duty-related shootings, some of which were fatal," I said.

"Yes."

"Any accidental discharges?"

"No."

"Any civilians or innocent bystanders hit by my bullets?"

"No."

"Then why am I here?" I asked as I leaned even closer towards her.

"I think I adequately explained that to you already," she coolly replied.

"I think I adequately explained that this is unnecessary," I replied with equal coolness.

"Your point is well taken, Detective. Now, rather than go back and forth with me about the purpose of my involvement, why don't you recognize that the police department that hired you, employs you, and de facto pays you, mandates you be here?"

"Obviously it's mandatory or I wouldn't be here."

She looked at me with dispassionate eyes. The room was silent again. "Let's try a different tact, shall we? Do you consider yourself a violent person?"

"No."

"Wouldn't you agree that using a firearm that takes a life is at its zenith, an act of violence?"

"I consider it a definitive solution to a violent situation."

"Meaning?" she said with a smarmy grin.

"Meaning that there is a matrix for the escalation of force. Verbal leads to physical. Physical leads to non-lethal methods. Non-lethal methods lead to lethal methods. The matrix is a real nice graphic on posters and thoughtfully printed handouts in the police department's training bureau. Nowhere on those glossy placards is there any mention of low-light situations, loud, distracting noises, people milling about in the background, adrenaline spikes, or the fact that I, who am now in the 'lethal' category, did *not* proceed through the matrix like I'm expected to do. They just started shooting at me or someone else putting me into the last stage of the perfect matrix right from the jump," I said through clenched teeth, feeling the anger percolating within me.

"Surely, you must have thoughts and feelings after such a traumatic event, or as you say a '*definitive solution*' occurs."

"I do."

"Care to share them with me?"

"No."

"This is a safe space, Detective Taylor. You can feel free to say what's going on inside of you without fear of judgement or reprisal," she said, leaning forward with eyebrows knitted in faux concern.

"Safe space. Free to say what I'm thinking, huh? Well, I think having fake plants in Miami is either a sign of laziness or thoughtlessness."

She was momentarily taken aback by the left turn the conversation took. Her face contorted, surely wondering where or why I would even mention the plastic plants. She recovered with minimal effort.

"It's neither. The nearest water source is the men's room down the hall by the elevators. There aren't any men in this office. The artificial plants are a sign of practicality. I felt a desire to soften the harsh lines of the walls. So, I placed the plants in the office. See? No judgement. No reprisal. Just a logical explanation to what you were thinking. Now my turn to let *you* know what *I* am thinking."

I silently braced for her to steer the *S.S.S Get All In Your Business* around my own personal Cape of Good Hope.

"Do you consider yourself the arm of God? Doing His will? Judge, jury, executioner all in one?" Now it was me taken aback by her haymaker of a verbal punch.

"Oh, I see we go from fake plants to a God complex?" I said defensively, knowing I was leaning back and away from her in a clinically cold manner that she'd ache to write down.

"To you it may seem like a bold leap, but it is what I am thinking."

"You need to think of something else. Do you ask everyone who sits across from you if they think they're doing the work of God? Notice I didn't say 'patients' because I'm a one and done in this little friendly conversation today," I said dripping with sarcasm.

"It's a legitimate question, Detective, and no I don't ask everyone who sits across from me because unlike you, not everyone has been involved in so many on-duty- influenced prolific acts."

"*Prolific*? When I hear that word, I think of the root of the word. Pro. As in *professional*. As in *proficient*. As in *procedural*. Did that ever cross your mind, Doctor? Maybe there is an upside to all of this. Did you stop to think of that?" I tersely said to her.

"When I hear that word, I too think of the root of the word Pro. As in problematic. As in *profusely*. Even as in *prohibited*. Maybe there is a downside to this. The root word 'pro' is also in projectiles that cause prolonged effects."

I eyed her all the while straining to control the contempt bubbling to the surface. Being second- guessed is nearly a contractual obligation in my line of work. She held her gaze upon me. She wanted me to don a miner's cap and dig into the dark tunnel of my life.

My mind could be like a bad section of town. Don't venture in there alone. If you do, keep the windows up and the doors locked.

I steadied myself internally, let a sense of ease come over me. She couldn't see the emotions settling inside of me. I reminded myself that I'm not responsible for the version of me that other people have in their heads. I'm only responsible to me.

"Doctor, have you ever fired a gun before?" I asked her with as much civil tact as I could muster.

"I was once close to someone who enjoyed target practice, and I accompanied him to the gun range."

"So, is that a yes?"

"Yes."

"Paper targets?"

"Yes, blue silhouettes. They looked like crash test dummies with little numbers on the torso and limbs. Now are you willing to answer my question?"

I cleared my throat and then began to speak. I was surprised that my voice naturally took on a lower octave.

"Shooting paper targets," I said, nodding like I was extending an olive branch. "The gun feels the same in your hand and operates the same whether you're shooting at paper targets or at humans. The sight alignment, the tension on the trigger, the loud blast, the blinding muzzle flash, and the jerking recoil are all the same." I paused to gauge her interest.

I detected introspection creeping across her mind.

"With just a few exceptions. Except paper targets don't scream. They don't wail. They don't soil themselves, they don't shake, and they don't cry in agony. With paper targets there is no blow- back. Blood doesn't splatter back on your clothes, bone fragments don't whistle past your cheek, and the putrid smell of gastric and methane gas don't fill your nose as they explode out of a human being's intestines. There is no eye and ear protection. Your senses are dulled to those around you. Just as well, I guess. Everyone around you is usually screaming and running. Tables get toppled, chairs fall over, water glasses shatter. Its combustible chaos. Isn't that something God can do? Create emotion? Upend tranquil days? Take a life? So, do I think I'm the arm of God? No, because I don't believe God would choose me repeatedly to do his bidding. I'm a detective in the Vice Intelligence and Narcotics Division, working in a less than God-favorable environment. It's a never-ending cycle. My life is a smoking crater. That's all."

It was now Dr. Rangela that was clearing her throat.

"I see," voice hushed. "Do you have job fatigue, or the feeling that what you do is futile?" she asked.

I was careful not to say anything that would be interpreted as career burnout or occupational despair. I stayed quiet for a moment.

"You did just say your life is a smoking crater," she pushed. I adjusted myself in the loveseat and leaned forward again.

"I will never lament being a dragonslayer when there are verifiable dragons amongst us. The battle is real. I don't get to say, 'time out' or 'hold on I broke my pencil.' I must stay in the fray, fight in the moment. Hard as it may be to comprehend, righteous brutality is sometimes needed against people who will use as much or more brutality to hurt me or others."

"Are you saying that to vanquish a foe you must be as tho?" she said in a Shakespearean way.

"I'm saying this is not a vocation for the faint of heart. I'm saying that I've been toe to toe with unrelenting heinousness on many occasions. I'm saying that I don't care how many times they send me here to see you, the result will always be the same. Until you walk in my shoes and see the world the same way I must see and confront it, you will always be on the warped B-side of the album of my life."

She put her pen and pad down and just looked at me for a moment.

"I've had to counsel many people in my practice. Divorce, death, job loss, family dysfunction, and yes post- traumatic issues like police shootings. While my optics on the world may be voyeuristic from your viewpoint, but I do know the trials and tribulations that people face. All the while parking my own problems and concerns. My perspective is far from the B-side of the album of life. In fact, I would say that not only am I on the A-side, but in many ways, I've sat in on the actual recordings that make the album."

"Then maybe you can see my perspective on all of this. My view of life," I said.

"Cade, what is your interpretation of life? Hypothetically, if someone were to come in this office right now and ask you to explain it all. Life and death. What would you tell them? What would you say?"

"In the end, the meaning of life can be distilled into one sentence."

"What is that?" she asked, wavering her pen over her pad poised to write my answer.

"Your mileage may vary."

Chapter Two

IT WAS STILL breezy outside as I strode out of the office to my car. Being so close to Biscayne Bay enhanced the blustery feel and I gulped in a few mouthfuls of the salty air trying to exorcise my visit with Dr. Rangela out of my lungs. Although infused with the aroma of new asphalt being poured somewhere around the corner, the air was a welcome relief to the stifling presence of the psychologist. The din of multiple leaf blowers a block away could be heard resounding off the nearby tightly packed buildings. One of the more glorious times to be in Miami is mid-February. March and April are divine, too. The weather in this ninety-day spate is normally unlike anywhere else in the United States.

I was still getting used to the car I was driving. In addition to driving seized vehicles, the drug task force rents cars from chosen rental car agencies in Miami. Ramon from the car rental agency had set aside an Acura RL for me, a 1999 model. I picked it up a few days ago. It was relatively new from the factory. The color was "Nighthawk Black." I wouldn't want a black car in the scorching Miami summer months, but this time of year it was devilishly fine. I settled in behind the wheel, took another deep breath, and I tried to put the shrink session in perspective.

Necessary
Cautionary
Exploratory

That's what I told myself. I tried to placate myself with those notions as being the driving decision that sent me to see her. Deep down I knew the lazy, sluggish way government agencies operate. I knew that there must have been multiple internal conversations about me at the police department before a decision was made to send me to a psychologist. I felt the push-pull within me as I grappled with theories on why I was sent there, and more than likely, the true reason why I was sent there.

"I am not responsible for the version of me that other people have in their head."

Right now, my responsibility was to my growing hunger. I decided to avoid eating anything near the downtown courthouse. Too many subpar eateries catering to a captive audience of attorneys, cops, and jurors who either can't leave the proximity of the courthouse or don't want to lose a prized parking space they fought each other earlier in the day to secure. I wanted to be away from the bustle of Brickell Avenue and concrete and glass canyon north of the doctor's office. I started driving west along the partially tree-shaded Southwest 3rd Avenue until it melded into Coral Way. I was just stepping out of the car in the lot behind the Old Lisbon Restaurant at 17th Ave and Coral Way when my cellphone rang.

It was the VIN office.

"Hello."

"Eh *oye* Cade, Major Broonsone say to have ju come to *la oficina ahora*."

The woman simultaneously massacring both English and Spanish was our VIN secretary, Ileana Portillo, a Cuban American twice divorced, single mother of two. Her preference to comingle Spanish and English words in the same sentence was known to everyone as "Spanglish." Her annihilation of the English language rivaled her uncanny way of doing as little as possible while appearing to be very busy. Her desk was prominently in the front of the VIN office, making her the first person that visitors and other police personnel saw when stepping into the office. Her ardent daily watching of Spanish

Language Telenovelas was legendary. She'd block off scheduled typing assignments and meetings around her television watching and become routinely overwhelmed with uncontained emotions, spontaneous shrieks, and drop-of-a-hat crying jags, engrossed in the farfetched plot lines.

"Broonsone," as she called him was Major Theodore "Ted" Brunson. Major Brunson tried repeatedly to correct Ileana's pronunciation of his name only to reach a point where he equally questioned his own sanity and the hiring decisions of the city's Human Resources Department.

Major Brunson had the distinction of being the longest-serving member of our police department. For a little over the last year Major Brunson had been appointed as our acting police Chief while our actual police Chief, Robert McIntyre, convalesced from a vicious, near-fatal stroke. Every month that our fiscally tight city manager kept Major Brunson in the interim position saved money on a nationwide search for a new chief, and the salary of hiring a new chief.

This financial maneuvering had only exacerbated Major Brunson's normally acidic, cantankerous personality. He was far beyond inflexible as a police administrator. Difficult and irritable don't even begin to explain his personality. With the fuzziness of a rabid porcupine, he was the one individual everyone in the police department consciously tried to avoid dealing with. His demeanor was sharp like a rusty nail just waiting to pierce through the bottom of your shoe. Salt-in-the wound abrasive, lacking in any basic courtesy, and frequently resorts to profanity, leading those unfamiliar with him to believe that cursing was his native tongue.

The entirety of the English language was purely secondary to him. He famously tended to express his frustration on inanimate objects, often kicking wastebaskets, slamming doors, and tossing crumpled wads of paper in exasperation. The palpable hostility that comprised his essence seemed to fuel his very existence. He had a literal consuming penchant for collecting hot sauces from around the globe. He'd gleefully sample each one regardless of its printed warnings and Scoville heat rating. He controlled a wide and equally enigmatic network of sources for information gathering. Like a clam with lockjaw, he had a vise- like grip on the pulse of the city and the department, and frequently reminded employees that he occupied the largest office in the building for a reason—that reason being his comprehensive understanding of the department, its personnel, and all matters pertaining to the agency.

All these things said, I would not want to be on his bad side.

I contemplated pushing Major Brunson off until after I'd sat down for lunch and eaten Old Lisbon's Thursday special: "*Costela de Vitela.*" The temptation was high. Still holding the cellphone to my ear, I started walking towards the Portuguese restaurant. With an eerie sixth sense of what I was contemplating, Ileana spoke in a sharp and authoritative voice:

"*Ahora mismo!*" [Right now!]

Her tone stopped me in my tracks. My hunger would have to wait. Frivolously jumping into the Spanish mood, I answered her back in Spanish. "*Entiendo.*" [I understand]

"Okay then ju have been told."

This conclusive remark was her frequent way of absolving her of any miscommunication.

I heard her say, "*Cabron*" as she hung up. I got back into my car and drove the short distance to the Coral Gables Police Department.

As I turned onto Palermo Avenue, I could see the Guldens Mustard-yellow police station looming in front of me. From a pure aesthetic perspective, it was one of the most poorly designed buildings in South Florida. It was a building contractor's homage to copiously poured concrete that was woefully absent the requisite structural integrity to support said copiously poured concrete. Entire sections of the parking garage were "recommended" to *not* park on, or for that matter, under. I often wondered if the bulk of the police department's allocation for crime scene tape was devoted to taping off segments of our own building. The concrete edifice had an abundance of windows on two sides of the building and was completely devoid of windows on the other two sides. The west side was ground to roof-framed windows that in the summer months broiled the building like an errant scorching solar flare.

The entire building was never sealed correctly. Heavy rains become floods, seasonally seeping down the walls. Mildew and mold were constantly being eradicated only to come back months later. Like the swallows of Capistrano, the mold and mildew reliably returned from either the monsoon-like afternoon rains or the humidity of the building's air conditioners laboring in the hot Miami sun. Coal black Saltillo tile laid in a bumpy, misshapen pattern on the interior hallways made every conversation, rolling cart, or click of a heel reverberate with the ferocity of an afternoon school bus ferrying sugar loaded elementary students.

I abhorred even being in the building for the slightest of reasons. Major Brunson wanting to see me was not a slight reason. But I'd learned to lump all reasons together with the same magnitude of disdain. I parked on the street, rationalizing that even if I had to be on the decrepit city property, my car didn't have to. My reasoning had fallen on the wayside of any logical construct. I'd adopted that if it made sense to me, well then so be it. Anyone who questioned it could seek the same level of acceptance on their own.

Outside, I passed a concrete planter that hadn't seen a living green plant for as long as I could remember. A dedicated mason labored to create the huge concrete planter only for it to become the biggest ashtray I'd ever seen. Countless cigarette butts flicked into the nutrient-deprived gray dirt found a final resting place in the planter. I say 'final' because custodians will pick up discarded trash and paper, but no one ever digs used lung darts out of barren dirt.

I took the dingy east side external staircase to the third floor. Inside the staircase one continuous, smudgy, dark, wavering line ran up the wall about four feet above the equally smudgy stairs—a traceable trail of where people leaned their bodies against the filthy walls as they descended, compounding the accumulation of grime. I stepped out of the staircase onto the third floor. I deftly ducked into the interior of the building. Major Brunson's office was at the end of the hallway. I walked straight towards Brunson's office, spotting Ileana at her desk through the open VIN office door as I passed.

"El cabron esta aqui!" I called out as I walked by.

She didn't respond but I'm sure she heard me announce that, "the asshole is here."

I stepped through Major Brunson's open office door, which is comprised of two offices. The one I stood in was where his secretary, Charlene Muscanera sat. Beyond that, the door to his working office was closed. Charlene was the gatekeeper whose chilly, taciturn attitude permeated the walls. She was engrossed in her computer screen, holding the telephone receiver in her hand. She looked up at me with the same disaffected dispassionate look a highway toll collector gives to the 1,400 car that has passed through the toll lane.

"Is he in?" I asked her.

She glanced back at her screen, then put the phone receiver back in its cradle. She must have developed second thoughts about whatever she was looking up or whoever she was trying to call.

"Is who in?" she said with a bored, deadpan affect.

A little power can really cloud a person's persona, I thought to myself.

"The Major. Is Major Brunson in?"

"Yes. He is," she said, showing no emotion or any compelling desire to inform him I was there.

"He wanted to see me. That's why I am here."

"Have a seat. I'll let him know you're here."

I backed away from her desk and back dropped into the earth tone couch across from her desk. Just as my butt contacted the faux tweed cushion, we both heard Major Brunson's distinct voice call out from the other office.

"Is that Taylor?"

Charlene picked up the phone and punched in his number.

Brunson bellowed through the closed door, "Goddamn it, Charlene! You don't need to keep buzzing my phone. It lights up and spastically blinks like the fryer at a fucking McDonald's. Just send him in."

With well-practiced demureness, she softly put the receiver in its cradle again. Without even looking up at me she simply said, "He will see you now."

The bottom of his door made a soft scraping sound as I pushed it open across the carpet. Major Brunson was standing behind his desk. He wore a blue pinstriped shirt with a blue necktie. He gave an anemic wave of his hand, devoid of any enthusiasm, indicating for me to sit down in one of the two chairs across from his desk. He seemed preoccupied, moving stacks and piles of paper across his desk. I don't know if it was managerial surrender or a needed break, but he placed a large stack of papers on the credenza on the side of his desk. I caught a glimpse of his dark cowboy style boots exposed below the cuff of his suit pants. I spied on his desk a bottle of hot sauce: *Belligerent Blaze Habanero Hot Sauce*. He settled into his chair and trained his eyes on me.

"Fun time with Doctor N. Sane today?" he asked me.

"You mean Dr. Rangela?"

"Yeah, her. She still has that crazy hair?"

"I guess so. How do you know her?"

He looked at me for a moment, stupefied. "Cade, I get her reports and evaluations all the time. I hate to pee on your hibachi and ruin your barbeque but you're not the only fucking employee in this cruddy place that has sat down with the Dr. Inner-Voice Whisperer. Instead of being a psychologist she should be a fucking surgeon since she charges an arm and a leg every damn time she sees one of us. Damn departmental protocol and that jabbering Lieutenant Maddalone demands that I send you fucking nimrods every time one of you steps in shit, takes a shit, wears shit, or has a shit out."

Lieutenant Charlie Maddalone oversaw police training in the Professional Standards Division. He was very rule-oriented and used his knowledge of directives and policies to enact what he considered proper adherence to those principles. I couldn't fault him for being a stickler. After all, we were in the law and order business. But there was no gray area with him. It was either black or white. He demonstrated increasing concern and agitation regarding my actions in every successive police-involved shooting. I'd become a tension point for him. Being on the side of righteousness, he had no compunction voicing his concerns about me to Major Brunson.

I didn't have any animosity towards Lieutenant Maddalone. He was just doing his job. Maybe a little too rigidly but just doing his job. The one factor that both Brunson and I knew was that it's easy to read chapter and verse from the directives of the agency when you yourself hadn't been on the road or in investigations for over a decade. In law enforcement, working on carpet versus working on concrete, is a whole different perspective.

"So, Lieutenant Maddalone advocated I be sent to Dr. Rangela?"

"Of course he did, and I gladly approved it."

"Gladly?" I asked.

"Gladfuckingly. Let me explain something to you. By sending you we met the criteria. No one can say that we didn't do it by the book. Her report, her analysis will be filed, and we'll all continue. The fucking moon will come out tonight and the sun will rise tomorrow. Nothing changes. That's it. Formality and obligation. Like a fucking New Delhi arranged marriage. Show up, say the right things, do the dance, and be done."

"That's it? I don't need to go back to her?"

"Are you spending your nights sitting on the floor in a dark house, rocking yourself back and forth, muttering crazy incantations and eating crushed lightbulbs?"

"No!"

"Well then yes, that's it. Now I'd like to move on to why I asked you to be here in my office." I just looked at him and as he is prone to do, he very quickly transitioned the conversation.

"I think you're a dasher," he said.

My blinking in confusion must have been noticeable.

"A dasher, Cade. You don't like being here so you try and dash in and dash out as quickly as you can."

"Well, unless there's anything pertinent, I just try to stay in the field, working the streets. That's where—"

He quickly cut me off.

"You think I don't fucking know where you work and what the fucking nature of your work is?"

I knew right away the forecast for today was going to be partly cloudy with a high chance of profanity. I waited to see where he was going with this expletive-laden conversation. He only said two words:

"Last Sunday."

I was becoming even more perplexed. "Last Sunday?" I repeated with an inquisitive lilt in my voice.

"Last Sunday. Super Bowl Sunday. Denver Broncos and Atlanta Falcons at Joe Robbie Stadium?"

I was even more confused. Just four days ago Miami had hosted the Superbowl. Brunson called Pro Player Stadium by its original name, Joe Robbie Stadium, revealing his own long history in South Florida. What was he angling at?

"You came by the office," he said with a steady gaze.

A memory flitted across my mind. I had come by the office in the morning to drop off overtime papers and to check my departmental mailbox. I preferred to do it on Sunday when there was very little personnel on the third floor.

"Yes, I did," I said.

"Yes. You did, Cade. Yes, you did. In fact, you parked in my fucking parking space."

Major Brunson's inexplicable way of knowing things in the department was proven again. Aside from having the largest and most desirable office in the building, Major Brunson also had the most coveted parking space—right next to the third-floor door into the building. I was still trying to comprehend what any of this was leading to. I started to speak. Before I could say anything, he snapped his hand up, the message clear: *Don't even try it.*

"Cade, the tradeoff of being over fifty years old is that you can't see letters up close, but you can spot bullshit from miles away. Don't even try and justify parking in my spot. I don't have a fucking yacht, or a goddamn Maserati, but in this splendid shitwreck we call the Coral Gables Police Department I do have my own fucking parking space. It's for *me* to park in. Not you or any other self-deluded, gun-carrying dickhead to park in. Understood?"

I nodded my head.

He continued to glare at me.

"I understand," I said quietly.

"Good. Now, moving onto the other reason you're here. I got word from the Secret Service this morning that Miami's Italian consulate general will be addressing an international press corps at some big fucking shindig at the Biltmore Hotel tomorrow. The Secret Service had a huge contingency here for the Super Bowl. They were caught off guard by this. Had the Secret Service known about this shindig, they would've left a few extra field agents here, but as it stands nearly all the Secret Service's outside resources are either back in place or on their way to their stations after the Super Bowl, quite literally as we speak. Actually, I'm speaking. You're hopefully listening. That's how I fucking like it. Anyway, the Miami field office has asked us to detach a few people to augment their needs for this event tomorrow. You immediately came to mind. Maybe next time you won't park in my space."

"I haven't done dignitary in a while," I said.

"Cade, I don't care. I really don't. The Secret Service are scrambling. They're doing it on the fly to organize the P.I. right now. They're working a skeleton crew and won't be doing their normal vetting, sealing, and countermeasures. They asked for help from Miami Dade and us. I have four detectives loaned out. You'll be our final piece, number five."

P.I stands for Protective Intelligence. At its barest definition protective intelligence is using people and information to identify and assess threats. It's a component of the advance work needed by the Secret Service to strategize threat mitigation for a protected individual or location.

"It's the consulate general. What's the big deal?" I asked.

"The consulate general is Baldassare Constantino. Today he's the consulate general at the Miami Italian Consulate. If my sources are correct, and they most certainly always fucking are correct, tomorrow at the Biltmore Hotel, Constantino will announce his candidacy to be the next Prime Minister of Italy."

"What time?"

"The event is at eleven in the morning in the Granada Ballroom. You'll need to be in place by 9:30am on the Biltmore Hotel property. Suit and tie. You have an earpiece?"

"I have a pigtail that fits the radios. I'm not cutting my hair for this midday Italian feast."

"Cade, I think I said moments ago that I don't care. Yes, I'm almost real fucking certain that is what I said. You ever just look at someone and get a fucking headache? You're my Excedrin moment each and every damn time I spend time with you, you know that? Your Secret Service counterpart is Special Agent Wayne Felton. Meet with Agent Felton at the Golf Pro Shop by the eighteenth hole of the golf course 9am."

"You said 9:30."

"That's everyone else. You be there at 9am. You have some distance to cover. You're not on the inside protective team—you're outer perimeter. We've assigned you by the dumpster near the eastside tennis courts."

"The dumpster!"

"That's right. The fucking dumpster. Someone could plant a bomb or something in there. In fact, that dumpster is right near a lot of parking spaces. Get a good look at those fucking parking spaces and then think better next time about parking in mine."

Chapter Three

I BOUNDED DOWN THE same filthy, decrepit stairs and was back in my car within minutes. Going from downtown Miami in the mid-morning, then back to Coral Gables chewed up a large part of my day.

And I was still hungry.

I opted to put in a pickup order from Havana Harry's. I was craving a *Pan con Bistec* sandwich but it wasn't to be. I was surprised it wasn't a menu option. My carnivore craving wasn't to be denied. I ordered a *Bistec De Palomilla, Arroz Blanco, Frijoles Negros y Maduros*, and added a Cuban sandwich for later. I knew I'd be hungry in the night. I always get hungry at night. If I put the pedal down and if the restaurant was quick with my order, I could beat the Coral Gables High School traffic on Lejeune Road.

The gastro gods were smiling upon me when I pulled into the nearly empty parking lot. I was in and out with a plastic bag full of delicious, aromatic entrees. On the drive south I mulled over the conversation I had with Major Brunson. At first, I felt chagrined that I was being relegated to watch a dumpster instead of being on the inside with the protection team. I recognized quickly that it really didn't matter. My longish hair, goatee, and earrings amongst all the short-haired, lantern-jawed, Ray Ban- wearing Secret Service agents would just make me stand. Besides, it's a *dumpster*. It should go smoothly. It might be one of the better places to be on the detail. No one to ask me for directions, literally stepping on my toes, or trying to engage me in small talk. Just me and the accumulated hotel refuse. The weather had been nice and there was zero percentage of rain for the coming days. As I often said, I get paid whether I sit or sweat. If I played my cards right, I'd be able to get a golf cart from the Pro Shop and have an easy day. It's all about patience. While away the time, just sitting and waiting for the radio transmission to tell us it's over, and we could all go home.

Speaking of home, that's where I was definitely heading.

Home.

It wasn't *my* home, per se, but it's where I'd called home for over a year. The condo was in southern Miami Dade County, in a bayside enclave called Paradise Point. It's what many of us refer to as "way down south" in the county off Coral Reef Drive and Ludlum Road. A doctor friend I'd met through the Miami Dade Medical Examiner's office had bought it for his mother who was living in the Dominican Republic. The day before she was to move to Miami, she broke her hip, severely delaying the move and leaving the condo unused. Shortly after the news, he kindly offered me the opportunity to stay in Paradise Point until she could make the trip. He'd tastefully decorated the condo for his mother, fully furnishing it with custom-built furniture and high-end artwork. My being a detective sealed the deal—he was happy to have a cop there as much as possible.

I was adrift in more ways than one. The flames of my divorce were still smoldering, and I leapt at the opportunity. His offer to let me stay there until his mother was healthy enough to move to Miami felt serendipitous. Transitional, but ideal for me and where I was in my life.

What started as a three-month arrangement had now stretched beyond a year. The doctor's mother had developed an attachment to her home health aide and refused to leave the aide in the Dominican Republic. The doctor didn't want to let go of the condominium and was now in a protracted battle with Immigration and Naturalization Services (INS) trying to secure a permanent visa for the aide to accompany his mother. The doctor's bureaucratic headache was to my advantage as I continued to call Paradise Point home.

It became home since my marriage took on the full aspects of sticking a metal fork into a live electrical outlet. After the burn, the shock, and the darkness I needed a new place to live. The home I had once, the one I once shared with my ex-wife Gina, was gone. As was Gina. The divorce was a serious gut punch and the ensuing carnage emotionally, spiritually, financially, and in some ways physically, was something I wouldn't recommend to anyone. In the game show of life, it's definitely not one of the top ten answers on the board. Flip the cards, spin the wheel, roll the dice, do whatever the game show rules say to either get another chance or get off the stage with whatever dignity you could salvage. If you lose and they offer you the home version of the Divorce Game, politely pass on accepting it. I saw no reason to reenact the loss and humiliation repeatedly in the confines of my own home.

Divorce, unlike campy, concocted, TV game shows doesn't allow for another chance. There would not be another chance with Gina. No further, future, or even futile chances. It was over. The marital wreckage, though it showed itself on the outside sometimes, was all my own to contend with. Only me. The salvaging of what was left of my soul was now in damage control mode. I needed to focus on the small victories, like today's win. A perfunctory meeting with Dr. Rangela, a hot steak from Havana Harry's filling my car with the wonderous smells of garlic and onions, and most importantly, the rest of the day to call my own.

The drive to Paradise Point was pleasant. The tree canopy over Old Cutler Road provided an ever-changing Rorschach Test of peek-a-boo light and shadow that danced across the road. I'd luckily slipped into the golden traffic seam that flows effortlessly before the marauding South Florida commuter crowd descends. Driving the final stretch of Coral Reef Drive to the complex is a botanists' dream. Delightfully bright fuchsia, fiery orange hibiscus, scarlet bougain-villea, fragrant frangipani, encroaching sea grape and mangrove trees line the road and vie for drivers' attention. The official title of the gated community is Royal Harbour Yacht Club, but everyone knows it as Paradise Point.

The spelling of Harbour is a nod to when the British ruled the Bahamas. Gun Cay is the closest Bahamian Island to the front door of my condo. The little island is only sixty-two nautical miles away. The security guard who mans the gate at the Royal Harbour Yacht Club was familiar with my odd comings and goings. He barely looked up as I used the remote attached on the passenger visor to open the gate. Midway down the stretch of lushly landscaped road I pulled into the doctor's condominium at 6211 Paradise Point Drive. My home for the past year.

The Royal Harbour Yacht Club are high-end row houses. Every row house is adjacent to the next row house by a shared external wall. Each residence is surprisingly long in depth, and all the units are at a minimum, two stories high. Most, including my unit, have a third level used as an outdoor terrace, from which I frequently could see all kinds of marine life, I'd watch manatees and dolphins frolicking and swimming in the narrow Cutler Channel that leads out to Biscayne Bay. The view from the rooftop was an unobstructed spectacular vista of trees, mangroves, and Biscayne Bay looking south towards Boca Chita Key, Elliott Key, Chicken Key, and the rest of Biscayne National Park. A refuge from all things VIN. All things. The white cocaine, the green money, and the bloody murders fall away when I see those spoiler islands in the distance.

I parked in the courtyard driveway. I never parked in the garage which the doctor used for storage. Verdant dark green ivy blanketed the staircase up to the decorative front door. The only portion of the edifice not obscured by thick, gnarled vine were the house numbers and the curved garage door which was aptly painted a deep hunter green. I took a deep breath when I stepped into the inviting condominium. I had the thermostat set for a comfortable level, but the ambient early low humidity of February in South Florida helped keep the place pleasingly cool. The good doctor generously provided for a housekeeper to clean the unit once a week.

That either said a lot about him or a lot about me.

The housekeeper had cleaned yesterday, and the entire three-story abode smelled like the olfactory kaleidoscope of lavender that was the disinfectant, *Fabuloso*. The purple-tinted cleaner is adored by nearly the entire Latin population of Miami, so revered that I wouldn't be surprised if some newborns were baptized in it.

The unit is appointed exquisitely with oversized comfortable designer couches. The polished Brazilian Camura wood built-in shelves accentuated the decorator's high-end taste. There were eye-catching pre-Colombian art pieces. There is a smattering of tastefully sized, imitation Botero pieces. Paintings from Sebastian Spreng, Alberto Pancorbo, and Connie Lloveras adorned the walls. The condo even boasted an imitation Wilfredo Lamb lithograph. The doctor left a laminated binder describing the artwork and the artists. If not for the binder I would have no idea who or what I was looking at. The interior is very spacious with large white ceramic tiles and eggshell white walls. In the daytime the towering custom-built windows permit natural light to bathe the walls and surfaces.

I put my keys, badge, and gun in a bowl on a waist high small table in the foyer. I'm sure the wood-working craftsman who created the table and the skilled artisan who made the bowl never envisioned their toil and hard work being a drop spot for a .40 caliber Glock, gold detective badge, and dirty keys. I put the Cuban sandwich in the microwave entrusting that if I forgot about it, I'd rediscover it sooner than later. I grabbed two Amstel Light beers from the refrigerator. With the chilled beers clanking against each other, I carried them and the full Styrofoam container from Havana Harry's up to the third-floor terrace. I collapsed myself into a cushy outdoor loveseat and listened to the soft, churning gurgle of an outboard engine slowly moving through the channel. I appreciated the boater obeying the *"No Wake Zone"* and *"Caution Manatee Area"* signs in the waterway.

I ravenously devoured the food and made quick haste of the beer. Two beers should have been enough, but I wanted at least a third. Comfortably satiated from the meal, I weighed getting up and going back downstairs against my desire for another beer. My mind went to the frequent thought of putting a mini fridge out on the terrace.

My yearning for a beer coupled with the sedentary comfortableness of the lounger made that notion take on deeper significance. A Great White Heron glided overhead, beak lowered, eyes scanning the channel for a fish just below the surface. It was one of those "only in South Florida" days with sunshine wrapped in soft murmurs. The faraway hum of a single engine airplane miles above, the rustling of palms in the afternoon breeze, water lapping against the docks below, and the nearly inaudible sound of a distant neighbor somewhere in the complex practicing scales on an oboe added to the lofty coziness of the afternoon.

The next beer could wait.

So could the next beer after the next one.

I slid further down into the plush sunbrella fabric of the chaise knowing full well I was heading towards a late afternoon sleep of irresponsibility. No children or spouse to demand my attention. My time in the office rendered and delivered. I call these moments "nap roulette," lulling myself into slumber without a set alarm. Will it be twenty-five minutes or four hours? I have no way of knowing. Afternoon beers, evening cocktails, and morning eye-opener Jameson Irish Whiskey shots can induce the chancy nap roulette to commence at any time. It can be risky, but I like it.

I awoke with a slight startle. No reason other than my own biorhythms conflicting with the experiences and moments of my past. My nap roulette clocked in at a tight two hours and seventeen minutes. For a moment I wavered between feeling guilty for sleeping, wondering what I'd do the rest of the night, and inwardly applauding myself for adding the Cuban Sandwich to my Havana Harry's pickup order. My night was set. No need to go back out with the teeming masses. I gathered up the messy remnants of the *Bistec de Palomino* and the drained Amstel Light beer bottles. Moving downstairs and after disposing of the midafternoon meal, I turned on the television. The local news came on the mammoth plasma screen. Miami television news has multiple segments that start at 5pm, continue through 5:30pm, and regurgitate it all again at 6pm.

It was 5:40pm. I'm sure that in the ninety-minute cycle of

murder, mayhem, and repetitive weather segments the news team had exhausted their effective ability to hold viewers' attention.

The news cycle can only sustain so much rehashing of stories before it trends into nap roulette- inspiring boredom. The local news producers are continuously seeking any content they can finagle to stretch the remaining twenty minutes before they amp up the 6pm broadcast with the A-team news anchors. The entire 6pm newscast thump-thumping the all-too-common theme of locally produced Miami news: *"Lock your doors and fear for your life."* The slick broadcast of carnage, corruption, and conflict are delivered with bright motion graphics and thunderous introductions. The only respite from the sensory overload are commercials for car dealers, HMOs, and air conditioning repair companies. A tourist watching Miami local news out of fear would never venture out of their hotel room. It was just background noise to me.

As I rummaged through the kitchen a news story came on TV that did catch my attention. It was a young petite Hispanic female reporter doing a stand-up story in front of the Biltmore Hotel. Behind the reporter the afternoon setting sun was casting cotton candy hues of pink and light purple across the sandstone color of the Biltmore's iconic thirteen-story tower. She seemed to be as busy keeping her hair from blowing across as her face as she was reporting the story. She said that Miami's Italian consulate general, Baldassare Constantino, would be making a major announcement tomorrow at the Biltmore Hotel. She didn't have much more to offer. When she threw it back to the studio anchors one of them made a comment that he hoped it had something to do with pizza.

I couldn't turn the TV off soon enough. I bounded upstairs into the master bedroom. In the enormous walk-in closet, I started to arrange all the things I would need for tomorrow: a crisp deep navy suit which I complemented with a white long- sleeve dress shirt. My necktie supply was sparse, but I did find a solid burnt orange silk one with a microprint of blue dots. I took a t- shirt out of the hamper and rubbed whatever dust had accumulated on my brown loafers. I put the suit, shirt, tie and shoes in the spare bedroom. I laid out my brown leather shoulder rig gun holster. I pushed two fully loaded drop-free ammunition magazines into the spare magazine pouches of the shoulder rig holster. I put the holster and the adaptive "pig tail" earpiece for radios with the suit. I wanted everything in one location so that in the morning I could just get dressed and minimize forgetting anything. Satisfied that the essentials for what I needed in the morning were ready I went back downstairs.

I poured a two-finger splash of Jameson Irish Whiskey into one of the etched crystal rocks glasses on the bar and took the drink back up to the terrace. I tuned the radio to 93.9 FM, *Love 94 Smooth Jazz*, and with the melodic music playing, I had my own little conversation with the rising moon. I thought about my appointment today with Dr. Rangela.

"The police department has asked me to talk with you and determine if the past events of your life are potentially shaping your future events."

What the hell was that supposed to mean? If a cop writes bushels of traffic tickets, does *he* get pulled in and asked if the past events of his life are shaping his future? Actually, they *commend* him and use him as an example for others to aspire for. Work narcotics in Miami and a drug dealer dies and suddenly grave concern for the safety and welfare of who? The public? Me? No, it's concern about if I'll do it again.

"Psychology is a Voodoo science."

I don't think I made any points with that comment.

It was getting late. I eventually ate the Cuban sandwich. Without fully realizing it, I filled my glass twice more as I languidly stayed on the terrace, taking in the movements of white puffy clouds sliding and gliding across the tranquil night. *"Moments in Love"* by the British Avant Garde group Art of Noise was playing on the stereo when the moon finally started to fully rise over the Atlantic, splashing the terrace in opaque striations of white light and ebbing shadows. It also foretold me that I needed to end my time on the terrace and get to bed.

"You'll need to be in place by 9:30am on the Biltmore Hotel property. Suit and tie."

Major Brunson's voice ran through my head, and it was one of the few times I thought about something he said to me that didn't contain profanity.

Chapter Four

THE WEST SIDE parking lot of the Biltmore Hotel had more available parking than most municipal stadiums in the U.S. Having been here for presidential visits, I knew that the most westerly row by the high hedge line was reserved for buses and large transport vehicles. It's also where the presidential vehicles will stage and organize "the package" that will be the president's motorcade. I didn't think the consulate general for Italy would merit nearly as much attention. I was very certain that many people at the hotel wouldn't know he was coming, nor would they probably care. Nonetheless, I chose to park in the middle of the open lot. When it came time to leave, I wanted the opportunity to go in any direction to avoid the traffic. The parking lot is situated between Anastasia Avenue and the world-renowned eighteen-hole Biltmore golf course. An eight-foot-high vine-covered chain link fence runs the length of the parking lot, separating it from the golf course.

The early morning walk to the pro shop was punctuated by the sounds of golf clubs being retrieved out of cars, Cushman vehicles puttering along on the other side of the fence, conversational voices, and the occasional clickety-clack of golf spikes walking across the asphalt parking lot.

I was the only person wearing a suit and tie. Just like my own assertions about the consulate general no one seemed to notice, no one seemed to care.

Sitting on a stool behind the starter's position window at the pro shop was a guy wearing a Biltmore name tag. It said Alan. My first impression was that Alan was a severely consumer brand confused individual. Alan was adorned with a Titleist visor and a Greg Norman windbreaker partially covering his Biltmore Hotel golf shirt with the visible Munsingwear Penguin logo.

"You with them?" he asked me by way of greeting.

"Them?" I asked

"The feds, the Washington guys. You know. Grassy Knoll guys."

"Uh well sort of, but not exactly. I'm with the Gables," I said.

"The Gables? Like the police department? You don't look like a cop."

"Has the city manager arrived yet?" I retorted.

It was an artful deflection. I never acknowledged or denied I was with the police department. By asking him if the city manager was on site, wearing my suit and tie, I let him make his own deductions.

"Oh, you're from City Hall. No, he hasn't been by here. At least not yet," was his cheery response.

"I need to get a golf cart. So, I can be more fluid for the city."

The omission of "manager" from my sentence was intentional. Alan had already formed the conversation and my position in his head. He heard what he wanted to hear. The city steadfastly retained a very cozy, if somewhat proprietary relationship with the Biltmore Hotel. A confluence of land rights, leases, and operating permissions created a complicated arrangement between private business and local government. Alan reached under the counter and lifted a box filled with identical keys and keychains. He looked past me at a row of parked golf carts. He then retrieved a matching key for the cart of his choice.

"Take 328," he said as he slid the key to me across the open window frame.

I looked behind me. In the gleaming morning light was a row of golf carts, and in the center was number 328. I thanked him as I put the key in my pants pocket. I looked to my left and there were three prototypical dark suit-wearing Secret Service agents in a loose huddle. They stopped their conversation when I walked towards them and looked at me inquisitively. They each had an identical lapel pin on their suits. The pin was a blue star centered within a fine line gold circle.

"Good morning, guys. I'm looking for Wayne Felton," I said.

The shorter of the three agents glanced at the other two and then said to me, "I'm Special Agent Wayne Felton."

"I'm Cade Taylor, with the Gables. I was told to come see you."

"You're not what I was expecting," he said, looking me over. "Do you have any credentials?"

I pulled back my suit jacket, exposing the detective badge on my belt. I simultaneously reached into my inside pocket and proffered my picture ID. In doing so I'm sure one, if not all of them, saw my concealed Glock in the shoulder holster under my suit jacket.

"You can call me Wayne. I'm a group supervisor in our Memphis station. I'm a remainder from the Super Bowl. You ever been to Memphis?"

"No. I haven't."

"You're not missing much. Think Mogadishu with a lot of Elvis Pressley tribute bands. Well, now you know who I am. This is Agent Tom Borges from our Palm Beach station, and we have another orphan from the Super Bowl here with Agent Louis Akicita from our Tucson office," he said.

"Call me Tucson Lou," Akicita said with a smile.

Felton gave me an abbreviated version of what the day's events were expected to be.

"The primary will arrive at zero ten thirty. He'll come in from the west parking lot. We will disembark just outside of the west courtyard. A small contingency of the *Carabinieri*—"

"The Cara what?" I interjected.

"The Carabinieri. One of the four branches of the Italian National Police is the Carabinieri. When it comes to foreign and domestic dignitary details the Carabinieri have authority at any time and in any part of the country that their protective assignment takes them. Yes, before you ask, they will be armed. They carry Beretta 92FS' A team flew in from New York City last night. They'll be in the package. When the package drops him at the courtyard, we'll join them. We'll walk through the courtyard on the path to the conference centers. Black curtains were hung last night in the lower lobby, and we'll escort the consulate general on the perimeter corridor we created with the curtains. We'll move across the lobby between the Palme d'Or restaurant and the Alhambra Ballroom. We're going straight in through the side door of the Granada Ballroom. We expect him to be on site for just under an hour, then back out the same way he came in. Once he's back at the consulate residence then we consider it to be 'wheels up' and we break it down here. Any questions?"

"No. Nothing I can think of," I said. "Good. You have a radio?"

"Yes."

"We set up a communications swamp box in the tower. It has a range of about a mile. We'll be on channel seventeen. Just check in as Gables whatever your unit number is—"

"923," I said quickly.

"Okay. Gables 923. Check in as Gables 923." He reached into an envelope that he pulled out of his jacket. He handed me a lapel pin with a palm tree on it. "Stars are agents. Palm trees are locals. Primary code name today is *Positano*. Sorry but I'm not authorized to provide you with a golf cart."

"That's okay." I replied knowing the golf cart key was in my front pants pocket.

Agent Felton moved on with Agent Borges and Tucson Lou. When they were sufficiently gone, I climbed into the golf cart. I began driving to my assigned location. I drove no further than twenty yards when I heard an unfamiliar, but very distinct clanking and clanging coming from the golf cart. I looked around for the source and discovered a golf sand bunker rake in a PVC tube holder attached to the back of the bar affixed to the roof. Surely Alan must have known the rake was there but either he didn't care, or he was messing with me. My posted location wasn't too far away, and I decided to keep driving. Me, my suit, my necktie, and my rake.

I continued around the backside of the hotel, past the center terrace and the crazily manicured back lawn. I followed the cart path around to the east side of the hotel and a lush canopy of trees. I parked the golf cart at the end of the path, squarely, snugly between two gumbo limbo trees with very thick trunks. Nothing would be able to pass in or out of the path.

I was facing the entire east side of the hotel. In front of me there was a small tropical landscaped island. Traffic moving west towards the center of the hotel diverted into a traffic circle around the landscaped tropical island. The roundabout led traffic back east and away from the hotel. Across from the island was the east wing of the hotel. The bottom of the east wing was delivery bays and pedestrian corridors that the staff used to enter the hotel. It was in the heavily traveled corridors that the hotel administrative offices were deeply tucked away. It was also where the hotel staff would punch in and punch out on closely monitored time clocks. I could see there was more than one dumpster—one inside the narrow passageway and the other outside of the arched entrances to the corridors. I looked up to my left and could see the rows of milled paned windows of the Palme d'Or restaurant and the adjoining Granada Ballroom.

I slipped the earpiece of the pigtail wiring system into my left ear, turned my radio to channel seventeen and I checked in. For forty minutes my ear filled with constant chatter about arrivals, stations, doors, hallways, alignments, estimated time of arrival, pushing on, pushing off, post check-ins, and a whole litany of inconsequential talking. Working in VIN and being removed from radio chatter, I quickly grew tired of the constant talking. The agents talked for what seemed like the pure joy of hearing their own voice. I opted to remove the earpiece from my ear. I let it dangle down across my shirt collar. I adjusted the volume on the radio so that instead of a cacophony of vox humana screeching in my ear it was now just faint ongoing dialogue gurgling up from around my neck.

Securing the golf cart was a grand coup. If I had to stand out in the parking lot the entire time, I would have been miserable. Maybe I should say *more* miserable. I was still not over-the-moon happy being assigned to such a pointless position. I was sure the three agents from this morning had already forgotten I was even out here amongst the trees. I lamented not bringing something to read. I decided to make the most of my time by watching the constant flow of workers entering and leaving the hotel. Most of them got on and off the mini shuttle buses provided by the hotel to ferry the workers from bus stops and designated off-site parking lots. Some of them got dropped off and picked up by private cars. Maintenance, Housekeeping, car valets, Food and Beverage—it made no difference what their job description was, they all passed in and out of the tunnel entrances. I tried to pass time speculating about their lives based on how they conducted themselves.

"*Positano*" had arrived on time, and he'd been in the Granada Ballroom for at least fifteen minutes. Once the package ferrying *Positano* had arrived, the voices on the radio went into operational mode. Channel seventeen was quiet. The day was going smoothly, and I was mentally counting down the time until *Positano* was gone.

The quiet I was finally enjoying was interrupted by a motorcycle roaring through the east tunnel that went through the hotel and connected Anastasia Ave to the rear parking lot. The engine growl reverberated off the arched ceiling, amplifying the sound. The motorcycle emerged from the tunnel with announced ferocity. The driver was dressed head to toe in black, including a full face helmet. The visor was darkly tinted and concealed the driver's face completely. The motorcycle itself—a Yamaha XJR 1300—was a shade of green so dark it was nearly black. The four exhaust pipes ran from the front of the motorcycle and spread out underneath the rider, converging into one large exhaust pipe in gleaming chrome that flanged out to the bike's back right side. The noticeable attribute of the motorcycle was its bulbous gas tank.

The driver eased the motorcycle into the open parking lot but instead of going towards the corridors he steered towards me. He drew closer quickly, stopping two feet from the front of the golf cart. I was so taken aback by the audacity of the driver that for a moment I just stared at the visor, looking for some sort of human features to focus on. He revved the engine and waved his arm across his body clearly indicating for me to move the golf cart out the way.

I started to unwind myself from my slouch in the golf cart seat. With confidence fostered from my authority I told him to "shut it down."

He responded by revving the engine, making the bike lurch forward a few inches. "Turn it off. Now!" I barked as I rose out of the golf cart.

Over the steady idling engine, I heard a muffled response come from somewhere inside his helmet.

It sounded like he said "Move."

"Look buddy, I'm telling you to turn off the engine! Lift the visor *now*!" I said louder. "Move now!" came a forceful reply from the rider.

"I'm a cop. Turn it off. Take off your helmet!" I commanded, now out of the cart.

I'd just started pulling back my jacket to reveal my badge when the rider released the brake and intentionally, forcefully rammed the cart, The golf cart was pushed back until its locked-in brake system caught hold.

I was glad I'd gotten out of the cart.

I moved quickly. I retrieved the rake from the back of the golf cart and shoved the handle of the rake into one of the wide gaps of the tire rim, immobilizing the bike. He'd have to turn off the bike and dismount to remove the rake from the wheel.

His reaction was odd to me.

He pulled back the sleeve on his dark shirt and calmly glanced at his wristwatch. It was hard to understand him with the full visor helmet on, but it sounded like he said, "motherfucker."

I moved closer to him with intent to pull the key from the ignition. I briefly debated reaching into my jacket and putting my hand on my gun. That debate was indeed brief because he deftly swung his right arm across his torso, reached aggressively into his black windbreaker and unsnapped a firearm from a concealed holster.

My brain went into hyperdrive. I wouldn't be able to pull my gun quicker than he just did. I needed to get my hand on top of his and try and lock his hand down so that he could not pull the gun further from his holster.

I leapt at him. I felt my feet leave the ground. I crossed his body with my right arm while my left hand jutted up under his right elbow, shoving his shoulder up at an unnatural angle, stopping his arm from pulling the gun out. It happened in an instant. An instant that felt like one of the slowest moments of my life.

The momentum of my dive at him caused us both to topple over beside the motorcycle. He landed on his left side with me on top of him. He couldn't pull the firearm any further but now my right hand was trapped under the weight of both of us.

The motorcycle tipped over, but the rake and the front end of the golf cart kept it partially upright, leaning precariously on its side. The bike loomed over us on the ground, the clamor of the idling engine making hearing nearly impossible. I wished I hadn't removed my earpiece. The radio was my lifeline for assistance. The plugged-in wire just limply flailed about on my chest.

The rider kicked and squirmed under me with all his might. There's an expression that if you control the head, you control the body. With his helmet still affixed, that was not to be. He was strong and fought with ardent determination. He bucked his body repeatedly trying to knock me off him, and I was sliding off him. I needed to get my own hand free to extract my gun, but I couldn't risk letting go of his hand.

My dominance was slipping. I screamed at him to let the gun go and to stop fighting, the repetitive hum of the engine inches from my head making my own voice sound foreign to me. He was on his left side and trying to roll towards the motorcycle. He was trying to get positioned on his back. It became apparent quickly that he had some Judo training. Most people aren't comfortable fighting from their back, but he knew enough not to turn away from me and try to get up from a kneeling position. As much as I was trying to lock his right hand down, he was equally trying to hold my right arm and maneuver me into a bone-crushing arm bar.

I needed to do something quick, or this was not going to end well for me and potentially just be the very actual end of me.

I couldn't tell if he was exhausting himself, but that was not to be with me. My strength was quickly sapping. Our fight had only started but I could sense I was outmatched. I couldn't head- butt him. I couldn't strike him in the head or face with him wearing that helmet. I was in a grappling, tussling fight with a superior trained opponent, and I was losing control of his arm and gun hand. I leaned on him with as much weight as I could muster. I got a moment of leverage and gave a left knee strike to his lower back and right kidney. If it fazed him, he didn't show it.

I bent my own left arm like a contorted chicken wing, earpiece continually jamming itself up under my chin. I frantically fumbled to unsnap my holstered Glock, each pass I made at it causing me to release whatever hold on him I had, and the whole time the same fearful thought ran through my head: What if the Glock is unsnapped and slides out, falling somewhere between our twisted bodies?

On my second attempt I managed to get the Glock unsnapped. I could feel the weight of the weapon immediately shift as it slid partially free. I hurriedly bent my wrist inward towards my armpit and grabbed whatever part of the gun I could, relieved to feel its heftiness transfer from under my arm to my hand.

He was nearly free from my failing attempts to restraint him, and much to his advantage, almost completely on his back. My hold on his left arm was gone. Instead of punching me with the newly freed arm as most would do, he grasped me behind the neck with an iron grip, trying to forcefully pull me into his chest and neutralize me with a submissive hold. I strained to lean my head to the left, giving me just enough space to wedge my hand between his chest and my head.

The butt of the Glock settled in my palm.

His grip was wrenching my neck, pulling me and my extended arm to the left. I began to lose hold of his gun hand but worked hard to pull my head back and turn the Glock in towards me. I quickly shoved it upward and away from my face placing it right up under his jawline.

With two rapid pulls of the trigger, I fired into his jaw and struck him just below the helmet's face shield. In an instant I was nearly concussed from the close-up loud noise. Blood, bone, and some sort of viscous membrane splayed across my neck and chest.

My bullets never exited the top of his helmet. Looking up through the helmet's bottom, all I could see was a splattered thick curtain of blood across the inside of the tinted visor, and a scorched powder burn under his jawline.

He was dead.

He died with his gun in his hand. I was panting, sweating, and still crazy wide-eyed when I pushed back from him. Blood continued to stream out from beneath his helmet while I tried to comprehend what just happened and how it unfolded so fast. The entire exchange had lasted maybe forty seconds.

I reached up and turned off the motorcycle. My sensibilities started coming back to me slowly. It was then that I heard three hotel housekeepers across the parking lot shrieking and screaming. They must have been screaming for a while because more people and workers were bounding out of the hotel. Three landscapers began walking cautiously towards me. One was holding a machete at his side. They were talking to each other excitedly in Spanish. Still holding my blood- smeared gun, I pulled my badge from my belt and weakly held it up in the air.

"I'm a cop. *Tabien. Soy policia*," I said in a fatigued voice.

Fortuitously that morning I'd snapped the holstered weapon retention strap to my belt to minimize my gun from swinging. That little strap kept my gun reachable and may be what saved my life. I fumbled for my earpiece with blood-coated fingers and just as I put it to my ear, I heard even more screaming and shouting on the radio.

"Shots fired, *Positano* down, agent down!"

Chapter Five

I WAS STUNNED HEARING that desperate radio transmission. For a second I thought I was hearing my own inner thoughts somehow broadcasting across the radio. My own heaving desperation now turned heavenly salvation. I turned my head downward and pressed the earpiece tighter into my ear. I listened intently. Then I heard it repeated almost verbatim on the radio again.

"Shots fired, *Positano* is down, agent is down!"

The sickening feeling in my stomach just compounded. I felt even weaker in the legs. I leaned heavily against the golf cart. My shoulders slumped forward. My mind reeled as though rational thought was unspooling in my head. That was the last discernible transmission I heard. What quickly followed sounded like fifty loud voices yelling and transmitting on the radio at the same time. Loud shrill emergency tones sounded off like errant rockets due to frantic agents pressing the emergency buttons on their radios. Each press of the emergency tone would override and cut off the hyperventilating, over-modulating, panicked transmissions, turning the entire radio into a garbled, frightened mishmash of interrupted sentences, blasting signals, and cut-off voices in one frenzied ball of confusion.

I had to keep my wits about me. I had another whole other dilemma here quite literally at my feet. I couldn't get on the radio. The radio was useless. Even if I'd been able to transmit, it would've confused everyone further. They had a full-on emergency going on inside the hotel a mere forty yards from my disaster.

I propped myself up against the golf cart and retrieved my cellphone and dialed 911. The Coral Gables emergency operators were in their own whirlwind as their switchboard lit up with an avalanche of calls from protection agents, hotel workers, hotel guests, attendees, and even a few golfers. Once I was able to finally get through to an operator and explain my own critical situation, I emotionally eased a little. Much-needed help was on the way. Adrenaline and cortisol started abating in my body. I began to feel queasy and lightheaded. My radio continued to be a conglomeration of excited voices. Finally, a commanding voice from somewhere on the thirteenth floor command center instructed all agents with *Positano* to go to channel sixteen, all agents with the fallen agent to go to channel fifteen. The commanding voice was trying to sectionalize the mayhem and triage it as best as he could.

I had no idea what had happened and what was happening. My assigned post had turned into an active homicide scene. The wail of distant sirens was getting closer. It was as if anyone with a siren on their car was on their way to the Biltmore Hotel. The golf cart and tilting motorcycle were like a kid's play fort, sheltering me from the waves of onlookers. I tried to keep them back and away.

"Stay back, police matter. *Quédate atrás.*"

By now the bravest of the bystanders had edged closer to me, only to see my violent struggle splayed out in front. He abruptly turned away and vomited. A blood-soaked corpse will do that to people. At least the blunt gruesomeness of his death was contained in the helmet. I guess I wasn't a pretty sight either. Glops of spinal fluid or brain matter caked my torn and filthy suit, as well as my chin, neck, and chest. I holstered my bloody gun. My badge had bloody smudgy fingerprints on it from me holding it up to the gathering crowd. I just clipped it back on my belt. The sirens were descending upon us. Police cars raced into the parking lot through the passage tunnel, causing a bottleneck. Officers jumped out of their cars, blocking the tunnel more, backing up the additional arriving police units onto

Anastasia Avenue. It was a clustered mess created by the confluence of everyone trying to help but doing so without any clear organization. At first many of the police officers neglected to turn off their sirens in the tunnel, making the decibels rise like twenty airplane engines at full throttle.

It was professional pandemonium.

Commotion compounded.

Collective confusion.

Ineffective inability.

Uniformed officers were running towards me. Seeing me ragged and bloody with the dead motorcyclist was spectacularly confusing to them. I knew the best thing to do was create space. Most of the officers recognized me right away but a few had never met me due to my undercover status. The officers who did not know who I was were quickly informed by the others that I was in fact a Coral Gables detective.

"Set up an overly wide crime scene to keep the hotel workers away," I instructed the first three officers on the scene, then, "Shut down the tunnel and all comings and goings by staff, including the shuttle pick-up," to the others.

Everything was to be done in the front of the hotel.

An arriving sergeant and I arranged for three more officers to sequester any witnesses and to check any cellphones that may have been used to take pictures. As more high-ranking officers and detectives arrived, I stopped directing efforts and tried to mentally chronicle everything that happened. It was surreal to see the scurrying of people and resources. I could hear the *thump thump* of a helicopter approaching. One detective told me that Coral Gables and Miami Dade police units were holding a landing zone on the golf driving range between the fifth and ninth holes so Rescue One— the Miami Dade Fire Rescue medical helicopter could set down and leave quicker there. Rescue One was a good sign that either the agent or *Positano* were not dead. I prayed both weren't dead.

A man in a suit came up from behind me across the golf course.

By the time I saw him he was rounding the cart path. He was harried, flustered, and eyebrows creased with worry. It was Secret Service Agent Tom Borges from Palm Beach. He was completely shell-shocked. His gun shook in his hand. Borges saw that the cavalry had arrived and wisely holstered his weapon. Still fighting to get my normal voice back, I hoarsely called out to him. He couldn't conceal the horrified look on his face when he saw me. He changed direction and made a beeline right to me. He hesitated in his walk as he tried to understand what he was seeing, stopping a few feet away to look at all the carnage.

"Borges. Borges! What the hell happened?"

He looked shattered. His gaze was transfixed on the dead motorcyclist. I think he was in shock.

"Borges. Borges! What the hell happened?" I asked again louder.

"Shooter is a white male. He was dressed as a hotel worker. He ran out the back onto the golf course..."

"He's not in custody?" I asked in total disbelief.

"No, he—"

I held up my bloody hand to silence him and urgently yelled as loud as I could to the uniform sergeant. "We got an unsecured scene! Shooter is still at large, last seen on the golf course. White male. Might be dressed in hotel uniform. Stand by for more," I yelled, my voice still gruff.

The sergeant went ashen white. He commanded everyone on the scene to go to an alternative radio channel as he transmitted that the scene was unsecure and that all units on the scene were to partner up. At least one in every pair was to have a long weapon at the ready and set a southern perimeter on the golf course to protect the officers actively working in the scene. Agent Borges stayed in place, transfixed on the corpse half-under the leaning motorcycle.

"Borges. Borges!" I yelled to get the agent to focus on me. "What in God's name happened, Borges?"

"Everything was normal. *Positano* was at the podium. A guy who'd been in the back of the room ran up and shot *Positano*. At a full sprint. He just ran up and fired two rounds and kept running. Shooting on the run. Hit the bank of doors in the back, shot one of the Italian protection guys and kept running," he said with a quaking voice.

"What? What do you mean he came running up from the back?"

"I mean the guy was in the ballroom serving coffee and tea and then boom, like a freaking gazelle he just made a mad run at *Positano*. It happened so fast that no one could react. I was just off to the side by the windows. I didn't even see him until he was a few feet away from the primary."

"On the run, he shot the primary?" I asked again seeking verification.

"Like a damn Olympic sprinter. Then right out the doors. I heard a shot, and the Italian guy was down. But Jesus Christ! What the hell is this?" he asked staring down at the dead motorcyclist.

I had my own portion of this complete fiasco to deal with. I didn't answer him but turned to one of our on-scene detectives. "Johan! You need to talk to this agent from the Secret Service. Get a full account of what happened before it gets all tangled in this mess we have here. Figure out what he can tell us about the shooter. He was there."

I turned back to Agent Borges. "This is Detective Johan Williamson, tell him everything. You and I will circle back about all this later." I motioned to the motorcycle and the mess around me.

Williamson guided Borges by the arm and led him to a more secluded place to get information.

I don't believe in coincidences. Whatever the motorcyclist was doing had to be connected to the Italian consulate being shot. I needed to take a moment and try and make sense of how such a quiet morning and easy assignment just became a near-death experience for me. I was weak in the knees and wavering unsteadily. I gingerly eased my sore body back into the golf cart seat. I was spent. Physically and emotionally depleted. I replayed the altercation over in my head. It came close to going bad for me in so many ways. If the motorcyclist had perfected the grappling hold he was trying to put me in, I do believe I was probably six inches from being six feet under.

Sensory overload gripped me further. Everything I could see, everything I could hear, even my sense of smell became incredibly distorted and murky. Around me everything moved in hyper- speed, and I was in a rapidly degrading slow fugue. There were police officers trying to maintain a complicated crime scene, detectives looking perplexed, crime scene technicians trying to understand the bloody scene, more cops at the ready with shotguns and assault weapons, scanning the tree line and fencing surrounding the golf course, incessant barking of K-9 dogs readying for a manhunt search, more Miami Dade helicopters searching for the gunman, and a smattering of late-arriving Secret Service agents with MP5 weapons walking amongst it all.

The processing of the scene was getting underway, but everyone's movements seemed aimless. I was feeling all of it. I was woozy. A cold sweat broke on the back of my neck and seeped under my collar. My mouth felt desert dry. I wanted to lie down. I just wanted to lie down. My brain kept telling me that if I could just lie down, I'd feel better. I slid over on the golf cart seat, banging my knee on the console, and that's all I remember.

Chapter Six

People.

Lots of people. That's what I recall first. People standing over me, their hands all upon me. I felt my knee bang against the console again as they pulled up and out of the golf cart. They wanted to lie me prone and then thought better of it as they tried to maintain the integrity of the crime scene. I was becoming more lucid yet still feeling very out of it. The police officers tending to me realized I was becoming conscious. Through hazy vision I saw the parking lot was a jumbled impassable maze of cars and people. One of the more enterprising officers commandeered a different golf cart and wheeled up as close as he could get to the death scene. With officers holding each of my arms, I staggered under their assistance to the other golf cart. They placed me in the seat beside the officer at the wheel. Another police officer clambered onto the back of the cart and held me in place firmly by my shoulders. There were a lot of encouraging words from both the officers as they sped me out of the parking lot towards the hotel.

"Hang in there, buddy."

"We got ya, bro."

"Almost there, dude."

A Coral Gables Fire Rescue truck had been staged just on the fringe of the hotel property. The paramedics quickly strapped me to a gurney and transferred me, saying they were taking me to Doctors Hospital, a short distance away. Since I was still armed the paramedics demanded the officer who commandeered the golf cart ride in the back with me. An oxygen mask was placed over my mouth and nose. Normally I would have rebelled, but the cool flow of the oxygen was soothing, and I wasn't in the mood to talk. I was awake enough to know that with the mask on my face most people would refrain from asking me questions. I took solace in that. The ride in the rescue truck to Doctors Hospital was a siren-blaring sprint. Within minutes of being placed in the back of the Fire Rescue truck I was summarily taken out of it and wheeled behind a barrier curtain that served as a poor excuse for a privacy wall in the Emergency Room.

Two attending physicians, a paramedic, and Officer Sampson whose name I learned by reading the name tape on his uniform, all crowded in with me behind the curtain. At first the doctors were taken aback by all of the blood and other still-unidentified sticky substances that were adhered to me. Officer Sampson told the doctors what he knew about what occurred at the Biltmore Hotel. Both doctors looked at me with their mouths agape. One of them let out a low whistle. The doctors conducted an assessment and checked my limbs and torso for any unseen injury. I was helped out of my clothes which were put into a red biohazard bag. They equally helped me into a hospital gown. A nurse sponge washed me, cleaning away the gore on my body, then she tried to draw blood from my arm. By the difficulty she experienced trying to locate a vein there was a collective hunch from the doctors that I could be dehydrated. Within minutes an I.V. on a stand was wheeled in by an orderly. For good measure the doctors added some form of a Benzodiazepine to the I.V. to counteract my certain anxiety. The doctors left. They said they'd return when the lab results came back.

I'd finally gotten to lie down. The paramedic got rudimentary information from me. Satisfied, he was the first to leave. I dozed off for an undetermined time and awoke to find that Officer Sampson was gone. Instead, sitting in a chair at the foot of the bed was the head of the police department's training unit, Lieutenant Charlie Maddalone. Like the patron saint of and rules and regulations. I looked at him with groggy eyes as I continued to stir from my stupor.

"I brought you a polo shirt and BDU pants from training so you can change. Miami Dade Homicide is on their way here to get your clothes. I figured you'd want your car. Homicide wanted to just "peruse it," as they say. They were a little miffed. They said it took them forty minutes to find where you parked it. I have your gun. It's in a bio bag because of all the blood. We'll test it and I'll get it cleaned for you. I also brought you a replacement firearm."

I saw the red biohazard bag on the rolling bed tray behind him. I was feeling much better, and I started to sit up on the bed. The I.V. bag was empty.

"Doctors say your blood test came back normal. They think you were just dehydrated. Maybe a little shocky. Mostly dehydrated. You ever eat anything other than an olive out of a martini?"

"Pizza," I said as I sat upright. "For the record, no, I don't drink martinis."

"Miami Dade Homicide is having a mess of a time with this one. They're investigating the one you killed. They don't think the Italian agent is going to make it. Rescue One took him to Jackson Memorial Trauma Center."

"What about the consulate general?"

"Baldassare Constantino? He's going to live. Doctors say he's lucky. One round hit the podium and splintered. A piece of the bullet went into his right wrist. The second round missed the lung but broke two ribs and exited out through his side. He might not be able to blow up any party balloons for a while, but he'll be okay."

"The Italian agent. How bad is it?"

"He took it almost straight on in the chest. Thoracic trauma. Midnight shift is going to Jackson Memorial Trauma to donate blood before they come on duty tonight. The Italian protection group—"

"The Carabinieri," I interjected.

He narrowed his eyes at me which abruptly morphed into an *'I'm a lieutenant, don't interrupt me'* look. Then he continued.

"Some of the Carabinieri are standing guard with their agent and some are holding it down with the consulate general. They're on high alert, bringing in another team from New York City as we speak. They're really freaked that this even happened."

"Any idea why he was targeted?"

Before he could answer I heard Major Brunson's distinct voice.

"What I fucking tell ya? They wanted him whacked because he'll possibly be the next fucking premier of Italy," Brunson said as he pushed aside the curtain around my bed.

"How ya feeling?" he asked me.

I was surprised to see him and answered with as much energy as I could.

"I'm feeling good. Much better."

"Doctor says you were dehydrated. How 'bout you start drinking more water and we can avoid this fuckshow next time?"

"Understood," I said

He looked at for me for a beat.

"I understand." He liked a clear response.

"Goddamn camels can drink 100 liters of water and go a full week without rehydrating. Me? I drink a fucking thimble of damn water an hour before bedtime and I'm waking up eight times to piss," said Brunson.

Maddalone said, "Maybe you should have your prostate checked." Brunson frowned at him. "Are you offering, Charlie?"

"Um...uh...no."

"Well then how about you keep your mind, and especially your fingers, out of my ass." Brunson turned back to me. "Homicide will be here soon. Give us a rundown of what happened before those pencil dicks get here."

I gave a brief account of how I encountered the motorcyclist, our physical altercation, and ultimately his death. They both listened intently without saying a word.

Maddalone updated me: "We don't know who he is yet. Miami Dade Homicide might know, but we don't know. He had a Heckler & Koch P7M8 nine-millimeter. The thing can't be more than seven months old; H&K just came out with it. It's from their latest line of handguns. We've never seen one before. It was fully loaded with one in the chamber. A literal point and shoot. You're very lucky he couldn't pull it all the way out."

When he said that I subconsciously looked down at my right hand. "Serial number?" I asked.

"We ran the serial number. It was part of a shipment that went to a trade show in Europe last March. Not all the guns came back from the trade show. His was one of the missing guns."

"Where in Europe?" asked Brunson. "Tiranë, Albania."

"Albania? What the fuck? How does a gun get stolen in goddamn Albania end up in goddamn Coral Gables?"

The room went silent while collectively we were thinking about how a gun stolen in Europe was in the possession of our mystery rider.

"The shooter vanished. I mean like, poof! After he shot the Italian agent, he just pulled a Houdini. No sign of him anywhere. Three-hour search. Locked down the hotel and Saint Theresa Catholic School a block away on Indian Mound Trail. Parents went berserk. We finally broke down the perimeter only an hour ago. If the Carabinieri had it their way we'd have run a perimeter from the Biltmore on down to the Florida Keys. Needless to say, the Italians are none too happy." said Maddalone.

"Tell me you got more than this?" said Brunson, turning his gaze directly on Maddalone.

"I wish I did. On a high note, Detective Johan Williamson was able to convince Miami Dade Homicide that for the sake of expediency they let our crime scene people process the motorcycle and fingerprint the motorcyclist. We have those in our possession and are sending them to the Automated Fingerprint Identification System with us attached as a rider."

"A rider to AFIS?" asked Brunson.

"That way we'll get notified of the results at the same time as Miami Dade Homicide. At the *same time.* This might be a Miami Dade case, but it's still a flaming international incident in our city. One I might add that nearly killed Cade."

"Good work. Good work by Johan," said Brunson. A compliment from Brunson delivered without profanity was a surprise. "I once had to fucking rip into Johan about writing tickets on his fucking drive into work, which automatically made him a fucktard in my shitlist book, but this was good work by him."

Being surprised can only last so long.

"Cade, while you were sleeping Major Brunson and I discussed our sending you to see Dr. Rangela yesterday. I hope it was beneficial for you. In light of what occurred today and what's occurred in the past with your shootings, I think we should monitor these things from a distance and provide you the knowledge that Dr. Rangela or any other psychologist is available to you."

"So, no more mandatory appointments?" I inquired.

"As it stands, no.. The gravity of your work and the situations that have necessitated you to take decisive action are at a level most in law enforcement may not see, certainly not in repeat fashion. There were a few witnesses that we interviewed. They said it was a very quick escalation and that you had no choice. I hope your meeting with Dr. Rangela was productive, but we won't pile today on top of it. We move on," said Maddalone.

"I never needed a grippy socks vacation," I said with a tinge of disdain.

Brunson said, "Cade, I told you yesterday we play it down the fucking middle. We meet the damn criteria. No one can say that we didn't do it by the fucking book."

"Your replacement firearm is already in your holster under the clothes."

"Charlie, do us a favor and step out while Cade gets dressed. When Miami Dade gets here buy us a little time. I need to talk to Cade." said Brunson.

I didn't know if this was a good thing or a bad thing but nonetheless, Maddalone stepped out. I took that as my cue to get dressed and whatever Major Brunson had to say I'd at least hear it without my butt hanging out of a hospital gown. I started to put on the BDUs and polo shirt.

"Cade, I don't need to tell you this is a really big fucking mess. All of our lives would be easier if the damn consulate general would've tested his popularity at his little coming out party at the Hyatt Regency on the Miami River. Instead, the little bastard decided to fucking grace us with his presence at the Biltmore. So now Coral Gables is smack dab in the middle of a scorching fucking hot news spotlight. The city manager is shitting calzones over this Italian fuck-up. The Secret Service is looking to blame anybody not wearing a suit and sunglasses. It's horseshit. I got everyone with a phone fucking calling me."

He stopped talking and gazed at the curtain. In typical Theodore Brunson fashion, he transitioned the conversation with nary an attempt at segue.

"In '92 when Chief McIntyre was still healthy, the department sent me to the FBI National Academy in Quantico for ten weeks. I'm talking ten long weeks of living in a dormitory. When it's over you finally get the fuck out of the God forsaken fucking Virginia countryside with a really formal diploma, calamine lotion for all the bug bites, and a gold brick."

"A gold brick?" I asked as I put on my pants.

"It's symbolic. The academy has a fucking six-mile hell run with obstacle course stations I truly believe were created by Satan himself. Everyone has to complete it. It fucking sucks. All the training in flat Miami cannot prepare you for the hills, ditches, and slopes of this fucking course. When you complete the run you get a gold-painted brick. They call it the Yellow Brick Road. Getting your brick tells everyone that you're either fucking brilliant or fucking stupid. Believe me, at my age the only reason I'd ever take up fucking running is just so I could hear heavy breathing again. The point is there are law enforcement commanders from all over the nation and the world who attend these fucking academy classes. At the academy you build bonds and connections. That's the fucking key, making the connections. I had a guy from the Carabinieri in my class. Pasquale Ferrante. Good guy. A little fucking hard to understand at first, but a good fucking guy. Anyway, now he's the Carabinieri's Director of Global Investigations. He called me. He wants my help on this. He's sending one of his agents here from Milan. The agent is flying in on *Alitalia* and gets in tomorrow. I need you to be at Miami International Airport to meet the agent."

"On Saturday?" I asked.

"*Saturfuckingday* Cade! As in, you work when the job dictates. Remember what I told you yesterday? Because I sure as fuck do. I said 'You think I don't fucking know where you work and what the fucking nature of your work is?' Well, this is the nature of your work. When I get the agent's name, I'll call you with it. I'll need you to assist the Carabinieri with whatever they need. Put whatever your plans are on hold for a few days. You hear me? If they need us to be a part of this case—which I'm sure they will—then *we are in.*"

"Understood."

"We've been through this before. I need to know that you understand."

"I understand," I said as I pulled the polo shirt over my head.

"Whatever they fucking need, you be their guy in Miami."

I nodded as I looked at the loaner Glock .40 in my holster. My drop-free spare magazines were still untouched in their pouches.

"You gonna be okay?" he asked me, genuine concern in his voice for just an instant.

"Like you said, we've been through this before. I'll be okay."

"Normally we like to provide a few days off, but we can use

you. Can you get back in the saddle tomorrow and be there for the Italians?"

"Yes."

Lieutenant Maddalone walked back in. "The guys from Miami Dade are here. Your car's parked on the center traffic circle in front of the ER." He tossed my car keys onto the bed.

"Two of them?" asked Brunson.

"Yes. Two of them. I told them you'd been medicated and sleeping most of the afternoon. They get it. They have witness statements. I don't think they plan to ask too much on this visit— they're still up to their eye sockets in this case. I think a few *hellos* and *how are yous'* are what they want. We all know it will be days, if not weeks, until they get down to a formal interview. Play the game, Cade. Be nice."

"I am nice," I protested.

Both Maddalone and Brunson chuckled at that as the Miami Dade Homicide detectives came in. They were supportive but also maintained professional detachment. The deep dive on how everything came to be was set aside for later. The main thing they needed to hear was me acknowledging that it was my gun that killed the deceased. I confirmed that irrefutable and obvious fact and their short visit was finished. They left with me assuring them I'd provide a formal statement in a few days after they waded through all the witness statements and forensic evidence. After they left, both Lieutenant Maddalone and Major Brunson departed with Brunson reminding me he'd notify me when he got more information about tomorrow.

"We'll let the nurse know you're ready to go and see if she can get you discharged."

A few minutes later a nurse who had the look of someone who's seen it all came into the curtained space with a folder under her left arm. I erroneously assumed it was too many sheets of paper to be related to me.

I was wrong.

The next ten minutes consisted of her informing me what each sheet of paper meant and how it all somehow related to me. After each recitation she proffered the sheet to me for my signature and a ridiculous demand that I write my initials across countless lines and boxes. When we were finished she reached in the front pocket of her scrubs and gave me two packets of pills.

"These are low dose anti-anxiety pills. They're prescribed, but it's up to you if you think you need them. If you choose to get your prescriptions filled these samples will carry you until you can get to the pharmacy. They're close to their expiration date so don't keep them for more than a month."

"That's okay. I occasionally live in the past."

"You should work on that," she said, never looking up from writing on her paperwork. "The main thing is the doctor wants you to drink plenty of fluids, like Gatorade."

"I've always thought Gatorade was created for exceptional athletes or hungover drunks who don't know how they even made it home. There isn't any in between. You either made the cover of Sports Illustrated or 'woke up in the county jail.'"

"The green and orange are the best flavors," she said, once again never looking up.

I slid down from the bed. She handed me copies of the papers and the prescription in handwriting I couldn't comprehend. She saw me gathering the Glock and shoulder holster in my arms.

"I cleaned your badge with peroxide and alcohol for you. It's just on the other side of the curtain on the stand."

I thanked her and said goodbye. I stepped past the curtain to retrieve my badge. It was clean, shiny, and gleaming—resting in a bed pan.

Chapter Seven

I STEPPED OUT OF the hospital and promptly threw my copy of the redundantly signed and overly initialized papers into the waste can by the automatic ER doors. Doctors Hospital and our health trust could argue over any future disputes without my involvement. I learned a few months earlier the importance of having a "go bag" with me at all times. It's called a go bag so that when a crisis occurs you can just grab the bag and go.

My car was parked exactly where they said it was. I retrieved my go bag from the trunk. In my bag I carry a change of clothing and other necessities when I find myself in need of being rapidly mobile. Extra pants, shirts, underwear, toiletries, some cash, and a Hartford Whalers baseball cap. After I misplaced my sunglasses a few months before, I started carrying an extra pair. I was okay for now with the BDU pants. They were a slate gray and looked more like a poor fashion choice rather than a poor career choice. I quickly took off the polo shirt festooned with the word "POLICE" in large script across the back and traded it for a long sleeve soft yellow Louis Phillipe shirt. I switched the Glock from the shoulder holster to a sleek leather pancake holster, concealing it against the small of my back under my shirt. The routine of being constantly prepared and ready to go made me feel more like myself after the hospital visit. Now my only obligation was to await a call from Major Brunson to provide me with the information about the Italian agent coming in tomorrow.

My cellphone had been turned off when they put me into the back of the Fire Rescue truck, and when I turned it on, I saw the phone's memory was full of too many incoming calls. I shrugged thinking it might be for the better. I'm happier when it's turned off anyway. Trying to garner whatever happiness I could muster for the day, I turned the phone off again and tossed it in with everything else. I didn't want it on the passenger seat with me. I just wasn't in the mood. Besides, Major Brunson wouldn't be calling until quite possibly tomorrow morning. I looked around at the roofline of the hospital. I saw the afternoon sliding away across the sky leaving color swatches of light glinting off of the parking garage. I debated going home or going somewhere else.

Somewhere else or anywhere else it made no difference to me.

There was still a gunman out there somewhere. He could be hiding anywhere. Somewhere. Anywhere.

He could be running. He could have gotten away in a waiting car. It didn't change the narrative. He was still out there. He was out there somewhere, and he needed to be caught not just anywhere but any way.

I drove out of the hospital and was facing the small concrete bridge that bisects Doctors Hospital and the University of Miami. Turning south would take me home. Turning north would take me back in the direction of the Biltmore Hotel.

Any investigator worth their salt will tell you that case solvability goes cold really quick. Tenacity and determined investigative techniques are necessary. I turned north back towards the Biltmore. For a moment I drove with my mind on autopilot. I didn't know why I should go back to the Biltmore Hotel or what use I could be. I drove anyway, asking myself if I was doing the right thing. Could I handle going back so soon to the hotel where I nearly died? Is this something *I* need to be involved in or is it something that needs *me* to be involved in? I drove without any discernable reflection. My mind was blank. I'd bet Dr. Rangela would say I was in shock and conducting myself in some sort of post-traumatic fugue.

A brain fog.

Repressed emotion.

Stagnant consciousness.

I imagined Dr. Rangela jotting all those terms down on her notepad as she sat amongst her fake plants. I didn't care. I truly didn't care. I was feeling null and void when it came to people's opinions, especially a psychologist who's paid by the hour for that reason alone.

The Biltmore Hotel is an impressive property that literally towers over the surrounding trees and homes. As I drove closer the Biltmore seemed even more majestic with its striking architecture, inspired by Italian, Moorish, and Spanish influences. The hotel's most prominent feature is the 315-foot tower rising from the center, modeled after the Giralda Tower in Seville. The storied hotel's opulence is accentuated by an abundance of hand-painted frescoes, travertine floors, marble columns, and meticulously landscaped gardens. All of that majesty fell away as I turned onto Anastasia Avenue. I was quickly overwhelmed. It was like media floodgates had opened and what poured out was every news truck in the Miami area. They looked like a child's toys plopped completely askew along the roadway, their uplink antennae protruding from the roof of each one like metal tinker toy rods. Each news truck had identical ineffective low safety rails encircling their roof edge. I'm sure they were intended for safety when it only served as a flimsy aluminum obstruction for a TV technician to stumble over. The raised antennae were all vying for equal stature and height as if competing with the Biltmore Tower for sky supremacy, only to be dwarfed by the hotel's ornate dominance.

I took deep breaths, sensory overload threatening to take over again as I slowly drove by the garishly painted news trucks with their bold channel numbers and wide striping. Naturally each truck came with a news reporter, many of them standing beside their truck, primping in the sideview mirror, awaiting their live shot. The full length of the avenue's grassy swale was full of unspooled cables, igloo coolers, humming generators, laid-aside equipment, and TV employees milling about. My car crawled through the suffocating congestion. I avoided the hotel's valet and maintained my previous policy of parking further away from the hotel in the west parking lot. I walked into the hotel retracing the same route I took in the morning.

As I entered the hotel everything appeared to be normal. It was as I came closer to the Granada Ballroom that I felt a sense of increasing intensity and congregated human vibrancy. I rounded the corner to find more police personnel, crime scene technicians, and lots of suits and pantsuits. No one was smiling. There were a few enterprising television network people who'd found their way to the edge of the area only to be held at bay to the opening of the corridor by crime scene tape strewn across two banquet chairs. I stood there looking none for the worse in my Gray BDUs and yellow shirt. I took in all the activity of what I can only describe as a teeming pool of humanity striding through and standing in a contained area. There were uniformed Miami Dade officers guarding the tape line. I was surprised to not see Coral Gables officers but given our department's smaller size as compared to the Miami Dade PD, it made sense to have our personnel attached to other duties. One huddle of suits stood off to the side. I stayed just outside the tape not saying anything.

"They won't let you in," said a distinctively female voice behind me.

I turned to see a very attractive woman, about five feet, six inches, with mid-shoulder blonde hair and a bright, dazzling smile. She wore black slacks and a chic black turtleneck under a stylish caramel colored mid-thigh, fitted jacket.

"I'm sorry, what?" I said.

"They aren't going to let you in," she repeated.

"Well..."

"No. I'm telling you they won't let you in," she said with a haute frostiness.

"I don't know if I really even want to go in there. But they might let me in if I ask nicely."

"Ask nicely?" she laughed. "Believe me, I tried every trick in the book."

"How many tricks are in the book, madam?" I asked her.

She quickly responded to my prostitution innuendo. "The media can be whores but that doesn't mean I'm one. Just because I'm in the media doesn't make me any less professional. I was just trying to save you the time. They will not let you in, Mr. Ask Nicely."

As she finished that sentence the huddle of suits broke apart. One of the suits was Tucson Lou. He saw me and made a direct line to me. He stopped a few feet from the crime scene tape telling the uniformed police officer to lift it.

"Cade, come on in. We could use you," he said, beckoning to me.

I dipped under the tape. When I straightened up I looked back at the woman.

"Sometimes I don't even have to ask," I said.

She eyed me with a mixture of suspicious contempt. I shook Tucson Lou's hand. He looked past me at the reporter on the other side of the tape.

"Let's go over here where we can talk." He motioned for me to follow him.

We stopped near a toppled-over palm tree in a decorative pot. The entire area was exactly the way it was discovered by the first arriving officers. Plates were still smashed in shattered pieces where shocked people dropped them. Chairs remained overturned from the panicking stampede of attendees fleeing the sounds of gun shots. The drapes had been completely pulled down from one large window and laid thickly crumpled on the floor.

"I'm surprised to see you. How are you doing? I heard it was a knock-down drag-out."

Tucson Lou was still holding it together but the sweat ring around his shirt collar and the rumpled aspects of his suit clearly spoke to his involvement in this fracas.

"Not exactly a knock-down drag-out, more of a serious 'Oh God' moment for sure. It was definitely rough," I said, trying to downplay it all.

He stayed quiet for a moment, studying me. I think he was contemplating what to say. Both of our lives had been greatly affected since he'd been introduced to me only this morning. Maybe he was still in some sort of disbelieving shock. I tried to steer him into a better head space.

"Tucson, I've been in this situation before..."

"You've killed someone in the line of duty before?" he asked me with inquisitive animation.

"Yes. More than once. It doesn't make today any easier. There will be a lot of investigations, inquiries, soul searching, reflection, and probably second guessing, but in the end I just have to make the best of a situation knowing that I'm still here and whoever he was, is not. He put himself—and by that I mean he put me...us—in this situation. Like my police major said earlier: We've been through this before. I just have to recognize that."

"Holy heck, what a mess. Have you ever seen anything like this?" he asked, glancing around at the disarray of the scene.

"In similar forms and incidents, yeah, sort of. Where were you when it went down?" I said.

"I was in the back. You ready for this? I drew post on the veranda. Right where the Italian guy got it! He asked me to switch with him forty minutes earlier. He was posted in the back of the room, said he was tired of New York City winters, and he wanted to feel the sun. I'm like, whatever I live in Arizona, no problem. So, we switched posts. That could have been me..." he said, his voice trailing off.

I listened to him and his own account of near-death. Like survivors from an airline crash we spent the next ten minutes comparing where we were when it all went down, what twist of fate had put us in those places, and a lot of discussion about "what could have been" and "if only."

"What do you know that you can tell me?" I asked.

"Better yet I can show you," he said.

I followed him into the Granada Ballroom. The grandeur and beauty of the room is stunning. Seven wide, smooth arches tower above the room with hand-crafted tray ceilings between them, all of them artisan painted. For such an expansive room, the attention to detail is mesmerizing, giving the feeling of standing in a Moroccan palace. Well, more exactly a Moroccan palace that's been strewn about by one of those gorillas in an American Tourister luggage commercial. Chairs were on their side and tossed across the parquet floor. Dishes and drinking glasses were upended on the hand-woven, intricate Persian carpets. The room looked like a beautiful smile marred by a black tooth. The panic that followed the shooting still lingered in the air. People must have been running for the exits, skittering behind the large columns in the room, diving behind every piece of furniture, and rolling underneath every upright table. I took in the vast room and tried to conjure the way the shooting unfolded.

"How..." I said as much to myself as I did to Tucson Lou.

"What we've been able to gather is our shooter is male. He was lingering in the back of the room right there by those tables." He pointed at three tables set in a wedge for journalists, with papers and press releases still stacked neatly on top.

I said, "So, while the other waiters were serving coffee and tending to the needs of the attendees, this guy was here in the back. What did he look like?"

"I gave him a decent look-over when I first got on post. He's about five-seven. Medium build. Dark hair, cut short. He wasn't completely unshaven, but he had a stubble coming on. Dark eyebrows. Bushy. You know? Like one of those Muppets." He looked away, voice softening. "I feel so guilty. Like I failed."

"Lou, you can't be feeling like that. It happened but it isn't anything to do with you or the team. That kind of guilt will eat you up over time," I said.

"They talked about mission failure at FLETC in Glynco. After my thirteen weeks in Georgia, I don't think I want to see Glynco, Atlanta, Athens...none of those Georgia cities. I've had enough of Georgia."

Lou was ruminating over his Secret Service academy time at the Federal Law Enforcement Training Center, often simply referred to as FLETC in Glynco, Georgia. I could see where his mind and the conversation were going. He was kicking the proverbial dog of today as well as his career because of this shooting. I needed to keep him from tumbling further down the well of woe he was creating for himself.

"Lou, this is one day. One day that didn't work out as planned. One day. The principal, *Positano*, is going to make a full recovery. Prayers and hopes are that the Carabinieri agent also recovers. We all want that Lou, but you can't think of this as some sort of lapse or failure on your part. Not now. Now we need you to focus. *We* need to focus. We need to get this guy and right this wrong. We need to be the ones. Help me to help us. Tell me what you're thinking. Tell me what makes you feel this way."

"His shoes," he said.

"His shoes? What about his shoes?"

"I should have known by his shoes," he said. I waited for him to elaborate.

"Every big hotel event I've ever been at, the staff gets a discount from a shoe company. The hotel encourages it. Helps with uniformity. Hotels with big fitness centers like they have here encourage staff to wear Reeboks because of the big *Step Reebok* fitness craze. No different here, I guess. Everyone was wearing black Reeboks...the entire staff. Busboys, servers, even the bartenders were all wearing black Reeboks."

"Okay," I said.

"Okay? No. It's not okay. Our shooter was wearing black Pumas.

Everyone else had Reeboks, he had Pumas. I should've picked up on that. I didn't. I failed."

"You should be taking a bow for your powers of observation, not chewing yourself up over this." I said.

"This'll be my Clint Hill moment. I just know it is," he said looking away as he studied the movements of the investigators in the room.

"Who's Clint Hill?"

"Special Agent Clint Hill. Dallas '63. He was the Secret Service agent that jumped onto the back of JFK's limousine trying to protect the president and Mrs. Kennedy. He spent years lamenting what he could have done differently. Did you ever see the interview he did for *60 Minutes* with Mike Wallace? It'll rip your guts out."

Two Miami Dade detectives walked by and Lou lowered his voice. "We were all in here. Me, Felton, and Borges. This shouldn't have happened."

"Where were they when this all went down?" I asked.

"Borges had the east side of the room by the windows. Felton was near the front. The Carabinieri wanted to be front and center. If you ask me, I say they wanted to be in the pictures so that when the photos hit the newspapers back in Italy, it will be as they like to say '*muro de azurro*'."

"What does that mean?"

"It means a 'wall of blue'. The Italians refer to themselves nationalistically as blue. More like azure to be exact."

"You speak Italian?" I asked.

"I was on the advance team when President Clinton went to Naples for the G-7 Summit in July of '94. Washington had all the assigned agents attend a six-week immersive language school. I can speak enough Italian to get myself in trouble but probably not enough to get out of trouble. With a name like Akicita there's no way I could pass for Italian."

"Akicita? What's that" I asked.

"Lakota. I'm nearly full-blooded Lakota Indian. Akicita means 'warrior.' I've been trying for three years to get reassigned to Chicago, but they keep holding me in Tucson. Somehow they think my Indian heritage can do more for them in the desert southwest, but the dumbasses don't realize that Lakota territory is closer to Chicago than Tucson."

A crime scene technician was setting up a laser level on a sturdy tripod. We stepped further off to the side to allow the technician ample room.

"Tell me more about today. You said our shooter is about five-seven. Medium build. Dark hair, cut short. Stubble. Dark, bushy eyebrows. What else can you tell me?" I asked him.

"He's left-handed."

"Left-handed?" I repeated.

"Yeah. He fired with his left hand. He ran up to the podium from the right side of the room. Like it was planned..."

"So, he wouldn't have to fire across his body," I interjected.

"Exactly. He went up the right side using the pillars of the room for partial concealment as he ran. At the last pillar he cut in and fired two rounds at the consulate, hitting him with both. He kept running, never stopped. He went straight out the door behind the podium. I was still getting my bearings on the consulate when I heard the shot from outside, where he shot the Carabinieri agent. Agent Felton and I did a quick Israeli peek. I saw the Carabinieri agent down. Jesus, there was blood everywhere. The other Italian agents went berserk, started yelling all at the same time in Italian. Everything from panic, to profanity, to praying."

"Weren't the doors behind the podium closed and locked?"

"They were supposed to be," he said.

"Let's retrace the shooter's steps," I said.

We walked to the back of the room where the three tables in a wedge jut out like the bow of a ship. Looking at the configuration, I could see the shooter positioned the tables to keep his view unobstructed. It was a natural flow. Reporters, attendees, and interested people picked up the press release and other documents then moved off to the side, away from the center point of the tables. This kept them from milling about in front of him. Tucson Lou and I walked along the right side of the room, staying in the eight-foot-wide space between the pillars and the wall. We walked halfway towards the podium and center stage area.

"Hold up. Just stay right here," I said.

I walked across the room past the tables all askew and the smattering of chairs on their sides. I stood where Agent Borges had been stationed and looked across the room. The obscuring pillars and refractive light cast by the tray ceilings diminished any clear view of Lou. From Borges' position there was no way he could have seen our shooter advancing on the Italian consulate. This was a detrimental and possibly deadly scenario that played out in real-time and real fast.

"What was that?" asked Lou as I walked back to him.

"I was curious if any of the protection detail on that side of the room could have seen our shooter running towards the consulate. From where I was standing, I think not. Plus, if the guy was running in the outer shadows, partially blocked by the pillars, I just don't see how even the front protection detail saw him until he was right up on the consulate."

"I saw him get up from where I was. He casually walked to the right side of the room. Staff were setting up the receiving area for afterwards, and a few were back and forth doing their stuff, you know? Back there in the rear. Tell ya the truth, I was thinking if it wrapped up maybe I could get my flight changed and be back to Arizona sooner. Boy, was I wrong about that. Agent Felton is in charge of this detail. We got a principal in the hospital. By Secret Service standards the detail is still ours. I was informed that I'm mandated to be here until we get a resolve. All of us are now on this. I'm not sure if I'll even see Arizona for at least a week."

"Where are you going to stay?" I asked.

"The Biltmore Hotel and the Treasury Department want this

settled quickly and quietly. They think having us here will do that. They booked a block of rooms for us and the Carabinieri at a big discount. I haven't even gotten my room key yet but I'm staying here somewhere."

We continued talking as we took slow, deliberate steps towards the staging area and the podium, scanning the carpet and walls for any clue or item that could help with the investigation. The stage area was a mess of used gauge bandages, their wrappings, blood-stained hotel towels, IV tubing, and other discarded medical litter. The paramedic's gurney wheels left a rolling tire impression in the long, congealed pool of blood. I didn't stand in the active crime scene directly behind the podium, but as close as I could to get a sense of what the consulate may have seen. The far right side of the room, which would have been on the consulate's left as he faced the gallery of people, was shadowy and dim due to the pillars and the low accent lighting. *He probably never saw it coming.*

Lou and I stayed rooted in place. Sometimes if you can't reason from the start, maybe you can reason from the end. We both turned our attention to the bank of doors at the rear of the stage. The same bank of doors that lead out to the veranda and golf course. The same bank of doors that the unfortunate Carabinieri agent had been standing on the other side of. The doors were identical, with the same glass inlays, the same hardware, the same overhead bunting, the same paint, even the same gauzy thin window coverings. Everything was the same.

"Were all these doors locked?" I asked Lou.

"They were supposed to be. We cleared it with the fire marshal in our briefing. So long as we had side and rear doors unlocked, we were good to go. We had an agent at or near every door."

"At or near?" I asked him, my wariness showing through in my voice.

"Our Behavioral Threat Assessment Unit put this at a mid-level threat. With our skeleton crew and working with the Carabinieri, this was a small, but well-trained detail. Door entrance and door proximity can be the same effectiveness when you have an outer perimeter to bolster the inside team."

"Well, somehow in this bank of doors our shooter knew the one that was unlocked. The one that someone intentionally left unlocked. We just have to figure out how the shooter knew which door to use to make his escape," I said.

"Me and some of the team from the back ran forward. I got hung up on a locked door as did some of the others. When the shots were fired the Carabinieri focused on the consulate and basically pig-piled on top of him. Once they knew one of their own was injured than it became a real fiasco. They were panic-stricken, moving back and forth between the consulate and their agent. One actually had rosary beads in his hand. I mean, seriously. Between all of them moving around and the commotion and treatment of the consulate, I'm surprised we even had a crime scene here to process."

"Let's focus on the doors. What set the unlocked door apart from the locked doors? Something had to make it stand out."

We examined the doors, noting each door handle position and the hinges. Everything looked exactly the same. There was nothing to set any one of the doors apart from the other. We stood back and studied the door the shooter fled through while a crime scene technician was on his knees measuring its opening. How did the shooter know this door would be the open one? How, on a full sprint with adrenaline, fear, and excitement all converging in his body at the same time, did he know this was the door to open? Did he count them? Did he know that somehow this particular door was the one that was unlocked? I couldn't see any discernible difference. I'm sure Tucson Lou was just as perplexed. The crime scene technician stood up from his kneeling position.

His pants at the knee were wet.

Chapter Eight

I STOPPED THE TECHNICIAN as he started to move away.

"Hey, how'd your knees get wet?" I asked him.

"I don't know, just happened when I kneeled here. Probably A.C. condensation leaking," he said with a shrug.

I got on my knees a few feet from the threshold of the door. It was dry. I looked up at the ceiling only to see there weren't any air conditioning vents above me. Lou leaned down with his hands on his knees like an offensive lineman in a football huddle. I scooched closer to the door. The carpet was still dry. I moved even closer—still dry. I was kneeling practically on the threshold with my face pressed against the door. Still, the carpet was dry.

Tucson Lou was bent at the waist, watching from behind me. I angled my leg back and leaned to one side, dropping my hand down to push down on the carpet and backing away from the door. There, my hand hit a cold wet spot. My hand was in a direct line with the right side of the door frame. I didn't want to mask what I was seeking so I used my left hand and put it in front of the left side of the door frame. It too was cold and wet. Both hands wet with cold water. Both hands had been in front of the door frame.

Backing away from the door, I ran my hands in straight lines along the carpet aligned with the door frames. The cold wet spot was only up near the frames. I stood up and looked at Tucson Lou.

"I think I might have an idea how the shooter knew what door to use."

"How?"

"Let's look at it from your job perspective. Your job is to protect the primary, right?" I said.

"Right," he answered.

"Do you hold doors open?"

"No."

"On a golf course, do you hold the pin flag?"

"No."

"You're at an event and someone drops a piece of cake on the floor, do you pick it up?"

"No."

"None of those things?" I asked.

"No."

"Why not?"

"My job is to protect the primary. Holding doors, picking up a dropped plate, detract from the mission. I need my hands available at all times and to stay focused on the primary."

"Assuming each of the Secret Service agents and the Carabinieri approach it the same way, would any one of you stoop down to pick up chunks of ice left here by the door?"

"No."

"Ice that probably was placed before the consulate entered the room but was still visible in its melting state when the suspect shot the consulate. Ice that was *placed* on each side of the door frame marking that it was unlocked. Ice that nobody noticed. Ice that soon after the shooting occurred melted into the carpet, concealing that it was used as a marker for the shooter to know what door to run through?"

Lou was astonished.

"Whoa. Are you serious?"

"It's wet, it's cold, and it's gone," I said.

"So, our shooter had definite inside help. Someone on premises before the event unlocked this door and put ice near the frame to signal what door to escape through. Unbelievable! I need to tell Felton."

"I'd hold off on that right now," I said.

"I *have* to tell him," he protested.

"Do you trust me?" I asked him, leaning in close. "Yeah. I mean damn, you killed that guy outside—"

"The main thing is *I was outside*," I said, cutting him off in mid-sentence. "You aren't from here. You're from Arizona. You got *put* here. You don't know these Carabinieri guys. You don't know these hotel workers. Hold this one in your pocket. It's not really relevant other than that it points us in the direction, I mean by theory, that there was inside help."

"Do you trust *me*?" he asked me.

"I trust no one. No offense. You were also inside here. It doesn't mean that anyone inside actually was an accomplice. He could have unlocked the door and placed the ice himself. Until we get through this, I'm down with you, Until I'm not. Right now, I'm in. Let's keep it going and hopefully we can catch this guy alone or together. I'm local. You're federal. Let's work what we can together and play to our strengths."

He gave thought to what I said. We both looked around the disrupted ballroom and knew we had done all we could in here. There were so many people dutifully toiling at their tasks, we were just in the way. The veranda where the Carabinieri agent was shot was being photographed and the technicians wanted everyone to stay clear of it. We left the ballroom, passing the few remaining bystanders who'd latched onto the tragedy like ghouls. I saw the same attractive blonde woman I'd seen when I entered. She looked at me contentiously, but I ignored her and kept walking with Lou. We went down to the lobby, and he went to the front desk. He spoke to the young, perky desk clerk, and she cheerfully provided him his room key.

"Let's get together later," I said as I shook his hand before he walked off to the elevator, leaving me at the front desk.

"Checking in, sir?" the polite front desk clerk asked me. The ornate table clock on the credenza behind her said 5:05pm.

"Maybe. My friend was just telling me the rate that he was provided and since we're both here I'd like to know if I can get the same rate for a one night stay," I said.

"One night?"

"One night. After all the commotion today, I think one night is all I can handle," I said.

At a little after 5pm, in my mind's eye I could picture the stagnant bumper-to-bumper traffic home. Major Brunson would be calling about the Italian Carabinieri agent flying in. I didn't want to face the ugly traffic going home only to face it tomorrow morning driving back this way to meet the agent at Miami International Airport. The desk clerk studied the computer screen closely and then with a beaming smile declared that for one night she did have a junior suite available at the deeply discounted Treasury Department rate. I provided her my undercover credit card and my undercover Florida driver's license. She read my undercover name on the license.

"Cade Daniels."

"Yes."

"Welcome Mr. Daniels. Room 1024. Elevators are around the corner. We're happy to have you with us on your stay here at the Biltmore Hotel. To your left is our bell stand. Arvin, our bell captain, can assist you with any bags you have. Here's a brochure of everything the wonderful Biltmore has to offer. I hope you enjoy your stay." She slid my keycard across the desk.

I thanked her kindly. With key in hand, I turned my attention to Arvin at the bell stand. I provided Arvin exact directions to my car in the west parking lot, my car key, and proffered a sincere, polite request that he bring my bag in the car's trunk up to room 1024 as I slid thirty dollars into his hand. He nodded with appreciative affirmation. I thanked him and decided to decompress a little at the aptly named Biltmore Bar.

A bar, by the way, I was more than passingly familiar with. I'd spent many boozy moments there. I took the wide carpeted staircase down to the lower level. The Biltmore Bar is decorated in a very masculine, storied motif with richly upholstered leather wingback chairs and couches, a matte black painted tin ceiling, and a deep mahogany wood bar adorned with accents in polished brass and marble. The walls of the drinking haven are exposed Chicago brick interspersed with subdued amber willow and thistle print wallpaper. Exotic black cherry ornate wood panels and pillars break up the steadiness of the wallpaper. Under the light from the gold gilded light fixtures, the entire bar has the appearance of a tasteful speakeasy. Curated artwork consists mostly of large black and white photographs of men in suits in urban city settings. There are enough carefully placed pictures of Al Capone to remind you that he was accused of directing the murder of a rival mobster in this very same hotel. In 1929 Thomas "Fatty" Walsh was viciously murdered in the hotel's 13th floor suite during a gambling dispute.

The bar was moderately full of people when I walked in. The pitch of their voices and their excited cadence led me to believe that the day's events were still the main topic of discussion. This was probably not the best place for me to try and assuage my thoughts of what transpired today. There was an open bar stool near the end of the bar adjacent to the wall. It had a little less light. I figured if I was going to be here I might as well be there, near the edginess of shadows. I settled into the ultra-comfortable padded high-back bar stool. I had a moment to look at the bar menu before a very affable bartender sauntered down to the end of the bar to serve me. I was expecting Deanna, who normally served me.

"Deanna here tonight?" I asked him.

"She's in Hawaii for the next month," he said. "Must be nice," I replied.

I ordered the black angus burger with provolone cheese, alongside a Jameson Irish Whiskey. Neat. As the bartender turned to leave I pressed a twenty-dollar bill in his hand.

"That's my don't-forget-me-at-the-end-of-the-bar business card. I know in my picture I look like Andrew Jackson, but the photographer told me it's just the lighting," I said.

He chuckled. "Yes sir, how could I forget a guy like you?" he said with a knowing smile.

The Jameson arrived promptly in an Acopa Gardenia Rocks glass. The artisan-etched glass felt comfortable in my hand. Sturdy. Something I hadn't felt like in the past few hours. I was feeling anything but sturdy. The tsunami of emotions was cresting the inner shoreline inside of me. My thoughts were like rising flood waters, at first slow and quiet, but rising, nonetheless. I couldn't be sure if Dr. Rangela and her little Socratic method of questioning and puncture-probing of my psyche was the crack in my own personal levee or if the erosion of this job had finally crackled and chipped the denial sandbags I'd been stacking against my heart.

Today was different.

It was different because it happened so fast. The arc of escalation went from a placid morning to a heart-assaulting pulsation of violence and death in seconds. Simultaneously a just-announced candidate for the premier of Italy and an Italian protection agent who only wanted to feel the sun on his face were both struck down by a phantom assassin's bullets. This was directed, intentional lethality towards the consulate and intended collateral murders of anyone who got in the way, including me. I had to remind myself of what I told Dr. Rangela.

"I feel like I was acting in the scope of my employment using the tools and training that were afforded me."

I needed to make this my mantra. Although told to Dr. Rangela in a cavalier manner may have suited the conversation yesterday, I needed to *know* it. I needed to believe it. I needed to believe that I acted completely correctly. It couldn't be just words. The taking of a life is never something I've relished, but if it's between my adversary and myself, my own survival exceeds any sympathy or even remorse I may feel. Today I had the briefest of moments to react.

"On the contrary I am full-on in the moment. Those instances you referred to were all in the moment. Actions and reactions."

Today was different than other police involved shootings I'd been involved in. The ambient sounds in the bar fluttered to a low murmur as I plunged deeper into my thoughts. The cascading moments of the day were chronologically presenting and then evaporating in my mind. Like cards being flipped from a deck, each thought, each moment held the briefest of anticipation and value until it was replaced by the next one, only to have the next one and the next one and the one after that all flit across my mind and then flip over. Seen, but now discarded. The value of memory even the fleeting and newest, is only in what we give it.

"Do you feel the detachment in your words equally detaches you from your emotions?"

I was adjusting myself to detach, not latch. To jettison away the things I could not change. I told Dr. Rangela that my life in the VIN unit was a smoking crater, a never ending cycle. And that's all.

An absolute smoking crater. Keep in mind that the crater of my life was often from things impacting me. Crashing into me. Targeting me. Hitting me. Colliding into me. There was an alleviation of thought and understanding of acceptance with that. The bullseye doesn't resent the arrow. It's the person that aimed the arrow, that intentionally chose to point the arrow, pulled back the bow, and hit the bullseye with the arrow. There lies the culprit. My life may have been a smoking crater, but it was the result of the onslaught of circumstance, calamity, and conscript. Sitting here in this comfortable bar, I felt like I'd been hit at and missed and shit at and hit.

I stared at the buttery, caramel-tinted Irish whiskey in the glass and knew this could very easily be the first of many this night. I didn't have to drive, and my bag was awaiting me upstairs in my room. I just needed to press the elevator button and have the good sense to get in it, and the even better sense to get out of it when it reached the tenth floor. The need to beat back the demons of the day was starting to surge and swell within me. I powered down the Jameson, feeling the warm rush coat my throat on its way down, and asked for a second round. The burger arrived hot and smelling as though it had been grilled on a wood fire. I was hungrier than I thought. I actually was surprised I had an appetite. I promised myself I wouldn't drink the second Jameson until I finished eating the burger. With eyes on the empty glass anxiously awaiting my second Jameson, I gobbled down the burger and fries.

The gathering people in the bar now becoming two and three deep. I was happy to have my seat faraway tucked in the nook of the bar, resplendent in anonymity. It was my intention to disengage from any thought process...and it was mission accomplished. Or so I thought.

Chapter Nine

ALMOST AS SOON as the calm that comes with drinking alone had settled upon me, the two seats beside me became open. I caught a glimpse of the stool next to me being pulled back from the bar.

"If I ask nicely, can I sit here?"

It was the same female voice from outside of the ballroom upstairs. Before I could even think of a way to respond she spoke again.

"Doesn't matter. I'm sitting here anyway," she said.

"I thought the hotel chased reporters off of the property," I said, barely glancing her way.

"They did."

"So how are you still here?" I asked.

"Let me indulge you as I let you in on a little secret. When everything went to hell today and every reporter from here to Chef Boyardee, Italy, started vying to be the first on the air, I went to the front desk and got a room. I'm a guest. They can't make me leave. I might be a correspondent, but now I'm what we call in the business 'embedded.' I've been filing stories from right inside here while every pumpkin festival queen-turned reporter is eating a Circle K sandwich sitting on the bumper of an uplink truck parked across the street. Advantage: me."

I'd just convinced myself to keep the past in the past, but I was sure lamenting the loss of peace from a minute ago.

"Arica Sweeten, Triad Broadcasting," she said, extending her hand.

"Nice to meet you, Erica," I said, trying to muster congeniality as I shook her hand.

"It's Arica. With an A. I can tell by your pronunciation you think it's Erica with an E, but's it's A-rica. Arica with an A."

"You actually mean two As," I said.

"Yes, I guess so. I haven't thought of it like that before. Two As."

"I have a friend named Gregg. Everyone asks him if it is two G's or one G. It's actually three G's," I said.

She looked at me expectantly.

I'd avoided the media my whole career and opted to introduce myself by my undercover name.

"I'm Cade. Cade Daniels."

"Cade Daniels. Nice to meet you, Cade Daniels."

She said my name twice in a poorly disguised attempt to try not to forget it. "Are you a grip?" she asked me.

"A grip?"

"You must be in the tech side of the business. A grip or gaffer or something. You're wearing BDU pants so you must be in the trade. I saw how they let you into the crime scene. You must do something. Dressed like that, I assumed you might be one of the below-the-line people. So, why'd they let you in the crime scene? Who are you?"

"I'm nobody. I was just..."

Just as I said those words the bartender came over, interrupting me as he placed the second Jameson in front of me.

"Can I get you something?" he asked Arica.

"What's the gentleman drinking?" she asked.

The bartender and I both answered nearly at the same time. "Jameson."

"I'll have a MacAllan 12 Year Double Cask. Separate ice in a chilled glass."

The bartender smiled and walked away to fill her drink order.

"I like my Scotch like I like my men. Twice my age and from Scotland," she said to me. I decided I wasn't going to wait for her drink to arrive and took a sip of own.

"Jameson. Oh, the dreaded Irish whiskey. It makes you feel single and see double," she said. I was already feeling tiresome of the intrusion.

"I like my whiskey like I like my women—kept in an oak barrel for three years with very little oxygen."

"You'd be much happier if you enjoyed your women and whiskey differently, I don't know like maybe...smoky, full bodied, leaving you gasping a little."

I studied her, trying to gauge what her angle was. She was even more attractive up close.

"You look like you could scare weak men," I said.

"Do I intimidate you, Cade?" she said.

"Not in the least. I'm afraid of fast-rising water, creaky roller-coasters, and a waitress at the Bagel Emporium named Irma. But not you."

"So, what do you do Cade? Why'd they let you in the crime scene?"

"They wanted my opinion on cleaning the carpet."

"I'm calling bullshit on that. C'mon, help a gal out. I could use a scoop here, something my rivals don't have. Tell me something. I can keep a secret. I promise."

"The carpets are fine; cleaning should be nothing out of the ordinary."

The bartender placed her Scotch in front of her next to a chilled glass filled with ice, placidly resting on a small plate.

Arica raised the scotch up and waited for me to raise my own glass and clink it against hers. A civil gesture of a toast. "A little détente for the moment. Salud," she said.

I swilled down the remainder of the Jameson. I was fortunate to catch the bartender's attention. I requested another.

"You seem like an experienced drinker," she said.

"Oh really? And you're not an experienced drinker? Miss Ice in a Separate Chilled Glass."

"Honey, I've sat on more bar stools then I have manicure chairs. I've seen more bartenders than I have priests, and I've probably had more drinks in airport lounges than should be legally allowed," she said

"Yeah? Well, I think my guardian angel drinks," I replied.

"Oh, I get it now. The suit with the noticeable, non-noticeable lapel pin was so eager to lift that crime scene tape today for you. You're one of them. Aren't you? Don't tell me. Let me guess."

"Guess what?" I asked her.

"Shhhh, let me see if I still got it. Let me guess." She squinted at me. "It's not FBI, you're not rigid enough. If you were Secret Service you'd be clean-cut with your own little lapel pin and talk into your sleeve. ATF! You're with the ATF! That's it, you're Alcohol Tobacco and Firearms!" she said triumphantly.

"ATF? Alcohol Tobacco & Firearms? Lady, here in Miami we call that a convenience store." She still looked at me with an expectant gaze. I tried to transition the conversation.

"You keep asking about me, but I think you really want to tell me about yourself. So, Arica, tell me how a vibrant, electric personality like you ends up at the Biltmore Hotel with Triad Broadcasting?"

She tilted her head slightly as if to say *Okay I'll play along.*

"We at Triad Broadcasting are new to the market. Triad sees a vast potential in news source and delivery via the new world-wide web. A whole new frontier. Truth be told, they hired a lot of us from other networks. Network television is very unkind to women as they age. I graduated from Vassar College with a degree in Political Science. I did an internship at ABC News in New York City. I learned a lot about cameras, news production, and how Diane Sawyer likes her coffee. I got a reporter stint with WLNE in Providence, Rhode Island. Actually, we were in New Bedford Massachusetts, but we covered Rhode Island. In '93 I got a Peabody Award for my exposé on divorce attorneys taking advantage of female clients. It was called '*A Matter of Trust.*' Did you see it?"

"Um. No. Sorry."

"Well from there I went back to ABC in New York and with my on-camera experience and my background in Political Science I became a London-based correspondent. I've been to sixty countries, witnessed two insurrections, attended three bullfights, and once fought off an angry howler monkey with an umbrella and an empty coffee can."

This was becoming too much information than I actually intended or wanted to hear. I tried to show interest and was tempted to ask about the coffee can and the howler monkey but quickly reasoned it was too much to take in, especially with the day I'd just endured. Arica finished off her drink and ordered another. I in turn threw back the Jameson quickly and ordered my fourth. The bartender cast a wary look but dutifully turned to fill our drink orders.

"Okay that's me. Now how about you?" she said.

"There isn't really much to say. I don't nearly have those cool experiences like you."

We both heard a voice from behind us call out my name.

"Cade!"

I turned in my seat and saw Secret Service Agent Felton a few feet behind us working his way through the crowd to get to us. I was stuck in my corner seat, unable to extricate myself to a more suitable place to have a conversation. When Agent Felton got to us, Arica sat silent. Her experience told her that there's information in eavesdropping.

"Hey Wayne," I said greeting the overworked and troubled agent.

"Damn, I didn't expect to see you in here. This has been a really bad day, Cade," he said with a haggard voice.

Arica still didn't say anything. I wanted to slink away in the worst way, but I was quite literally stuck in place. I tried to devise a delicate way to get Felton to stay quiet about the day in front of Arica. Before I could say anything, she put her hand on my thigh. That overtly forward gesture inferred to Felton she and I were together. I had a momentary brain freeze between removing her hand and telling Felton not to say anything in front of her. Felton fell for her cozy gesture like a widemouth bass gobbling a fishing worm in a Louisiana bayou.

"One of our agents may have some intel on that guy you killed today. You available to meet tomorrow morning at ten in the 19th Hole Bar and Grill? Stay by your phone. I'll call you. Seriously, I'm really surprised to see you after all the shit today," he said before looking around at the bustling crowd around the bar. "Damn, I could use a drink!"

"How about a twelve-year-old Scotch?" Arica offered as she lifted her newly poured drink from the bar and handed it to him.

"Are you sure?" he graciously asked.

She smugly nodded and he took her drink, swallowing it in one quick swoop. He winced and his eyes opened a little wider.

"Leaves you gasping a little, doesn't it?" she said slyly looking at me.

Chapter Ten

A GENT FELTON DISAPPEARED into the teeming bar crowd but not before earnestly advising me that Arica was "a keeper," and how "I'm a lucky man."

I looked at Arica. "We're about to find out if like you said, you really can keep a secret."

"What the actual fuck! This is incredible. You *killed* someone! Was it the guy we heard about that was shot outside? The one with the motorcycle?"

Her exuberance, although fostered in her professional nature to get right to the heart of news story, was still disconcerting.

"If it's any consolation, I didn't use an empty coffee can," I said.

"Who in all that fucking matters are you?" she said with bulging eyes.

"My name is Cade Taylor. I'm a police detective here in Miami."

"Cade Taylor. Not Cade Daniels. Well, that explains the caginess. Exactly what kind of a detective are you? Looking like you do I doubt you're giving Officer Friendly talks at the local elementary school."

"I'm a VIN detective. Vice Intelligence and Narcotics. I'm on a DEA task force and now that you know, do not—under any circumstances—blow my cover. I mean it. I shouldn't have even been here today," I muttered at the end.

"If you tell me what happened it makes it harder to inadvertently blow your cover. It's stumbling into some part of the story I was unaware of, that's how something accidentally comes out. It's when I don't *know* the story that something slips out. There's containment and control in knowledge. Feed me. Feed me," she implored with pleading animation.

I simmered with anger at Agent Felton for being foolish enough to call out to me and approach me in public. I guess watching elevators, running alongside limousines, and standing in the rain outside a patio door for a living will diminish understanding the need for confidentiality. I was compromised by his carelessness. I was now tasked with trying to say enough to satisfy her without saying too much. I could just see her standing in front of a camera.

"Arica Sweeten, Live from Coral Gables reporting for Triad Broadcasting. Sources have told me exclusively..."

I contemplated what to say as I very slowly spun my glass on the bar top, staring at the alcohol trembling as it turned. I felt it was better to let her ask the questions, and I could decide whether I wanted to answer.

"Arica, what do you want to know?"

"You said you shouldn't have even been here today. What did you mean by that?"

"This dignitary assignment isn't what I normally do. My supervisor was pissed at me for something stupid and this was a convenient way to augment manpower shortages and jam me a little by assigning me to the detail today," I answered.

"Manpower shortages? Is there a budgetary problem with the Secret Service? What does that mean exactly?"

"I think they're financed appropriately. Hell, a bunch of them are as you say 'embedded' here at the Biltmore with you. That ain't cheap. The Super Bowl demanded a lot of local, state, and federal resources. This impromptu press conference was unforeseen. With the lack of time for full planning I think it was staffed appropriately."

"Yet two people were shot, one of them being the Italian consulate. How do you reconcile that?" she asked.

Three drinks in with a fourth resting in front of me and I still had presence of mind to be vague and nondescript.

"Proper planning and implementing the plan are vital to a safe event, but there are times when even the best plans and an abundance of trained personnel may not stop a determined assassin. It's happened countless times before and it will happen again."

"Okay. Let's talk *today*. Who was the motorcyclist?"

"I don't know."

"What did he look like?"

"I don't know."

"Did he say anything?"

"I'm not sure what he said."

"Cade Taylor. You're purposely being avoidant. This isn't fair. I have a stinger of a story here, and it can be told with or without your input."

"I'm not avoiding anything. He had a full-face motorcycle helmet on. I never saw his face. Whatever he said, it sounded like 'move' or something, and as far as your 'stinger' of a story? He had a gun and tried to pull it. We fought over the gun, and I shot him. That's it. What's avoidant about that?"

"Do you think he's related to the assassination attempt of Baldassare Constantino?"

"Yes. He was geographically and chronologically present when Constantino and the Carabinieri agent were shot. I mean there's coincidence in the world but not like this."

"Geographically? Chronologically? I mean, can't that be said about all of us here today?" she asked.

"We were here with purpose. Don't you see? There is no coincidence everyone was here for a reason. Including the motorcyclist. Place and time. Don't you get it? Place and...time..."

My voice trailed off as I drifted deep into my own mind. That part of the brain that holds the things that don't seem to matter, where the important hides amongst the inconsequential.

"What is it, Cade? What are you thinking about?" she asked, leaning close to me.

"Time..." I muttered to myself. "It was getting heated between us. I was telling him to turn off the motorcycle, but he didn't even care. Like I wasn't there. Like I was an apparition or something. Then he did something strange."

"What?" she said with wide eyes locked on me.

"I'm all up in his business and he pulled back his shirt sleeve... and calmly glanced at his wristwatch. Like he was waiting for the bus or to board a plane."

"Like something scheduled?" she asked.

Then it dawned on me. The reason why the motorcycle was there in the east parking lot. The hit on Constantino was *scheduled*. It was timed. I was throwing off their schedule. He wanted to drive on the golf course because he was supposed to meet the shooter. He was supposed to pick up the shooter! The revelation had sunk in. The shooter knew what door to flee the scene from, and the motorcyclist was supposed to be waiting for him, the shooter's getaway driver. They hadn't counted on the Carabinieri agent being on the veranda. They were expecting someone else.

Someone else, like Tucson Lou!

I ardently caught the bartender's attention. I needed to put some quick distance between myself and Arica, and I needed to make a call or two in private. This was important. I charged the drinks to my room. I'd settle it tomorrow with our in-house task force accounts manager, Gary Fowler. I tried to not be rude or intentionally evasive, but she was the media, and I could *not* allow her to make the connection through any conversation she gleaned from me. That was an inside investigative deduction that wasn't ready for hungry journalists and the public. I slid off my barstool and wiggled away from her.

"Where are you going? We're just getting started!" she cried out.

"I have to make some calls. It was nice meeting you," I said as I started to push through the crowd.

Arica reached out and grabbed my arm as I was making my exit.

"Make some calls? Like what some 800 sex line? Nice to meet you? That sounds like something a miserable parent says to another miserable parent on parent-teacher night. What gives? You can't just up and leave, we have things to discuss!"

"Sorry, I gotta go," I said as I eased further away into the dense crowd.

"And I thought you were an experienced drinker!" she shouted at me.

"Arica, you know what they say about drinking. It's fun, then fun with problems, then just problems." I called back as I turned away.

I was absorbed by the crowd, the cavorting drinkers making it difficult, but I finally got out and away and to the bank of elevators. I pushed number ten on the panel and noticed that in utter defiance of architectural superstition, there was a button for the thirteenth floor.

Once in my room, I sat on the settee, breathed a sigh of relief to see my bag had made it up, and called the Coral Gables Police Department.

"Coral Gables Police and Fire, Operator J.R. Richards, how can I direct your call?"

"Jeanie Rae, this is Cade Taylor."

"Cade! You scared everyone half to death here. Oh my God! I'm so glad to hear your voice! We heard what happened, we're pulling all the 911 tapes right now for Major Brunson. It was absolutely crazy here, but my God, I'm so glad you're okay."

This was quite a surprise to me. Jeanie Rae was one of our most tenured communications operators. She was routinely not very thrilled when I called, because I was often looking for some sort of collation of information, distracting her from her already hectic workload.

"Thank you, Jeanie. Thank you very much. Jeanie, I'm sure you're super busy but I need to ask you something."

"What is it?"

"I know you're pulling and sorting the 911 calls from today, but can you see if there were any suspicious vehicle or suspicious persons calls near the Biltmore Hotel at the same time today?"

"You do realize I said *we are pulling* the calls. Not just me. There were so many it seemed like it would never end. Then all of the 'why are there helicopters over my house' calls. What a regal mess."

"I know, Jeanie. I know. Sorry."

"Let me see. You mean anything in patrol zones five or seven?"

"Yes."

"Hold on."

She came back on the line after a five-minute wait.

"Only one. It was at 1275 Mariola Court concerning an Enterprise rental box truck parked in front of the caller's house. We held that call for at least ninety minutes before we could get a unit there. The call notes says that when the unit arrived it was GOA. No report"

GOA. Gone On Arrival. Jeanie essentially was telling me that calls were backlogged with the shooting and by the time an officer arrived at 1275 Mariola Court the box truck was gone and there wasn't anything to report. More than likely the officer drove by, saw the truck was gone and kept driving. Never stopped and went about clearing more backlogged calls.

"Who was the complainant?"

"The call notes say the homeowner, Flora Hughes."

"Flora Hughes. 1275 Mariola Court," I repeated. "Thank you Jeanie."

I hung up. I took a shower and emerged from the steamy bathroom to plop right into bed, praying the Jameson would help me sleep.

THE NEXT MORNING, I awoke at 8am to sunlight streaming through the windows. I called the front desk and asked for a late checkout then got dressed and went downstairs. I kept a watchful eye out for Arica Sweeten but I thankfully didn't see her. I wound my way through the lower lobby and outside towards the pro shop. I could see Alan through the large pass-through window of the pro shop tending to his duties. After trashing the golf cart he gave me yesterday, I sure as heck wasn't going to ask him for another one. Besides, I just needed to borrow one for an hour or so. Walking amongst the bushes and pathways I was able to avoid Alan. I went to the row of neatly lined carts, awaiting the day's golfers. I was confident that I would find at least one golf cart with the keys in their ignition.

Luckily, the golf cart at the end of the line had a key in its ignition. Being furthest from the pro shop thwarted Alan seeing me take the golf cart without authorization. From the back of the hotel, I knew that Mariola Court was a straight line south across the golf course. I didn't know the layout of the golf course, but I did know how to drive south. I took off driving south and within minutes I was on the southern edge of the golf course. There were no fences or barriers. The border was just a few backyards and some intentionally planted trees along the boundary. 1275 Mariola Court has a property line of palm trees, easy to traverse, and Ficus trees separating it from the golf course. I drove through the gaps in the trees right up to the home's driveway. A tall woman was watering a bed of rose bushes outside.

"Mrs. Hughes? Are you Mrs. Hughes?"

She turned off the hose and cast a wary eye at me. My approaching her from a clearly identified Biltmore Hotel golf cart may have helped to put her at ease.

"Are you looking for your golf ball?" she said as I drew closer.

"No, ma'am. I'm Cade Taylor. I'm a detective from the Coral

Gables Police Department. You called yesterday about a suspicious truck," I said as I held out my badge and credentials for her to see.

"You don't look like any police officer I've ever seen, and I've seen plenty in my day."

"Yes ma'am, I've ruined a lot of family pictures, plenty in my day," I said, parroting her southern inflection.

She wasn't frightened but I could see she was mulling over whether to keep talking to me. I decided to try a softer approach.

"Mrs. Hughes, how long have you lived here? I'm sure you've seen a lot of changes in the city."

"Flora. You can call me Flora. I moved here from Gulfport, Mississippi in 1977. Did you know Bob Griese used to live just around the corner?"

Invoking the name of the former quarterback of the Miami Dolphins is a sure sign of resident pride and longevity.

"I think I heard that once before, Flora. There was a truck that concerned you yesterday. Can you tell me about that? What made you to decide to call the police?"

"The first thing that riled my dander was that they parked on our charcoal," she said.

"Your charcoal? Like a firepit?" I asked, confused.

"No! Charcoal was our black Lab! He died six years ago. He's buried over there by the curve at the tree line," she said gesturing towards the golf course.

I looked back towards the golf course. "I see. Anything else about them you can tell me?"

"They were flighty. Nervous-like. It was two of them. Dark hair. Carbon copies of each other. One of them sat in the driver's seat, the other one kept pacing around the truck looking towards the golf course. I thought they were landscapers because they had the back of the truck open and the ramp down. Not a liftgate but an actual ramp. I kept expecting them to roll out a lawnmower, but they never did. They were in a white and green truck."

"My people told me it was an Enterprise rental box truck," I said, hoping to nudge her narrative.

"I was getting to that. Yes, it was an Enterprise rental truck. I didn't see the license plate because of the ramp but the truck number is 6082."

Flora Hughes was turning out to be a very good witness.

Mariola Court curves around to the much busier Bird Road. This was an ideal spot to rendezvous with the shooter. Flora telling me that the ramp to the box truck was expectantly lowered reinforced my theory that the motorcyclist was supposed to pick up the shooter, make a mad dash across the golf course, and ride right up into the truck. Once inside the truck the occupants, the shooter, and the motorcyclist could be out to the much busier thoroughfare, Bird Road. They would have blended into the midday traffic and disappeared. It was almost foolproof. Except Major Brunson got a wild hare up his ass about me and by chance he stationed me right where the motorcyclist was intending to enter the golf course.

"The one in the driver's seat was acting really fidgety. He was smoking cigarettes," Flora went on. "He kept looking at some papers and glancing up, real impatient like. The one walking around was high strung, too. He started pitching a fit with the driver. They were arguing in some language I've never heard before. It wasn't Spanish. I've heard enough Spanish in my life to know. This was some sort of guttural speak. It sounded harsh and they were yelling at each other. The one guy was leaning in the truck window pointing his finger at the driver and the driver was yelling back at him. The driver got really hot, and he threw the papers at the other guy. The papers went all over the cab of the truck, and some went out the window. They both really lost their marbles when their friend came running up all out of breath and sweating."

Chapter Eleven

"I WANT TO BE sure I'm hearing you correctly. A *third* guy came running up to them, out of breath and sweating?" I asked her. She pushed her glasses up on her nose, her magnified eyes clearly telling me that she thought I was incapable of following the conversation.

"That's what I said. All bug-eyed and frantic too. Then it was like they all started talking at the same time. The driver smacked the outside of the truck door like it was a fat hog, he was yelling something and they all got in the cab like three pissed-off crammed sardines. They blasted out of here out to Bird Road."

"Other than what you told me, is there anything else?"

"Only this." She reached into the front pocket of her gardening smock.

She handed me a folded piece of paper.

"I picked it up after they left. It was one of the papers that flew out when they were arguing. I can't understand the scribble scratch, but litter bugs really irritate me. If you find these guys, are you going to fine them for littering?" she asked hopefully.

"At the very least. Thank you, Mrs. Hayes," I said as I got back into the golf cart. I was dying to read that piece of paper.

I drove slowly along the tree line, scanning the area the truck had been parked at. There weren't any cigarette butts or loose papers to be seen. I gave Mrs. Hayes a final goodbye wave and then darted back across the golf course to the pro shop. I slipped the golf cart right beside the last one in the line and quickly got out. I don't think Alan from the pro shop ever noticed it was gone. I made my way into the opulent hotel. The hotel was busier than when I'd left an hour ago. Then I got a call on my cellphone. I ducked into a quiet alcove and answered.

"Hello?"

"Cade, do you know that the older I get the more I understand why roosters just scream to start their fucking day?" Major Brunson said by way of greeting. "Coffee ain't cutting it anymore, I need to eat batteries. It's been a mell of a hess this morning with every news organization camped out in front of the station. I have everyone in on this fine Saturday morning and I do mean every fucking one! That hasn't helped my stellar shitty likability factor here but then again how much worse can it really fucking get? Charlene took my phone off the hook at 7am. Anyway, I heard back from my Italian friend. Their agent touches down at 10:20am. *Alitalia* flight 1970. Guy's name is Cosima Verratti. I figure by the time he gets off the plane, clears Customs and all that happy horseshit it'll be around 11am. Be there, in Customs lower level. Find this guy and bring him back to the Biltmore Hotel. They got him staying there with the other Carbozzinis."

"Carabinieri," I corrected him.

"Cade, I woke up in 'fuck you' mode. I have three fucking press conferences, a meeting with the damn city manager, which I suspect will be a long-winded balls-to-dick rant from Lieutenant Maddalone, and then I have to sit in on a conference call with the assistant Secret Service director. All before noon today. So, pardon the fuck out of me if I call some foreign agency by a name that sounds like a goddamn Baskin Robbins flavor!"

"Okay," I said.

"You got his name and flight, right?"

"*Alitalia* flight 1970. Cosima Verratti. I got it. I'll be there."

"I know your ass will be there, I just needed to hear that you got the information straight. Charlene and I will be too busy to fucking handhold you if you forget. I don't see myself having the time to meet him today. Show him a good time. Don't worry about the U.C. credit card, just use it for what you need. I don't know why I even fucking tell you that since you do it all the fucking time anyway."

"Will do," I said.

Click.

I couldn't be sure if he hung up on me or if we got disconnected so I immediately called him back. It rang once.

"What, Cade?" he said gruffly.

"We got cut off. Or did you just hang up on me?"

"I don't know. Did it sound like this?"

Click.

I looked at my cellphone. I shook my head and just grimaced.

I made a call to Gary Fowler, our financial administrator. Gary had a surfer mentality and a Finance MBA from Florida International University. He had a blond buzz-cut and the straightest, whitest teeth I think I've ever seen. He also had a barcode tattoo on the back of his neck, and another small tattoo of an "F" on his finger. He once confided in me that the F was meant for the many times he'd been given an unpleasant task; he'd wave his hand as if to say, "I got it," but the actual reason was a silent "I don't give a flying fuck. I always called him "Big G," and it had nothing to do with his size or girth—simply a nickname I coined after I heard a guy once call his buddy "Big G" in an elevator in Chicago. I dialed the VIN office. Ileana answered the phone.

"Veen."

"Good morning, Ileana. It's Cade. Sorry you're working on a Saturday."

"*Esto es una cagada! Digme.*" [This is a mess. Talk to me.]

"Is Gary there?"

"Two minutes. I have to check first the *desfibradora*," she said.

"The what?"

"The theen that hatchets paper! *Como si Dice?* Cheredder."

"You mean check the shredder?" I said

"Yes. Cheredder."

While waiting, I tried to figure how a paper shredder interfered with Ileana putting Gary on the phone. My wait was shorter than expected. Gary's voice on the phone was the only pleasant one I'd heard on my phone this morning.

"My Bromigo," he said.

"Hey Gary. I don't know if you heard—"

"Heard? Did I *hear*? Why do you think I'm sitting here instead of home? It's like a Hollywood backlot with all the TV people here. The streets are full of trucks. I had to dodge three of them putting microphones in my face on the way into the office. They think everyone who works here is a cop. They have no clue. Speaking of which, how ya doing, man?"

"I'm okay. Thanks. Yeah, I'm okay. Hey buddy, I got favors to ask."

"Shoot. No pun intended," he said.

"Can you call Enterprise Truck Leasing and see if they have a record of who has box truck 6082?"

"That should be easy. What else?" he asked.

"I have some charges at the Biltmore Hotel and some other places. Major Brunson is cool with it."

I chose to omit that fortunately my discussion with Major Brunson came post-dinner and drinks from last night.

"Cade, no one ever checks your charges. The money laundering cases alone brought in millions last year. No one cares," he said.

"Good to know. Didn't you once tell me you took German in college at FIU?"

"Yeah, what a mistake that was. I try and impress the Cuban waitresses at Fritz and Frantz Bierhouse. When I order they look at me all confused and stuff because none of them speak German. I have to resort to my broken Spanish to order *Jagerschnitzel mit spatzle* in this so called all-American town."

"I'm holding a piece of paper here with some language on it. I think it's Albanian. Can you try and translate it?" I said.

"Sure, Cade. They're only different countries and languages about 1200 miles from each other. But send me the paper since Germany has absolutely nothing to do with Albania."

His voice was dripping with sarcasm.

"I know, Gary. I know. I was hoping maybe you knew someone at the language school at FIU or the University of Miami, or you could do that Gary Fowler magic and find a way to translate the writing on this paper I'm holding."

"Fax it over. I'll see what I can do," he said.

"You're the best."

"I know," he said and hung up.

I walked up the wide regal staircase to the upper lobby and the front desk. The front desk clerk was kind enough to fax it to Gary. I sat in one of the lobby's plush chairs and looked at the writing on the paper. It was a handwritten numbered list of some sort.

1. Hidheni biçikletën 2. Thirrni Tazzi 3. Pastroni kamionin

4. Ndërroni telefonat 5. Hidhni Coldstream

It was getting near ten o'clock. Time was getting away from me. I got my bag from my room and went downstairs, ready to check out if the Italian agent was delayed or had plans. I still had concerns about Tucson Lou switching positions with the Italian agent—not something that happens often, especially without a supervisor's approval. This thought had me developing doubts about both Wayne Felton and Tucson Lou. I decided that I'd hold this information about the truck and piece of paper until I heard what they had to say at the morning meeting.

With bag in hand, I walked into the 19th Hole Bar and Grill a few minutes past ten. I was late. Agents Felton, Borges, Akicita, and another Secret Service type guy were sitting at an outside table with a noticeably empty seat. My seat. There was another noticeable seat, but it was at an adjacent table and filled by Arica Sweeten. I slowed my approach upon seeing her.

"Cade, we were just getting started," Felton called out to me as I approached them.

Although I was wearing sunglasses, I'm sure Arica could feel my eyes burning a hole in her.

"Good morning, darling," she said with devious perkiness.

Felton had his back to Arica's table. He hadn't noticed her at first. He looked over his shoulder and saw Arica when she spoke to me.

"Well, hello again, and good morning," he said, beaming at Arica.

Felton was obviously still taken by Arica's arresting good looks and engaging demeanor from the night before. This was a quandary I did not want to be a part of. She was too close to be ignored and clearly not invited to this meeting. She was also too close not to overhear what we were discussing. I was in a bind. I couldn't tell the agents that Arica was the press, determined to gather whatever information she could from us. I'd appear complicit. Wayne Felton would surely not recall that he compromised me last night at the bar. The rest of them would think I brought Arica along with me this morning. Felton would also not recall what he said right in front of Arica last night.

"One of our agents may have some intel on that guy you killed today. You be available tomorrow morning at ten at the 19th Hole Bar and Grill?"

Arica picked up on that invite and decided to invite herself. This was not good. I knew before I showed up for the meeting that I'd have to leave early to pick up Agent Cosima Verratti. Early is early, right? Whether it's ten minutes or twenty-five, I would still have to leave. I saw the proverbial scoreboard in my mind, and I decided to punt.

"Good morning, everyone. I wanted to personally come down and let you know that regrettably, I can't stay for the meeting. Can I catch up with one of you later? I'm so sorry, but duty calls." I quickly turned my attention to Arica at the next table. "Right, sweetheart?"

I just as quickly turned to the table of Secret Service agents. "Sadly, something that she has had to endure during our whole relationship," I said as I pulled out Arica's chair and helped her rise from the table. "They have our car waiting at the valet stand, we need to hurry." I clutched her arm and guided her towards the exit.

When we'd cleared the exit of the restaurant I blasted her.

"What the hell do you think you're doing?

"My job!" she snapped back.

"Learn to do your job without getting in the way of my job!" I yelled. "I don't need you to do my job. Need I remind you that I earned—"

I cut her off. "—a Peabody Award. I heard you last night. I'm not some slimy Rhode Island divorce attorney—"

"No. You're a slimy—"

"A slimy what? What?" She stopped and looked at me with childlike petulance. I was trying to maintain my composure. "A slimy what? A slimy cop? A slimy Miami detective? Is that what you want to say? Really? After the day I had yesterday you have the unmitigated gall to even think that?"

"Cade. It's not what I meant," she pleaded.

"I need to take care of something. I have to do my own job. My job! You know the one without theater lights and makeup! The one that creates something for you to report about. The kind of job where decisions aren't based on TV ratings. The kind of job that can have terrible consequences. Listen lady, I'm involved here way more than your viewer's curiosities. So, how about you conveniently find a way to get out of my way," I said.

I stepped back and before she could reply I'd turned on my heels and headed for the exit. Frustrated, and more than a little disappointed, I tossed my go bag in the trunk and drove to the airport where, as directed, I waited in Customs for agent Cosima Verratti.

I grabbed an envelope from one of the rental car counters in the baggage section. I was challenged for space but managed to write COSIMA on it. I held the envelope near my chest as people funneled past me, scanning the crowd for what I suspected the agent looked like. He was probably travel-weary, bleary-eyed, and unshaven from the long international flight. I felt sheepish as each person that walked by looked at the envelope and continued walking, as if expecting some divine transportation miracle, a limousine awaiting them instead of their own rat trap of a car parked in the parking lot. The Customs area was clearing out and the amount of people walking by was dwindling.

This was becoming a zero-sum game that Major Brunson had put me in. I was losing valuable time waiting on this no-show Carabinieri agent. Their misdirection of me started as soon as they sent me to Dr. Rangela—a punitive decision by Major Brunson that put me quite literally dead center in this catastrophic case. Now we got one dead, a Carabinieri agent fighting for his life in a trauma center, and one Italian consulate whose aspirations to be the Premier of Italy were either politically hero or zero because of this shooting. Not to mention the gunman with at least two confederates in an Enterprise rental truck and a snooping TV reporter all in the mix. Plus, my suspicions about Tucson Lou switching his post and avoiding being shot were gnawing at my brain. All I could think was *there ya go Cade, welcome to the party!*

The agent never showed. A definite time-wasting, GOA moment for me. I turned to look for a garbage can to throw my handwritten Cosima sign in when I bumped into a startlingly attractive woman. She had green eyes and raven black hair that cascaded past her shoulders over a chic violet Dolce and Gabbana jacket. She saw the sign in my hand and with an Italian accent as captivating as a gentle breeze from the Amalfi Coast said:

"Cosima? Is that for me?"

Chapter Twelve

S HE WAS NOT anything like I thought Agent Cosima Verratti would look like. She didn't appear to be travel-weary, bleary-eyed, and was very obviously not a man. I was momentarily caught off guard but reminded myself to play it cool and keep my sensibilities.

"Verratti?" I asked her.

"Yes. I am Cosima Verratti. Are you Cade Taylor?"

Her accent was very captivating. I answered her and said the first thing that came to my mind.

"Welcome to America. You speak English?"

"This part of America is new to me. I obviously speak English. I also speak Sicilian and Friulian," she said.

"Okay," I squeaked out.

"And you? Do you speak English?" she kidded me.

"Only when I have to."

"Not a big communicator I see." She laughed.

She'd brought two medium-sized black bags which she allowed me to carry for her to the car. "You said this part of America is new to you. What parts of America have you been to?"

"I've been to New York City, Chicago, and Boston. All because of case work."

"What did you think of those cities?" I asked her.

"I liked them I just didn't see a whole lot because of my work," she said.

We stepped out into blue skies, the warm bright Miami sunshine, and tall green palm trees.

"This is gorgeous," she said gazing at the sky with a soft smile on her red lips.

"It's still just the airport. Wait until you see the rest of Miami," I said, even smiling myself. I placed her bags in the trunk.

"Wait," she said, and unzipped one of her black bags. She pulled out a small aluminum gun case, retrieving a Berretta 92FS. She loaded it with a full magazine and slipped it into a Bianchi M12 holster on her belt under the jacket.

"I'm here to work and I'm in Miami! I shouldn't have to explain," she said with an impish grin.

As we left the airport, I opened the sunroof flooding the car with dazzling sunlight. She was marveling at the deep greenery of Miami and the vibrant tropical hues.

"I don't want to appear bossy. I'm just very decision oriented. It was a long flight; can we sample some of the authentic Cuban cuisine I hear so much about?"

It was Saturday. Versailles and Sergio's Cuban restaurants would be full of tour buses and gawking out-of-towners. Cosima fit all of that criteria, but I opted for a smaller, lesser-known place. Within minutes of leaving the airport we walked through the doors of *Caribe*. The long- established Cuban café was filled with mostly local clientele, all speaking Spanish. Cosima asked me to order for her as she was not familiar with any of the dishes on the menu. As we waited for our meals she told me about life in Milan. She said the agent that was shot was from their Rome office and that she had never met him but nonetheless was determined to assist in the investigation, as she said, to her "utmost." I briefed her on the events that transpired when the agent and consulate were shot. Most of it she was familiar with from reading the investigators' notes and reports on the plane.

I felt it best to delay mentioning the Enterprise box truck until I spoke to the Secret Service. It might disrupt everyone if they knew that I could have informed them this morning but withheld it only to tell the Carabinieri first. We had a delicious lunch of *boliche asado* and *pechugo de polo a la plancha*. Cosima raved about her first taste of Cuban food. She was very engaging and asked a lot of questions about Miami and my background. We finished lunch and were soon on our way towards the Biltmore Hotel.

"I think you'll really like the Biltmore; it's a very Italian and Spanish-inspired hotel."

"I guess we will see, won't we?" she said.

It was then that my cellphone rang. It was Lieutenant Maddalone. I was surprised to hear from him on a Saturday. I answered the phone with the speaker on.

"Cade, we got notification about the motorcyclist you put down. We don't have an exact I.D. yet but get this...his prints came back to one of our unsolved cases from three years ago!"

"What? What case?"

"11027 Girasol Avenue. The home invasion. Don't you remember?"

"I'm in VIN. I miss a lot of our in-house cases. What happened?"

"Some big-time banker and his family live there. One early morning four guys broke in and held the family hostage. Two of the robbers took the banker to his bank and forced him to take a boat load of money from the vault. After they got the cash, they released him down in Homestead somewhere. The rest of the crew left the home. The family was unharmed."

"What are the names of the victims?" I asked.

"Matthew and Janice Gordon."

"Do they still live at 11027 Girasol Avenue?" I asked.

"Far as I know. The print from the guy was found on the kitchen faucet and the gate entry button, so he was definitely there, inside and outside the house. The medical examiner's still working on getting more identification. I don't need to tell you that your guy's cause of death was sudden, unforeseen lead poisoning. My words not the M.E.'s."

"Okay. Thanks. I'll brief the others when I meet with them later today."

I hung up the phone. Cosima appeared to be detached looking at the scenery outside of the car window. "We should be at the Biltmore in a few minutes. I'm sure you're anxious to get checked in and relax from your trip," I said.

Without missing a beat and with a definitive resolve in her voice she let me know that was not what she wanted to do. She repeated her statement from earlier.

"I'm here to work," she said.

I glanced at her, still a little surprised by her candor when it came to her job. She noticed.

"Would you want to go to a hotel and relax if one of your designated Consulates had been shot and one of your agents was nearly killed? Take me to this Girasol he mentioned. It's a good opportunity to talk with the homeowners. They might be home on a Saturday."

From an investigative perspective, she was correct. I knew that I'd be paying a visit to the Gordon household at some point today. Having Cosima with me would just be an additional set of eyes and ears to my visit. I altered my route and continued driving south, becoming even more lush and green as we reached Old Cutler Road. I could sense that Cosima had heard about the scenery in Miami but was probably not expecting such eye-popping natural beauty. Coral rock walls, thick Banyan trees, majestic palm trees all filled the panorama as I drove further south. Girasol Avenue was one of the newer streets in Coral Gables. The developer of the smattering of homes on Girasol Avenue was one of the few who provided a generous budget for the planting of mature native trees and flowering shrubbery. The result was that Girasol Avenue was one of the prettiest places to live in Coral Gables.

The house was halfway down the avenue with a center island splitting the road right in front it. A weathered, wrought iron fence lodged into a low coral rock wall rimmed the entire property. The eight-foot ornate front gate was open as we pulled up in front of the house where an older woman was in the courtyard hosing down the expensive coral rock driveway. Neat, hand- trimmed Zoysa grass created a two-inch buffer between each slab of coral rock. Cosima and I got out of the car. The woman was a little leery of me. She cut off the hose and stopped spraying the driveway. Cosima being with me helped to ease the woman's concern.

"Mrs. Gordon?" I asked her.

"*Adentro.*"

"She says she's inside," I told Cosima.

"Yes. I heard her. Spanish and Italian are very similar in many ways," she said.

We went to the front door and rang the doorbell. The front doors were tall and ornate with customized beveled glass and decorative black iron detailing. I saw the shape of a woman approaching the door. She became more clearly visible as she approached the door. I already was holding my badge and credentials up at eye-level when she opened it.

"Mrs. Gordon?" I asked.

Mrs. Gordon's natural beauty had stayed with her without inter-ruption. Her blonde mid-shoulder hair was cut in a fashionable style, and she wore tailored slacks and an eye-catching orange blouse. She was holding a cellphone in one hand. She told the person on the other end to hold on, then she asked me "Yes?"

"Mrs. Gordon, I'm Cade Taylor and this is Cosima Verratti. I'm a detective with the Coral Gables Police. I was hoping you'd have a few minutes to talk with us."

Confusion knitted her brows together. She put the phone to her ear, looking at us across the open threshold of her house.

"Did you send the police here?" she said into the phone. After a moment: "Well, they're here. Yup. Standing right in front of me. You're not scaring me," she said and hung up.

"I'm sorry, who are you again?" she said with slight agitation in her voice.

"Cade Taylor. I'm a detective with Coral Gables. I was hoping to speak with you about the incident that occurred here four years ago."

"Four years ago? You mean the robbery?" she asked me. "Yes ma'am. The home invasion robbery."

"Oh. I'm pretty sure I told the police everything I could then," she said.

"I'm sure you did but sometimes a revisit helps unlock something missing. This is still an unsolved case for us," I said.

"I guess so." She stepped aside, allowing us to enter.

The house was very tastefully furnished. On a credenza just inside of the front door were pictures of her and what I gathered were her three children at various stages of their lives in expensive frames. The home was comfortable, with a loving, calming aura about it. She led us to an expansive, tall-ceilinged room. Columns of sunlight streamed in from the row of transom windows. Curated artwork creating a tropical aesthetic adorned the walls. The room looked out over a custom swimming pool, decorated with ornate plaster koi fish, water pouring from their mouths back into the pool with a nearly inaudible gurgle. She motioned us to sit on a love seat, giving us a mesmerizing view of the pool. The entire house felt serene and peaceful. I could tell Cosima was definitely feeling the same way.

"Mrs. Gordon, thank you for allowing us to be here with you. Can you tell me what you remember about that morning?"

She released a short breath.

"It was a normal morning. Same as always. The kids were younger. They're in their teens now. It was breakfast, backpacks, carpooling for school. You know? A regular day. My husband was getting dressed for work, still upstairs. There was a knock...no...wait... it was the doorbell. Yes. I heard the doorbell. You met Esperanza, my housekeeper outside? She wasn't here then, so I answered the door. I don't answer the door now but since today she was outside I answered for you."

"You heard the doorbell, and you answered it," I confirmed.

"Yes. I opened the door and no sooner had I turned the latch when it was pushed hard against me. The first guy put his hand over my mouth, pushed me up against the wall right by that umbrella stand." she said motioning towards the foyer. "It really hurt. I mean, he really shoved me. Two of the other guys went right upstairs. Real quick-like. Ever see that Dr. Seus cartoon where Thing 1 and Thing 2 run around the house? It was like that. They ran up the stairs like rockets. I couldn't warn Matthew. I couldn't say anything, the guy had my whole jaw and mouth covered by his hand. He was right up close to me.

"Matthew? Your husband?" asked Cosima.

"Yes. Like I said, Matthew was upstairs. I heard a struggle and some shouting and then nothing. I started crying. I was so scared for our children. The kids were in the kitchen eating cereal. I thought these filthy marauders had killed Matthew. One of the two with me had a can of black spray paint. The police...you guys ...said the can of spray paint was to black out our surveillance cameras, but we didn't have any then. There's a whole system now! It seemed like forever, but it must have been rather quick. They came down with Matthew. He had duct tape over his mouth and his hands tied with those plastic things... what are they zippy ties?"

"Zip ties. Where his hands bound in front of him or behind his back?" I asked her.

"In front."

"What happened next, Mrs. Gordon?"

She put her hand to her forehead and squeezed her eyes shut. "I'm sorry, I'm a little loopy about remembering everything. I didn't sleep well last night. We have a health crisis here with a dear friend and it's taking a lot out of me. Where were we?"

"You were telling us that they had brough your husband downstairs," I said.

"Oh right. They were shoving him really hard towards the front door. I was able to reach out with my hand and I tried to grab him by his suit jacket, I just wanted to keep him here. We needed him here. Me and the children," she said as the memory started to make tears well in her eyes.

Cosima stood up and sat on the loveseat next to Mrs. Gordon. She put her hand on top of Mrs. Gordon's hand.

"Why are you both here now?" she asked us again.

"Mrs. Gordon, we don't have a positive identification, but we believe that one of the men who was here, who terrorized you and your family, is deceased. His fingerprints matched one of the fingerprints gathered here by our crime scene technicians."

"One of the bastards that left with Matthew?" she asked.

"With what you've told us. I think it may be one of the ones who stayed here with you and the children. The fingerprint was found on your kitchen faucet."

"So, you know the story."

"Somewhat. I was given a few of the details but it would be beneficial to hear anything you have to say," I said.

"Detective, what would you like me to tell you? Can you imagine how violated we all felt? My youngest was still in his PJs! He thought these animals were friends of ours at first. The way they looked at me...it was disgusting! The way one of them looked at our eleven-year-old daughter was beyond reprehensible! I wanted to pull his eyes out of his head. They herded us all into this exact room. Right here! I sat right on that very couch with my kids while one of them stood over us. The other kept pacing up and down holding a phone. I wanted to break that phone over his head."

"Can you tell us about them?" asked Cosima softly.

"You want me to regale you with the worst memory and time of my life? Sure, why not," she said snippily. "They weren't American, and they weren't Spanish. It was like Armenian or something."

"Could they have been Albanian?" I asked nudging her.

"I don't know, I just know they weren't American or Spanish," she said with exasperation starting to set in her voice. "The hours seemed like days. The one holding the phone received a call. He smiled and laughed. I remember he did this little jig like he won a prize or something. I was so scared. I thought at any moment they were going to kill us all. When he got that call I thought here it comes, no witnesses, they're going to kill us..." Her eyes misted again as her voice trailed off.

"Then what happened?"

"They took us upstairs and shoved us into my master bedroom closet. They tied the door shut with nylon rope. They ran the rope all the way to the bathroom and tied it tight to the drainpipe under the vanity. It took about forty-five minutes for me to get us out of the closet."

"How where you able to get out?" I asked her.

"I used the heels of three of my boots to bash out the doorknob. The nylon rope was still tied to it and holding it in place, but I got the door open enough to push my youngest through. He ran and got scissors, and we cut the nylon then ran downstairs and outside. I didn't know if they were still in the house. We ran to our neighbor and called the police."

"And Matthew? What about him?" I asked.

"They took him to a branch of the bank on U.S.1 in Pinecrest. Matthew was chairman of the bank. He had a master access code to the vault. They forced him into the bank an hour before they opened, when there weren't any employees there. Matthew was told if he didn't do exactly like they said the two men here would kill us. Matthew turned off the alarms, went in the vault and gave them all the vault's cash."

"Do you know how much money they took from the vault?"

"The FBI was concerned about copycat crimes. The bank didn't want the bad press. The official response was 200,000. But I know it was more like six million."

Six million? "Mrs. Gordon, is your husband Matthew available to talk with us?" She hesitated and then simply said:

"Matthew is not here anymore."

Chapter Thirteen

"I'M SORRY. DID you say he's not here anymore?" I asked.

"Yes."

"As in you're divorced?"

"No. As in he left. He left me, and he left our family. He is not here anymore."

"Mrs. Gordon, I feel that this may be a bit personal, but can you help me understand what you mean? Where is he?"

"I wish I knew. It would be so much easier on me and especially the children if they knew where their father was. This robbery affected Matthew deeply. He felt hopeless to protect us, he blamed himself for not having taken stronger precautions to make us safer. He blamed himself for not having more stringent policies at the bank to prevent something like that happening. He eroded. As a man, he just fell into himself. He was never the same after that day. He mentally went into a decline that he never seemed to get out of."

"It must have been so difficult for you. How long was this mental decline?" asked Cosima.

"At first, he took time off from the bank. The bank wanted him back. They told him the money was FDIC insured. They said they understood. They said *he* was the steward they wanted leading them. Except he wasn't feeling like a leader. He felt...desolate. He'd just sit right there on that couch, staring out at the yard and the bushes, just spinning. He was in a deep spin. He kept talking about Australia for some reason. It was Australia this and Australia that. Constantly obsessing about Australia. After five months I came home from a meeting, and he was gone."

"Gone?"

"Gone!" she blurted angrily. "Yes, do I need to spell it out? Gone. He left us," she said with ire rising in her voice.

"Do you know the last day you saw him?" I asked her.

"April 19th, 1995. Six-thirty in the morning. I'll never forget that day. The kids were all at a sleepaway camp for spring break. I was hoping we could rekindle our marriage, our love for each other. He was still obsessing about Australia. 'Down under' this and 'down under' that, it's all he ever talked about. He ordered maps, brochures, travel catalogs, anything Australia. Obsessed! He said it was his destiny. One night he even asked the manager at the Outback Steakhouse if he could tell him about Australia. Can you imagine that? The chairman of an international bank thinking the manager at a restaurant chain could effectively talk about a country a world away. He was losing it in so many ways."

I tried to be sensitive to her, not upset her anymore, but there was more to this, I could feel it.

"You said you came home from a meeting, and he was gone. What time did you come home from the meeting?" I asked her.

"Is that really relevant?"

"Yes, I can go check with the airlines and see if there were any feeder connectors from Miami to Los Angeles or San Francisco that continued on to Sydney or Melbourne," I answered.

"Oh. Right. Yes of course. Please pardon my irritation, it's just a lot of emotion going back and trying to recall sad times. I didn't sleep much last night. This family friend being ill has me all off kilter. Back then I was the vice chairperson for the New Republicans of Miami Dade. My second four-year term. We were hosting a 9am brunch on Grove Isle. Bob Dole was speaking, and we were excited about the rumors that Jack Kemp would be with him on the Republican ticket. Kemp was the quarterback of the Buffalo Bills in the 1960s and he was still very dashing. We had breakout sessions after the brunch. It was nearly a full day. I arrived at 7am. We had to get wanded in by security. They even checked my purse. Can you imagine? I got home about 7 that night and the house was empty. Matthew was gone."

"If you had to guess, what do you think happened to Matthew? Or better yet was there a specific place in Australia that he spoke of?"

"I don't know, everywhere on the continent..." she said with a sad, audible exhale. "I thought he'd reach out on our son, Keaton's birthday, but he never did. The not knowing is slowly killing all of us. It's total radio silence. He's like a submarine running silent under the surface. I still console myself that he's in Australia. That's what I tell myself. To me he's down under and I hope he's found his peace."

We sat in silence as I struggled for the right words to say to her. Cosima sensed my wavering, and she stepped in.

"Mrs. Gordon. Thank you for seeing us today," she said throwing a hint to me that we had run as far as we could with this interview.

"Detective. I have something for you" Mrs. Gordon said as she rose up from the loveseat.

She went to a closet under the staircase. We could hear her moving some things around. She came back with a storage box, oddly enough often called a banker's box. It had the word "Oz" written on the lid.

"If this helps in any way, I want you to have it. In this box are all of the pamphlets, travel inquiries, brochures, whatever. All the stuff Matthew sent away for about Australia and had delivered here. It's all there. I don't even know why I saved it, but I guess I just thought it would magically lead him back to us. Maybe you'll find something in it I couldn't."

"Thank you. I'll be sure it gets returned to you."

We started to make our exit but not before I asked her about the phone call we interrupted when we arrived.

"Mrs. Gordon, when you opened the door, you thought that

whoever you were on the phone with had sent us. Is that something I can help you with?"

"I doubt it. It's actually the city. More precisely, Building and Zoning. They are complete Nazis about everything. I've been fighting with them about permits, it seems like forever. They keep claiming we do or don't have the right inspections, do or don't have the approved plans... It's a constant battle with Coral Gables or as I call them, Immoral Gables."

"Well, yes, like they say, you can't fight city hall. I wish you luck with that." She opened the door for us.

She had walked us to the front door and opened it. We were now at the open front door.

Cosima smiled and asked, "Mrs. Gordon, I must say that blouse you're wearing is beautiful. You must tell me where you got it."

"It's a Robert Varga. I call him Bobby. He's one of my select designers."

"Varga? Is he Italian?"

"Well, if you count Trenton, New Jersey as part of Italy I guess he could be. Bobby brings me fabric samples and sketches and then flies back to New Jersey and does his magic. Each piece is an original Robert Varga and one of a kind."

"No. I know Italy and Trenton, New Jersey is not in Italy," chuckled Cosima.

"She definitely knows Italy. Cosima is with me for today, but she's actually a member of the Carabinieri, the Italian National Police," I said.

"The Italian police? I thought you were both the Coral Gables Police?"

"Agent Verratti is on loan to us for a few days."

"On loan? What does that mean? Why the Italian police? This is a surprise."

I glanced at Cosima, whose eyes I could feel on me, worried I'd say too much. But if I said too much, maybe Mrs. Gordon would talk some more. "The deceased man whose fingerprints connected him to your robbery is also connected to a case of high importance to the Italian authorities. I'll let you know if anything comes up concerning Matthew," I said.

"But how is Matthew connected to this...Italian concern?" she asked.

"I don't think he is. We just learned about Matthew being missing from you."

"Missing?" she scoffed. "I'm past 'missing.' He left us. He's gone and he is never coming back. Time has shown that to me." And with a polite smile, she closed the door.

I opened my trunk and laid the box next to Cosima's suitcases. I couldn't wait for just a glance, so I lifted the top of the box. It was filled to the brim with every possible brochure, vacation enticement, investment opportunity, time share plan, and real estate listing for Australia. Western Australia to the Gold Coast, it made no difference. Any investigator tasked with looking for Matthew Gordon in Australia would need to go everywhere from Perth to Cairns and every city and dusty outback town in between. I shuffled through the box; every piece of paper was mailed to Matthew Gordon. If an obsessive mind could be represented in a box, then this was it. Both Cosima and I perused the items. We saw no quick end to the depth and variety of the material and decided to just keep it all in the box to review later.

"So, what do you think?" I asked Cosima as we drove north on Old Cutler Road. "I think it's beautiful here," she said.

"No, I mean what do you think about our chat with Mrs. Gordon?"

"She's obviously in a frazzled, sleep-deprived state. Grief and loss can do that to you. She appears to have a semblance of reconciliation with the violation of her life. Although she may never get over it, the loss of her husband is a bigger loss than the loss of serenity."

"The house felt pretty serene to me. There's a lot of intentional calmness with the décor and landscaping," I said.

"Cade, you of all people should know that manufactured tranquility cannot mask the storms within yourself."

I pulled the car over hard right in front of Fairchild Tropical Gardens. "What do you mean, 'you of all people'?"

"Exactly what I said," she said firmly, eyes piercing mine.

"Meaning what?" I said, raising my voice.

"Meaning that I am *de arma dei Carabinieri*! We are global and we have designated contacts. Do you think they sent me here to Miami without any intel?"

"Intel on *me*?"

"Intel on everyone. Including you," she replied. "What the hell..."

"Cade, one of my agents is in Intensive Care and a dignitary official from our country is lucky to be alive. The Carabinieri is not some low-tier organization. We are the national police of *Italia*! Now you may be what you say in America...all *squared away*, but the turbulence of your life, the violent situations, the upheaval you've been a part of is known and documented."

"Upheaval? What upheaval?"

"Your isolation, your pathological aversion to authority, your divorce. All of it. What did I say to you earlier today? I'm here to work." She punctuated each of those last words bitingly. "How much clearly must I say it? I'm here to work and I'm in *Miami*! I shouldn't have to explain. In all of that violence yesterday you are the only one who fired his weapon and killed what I suspect is a member of the assassin team. *Sei un canone sciolto ma ottieni risultati!*"

"What does that mean?" I asked feeling my anger growing.

"It means you're a loose cannon...but you get results. It means that we have a monumental task in front of us and I need you to be in line with me. It means that researching a potential partner is not a bad thing but a necessary thing to build a bond."

I stared straight ahead at the road. We both sat silent, the only sound the idling engine.

Deep down I knew that I would've done the same thing if I were her, researching the partner I was paired with. Being thrown with Agents Felton, Borges, and Tucson Lou was not how I normally operated. Now I had Cosima in the mix. I relented and put the car in drive and eased us back onto the road.

"Marriage is tough," I said, reflecting on our time with Mrs. Gordon.

"Are you talking about yourself or Mrs. Gordon?" she asked.

"Both."

I thought about what Lieutenant Maddalone said: *"That way we'll get notified of the results at the same time as Miami Dade Homicide."*

If Maddalone knew about the fingerprint, then Miami Dade Homicide knew as well.

Traffic was light as we drove north. I wasn't mad but I wasn't looking to have a conversation with Cosima either. Regardless of what she may have been told or knew for certain about me, she appeared to trust me. If not, then she and the higher-ups at the Carabinieri would have nixed my meeting her at the airport. I felt disadvantaged. Ridiculously so.

We were approaching Cartagena Circle when I decided to call Gary. The VIN line forwarded right to him. Ileana must have been away from her desk.

"VIN this is Gary."

"Big G! Anything come up with that Enterprise rental truck?"

"I was just about to call you. I might have something, but it's kind of involved. You got time for the rundown on it all?"

"Hold it. I'll be there in a few minutes," I said as I hung up. "That was Gary Fowler, a civilian employee in our office. He's looking into a rental truck that I think the shooter used as an escape vehicle," I said to Cosima.

"There wasn't any rental truck in any of the intelligence reports I saw," she said.

"That's really odd since you're *global and you have designated contacts*," I retorted. "Now before you get all Benito Mussolini on me and accuse me of withholding information, you may want to consider that although you came here to work, I didn't come here to work for you. Eventually your work vacation here in Miami will come to an end and I'll still be here dealing with this case. So, before you ask when did the information about the rental truck come to light, I learned about it before I picked you up at the airport. It's still hot off the presses."

"When were you going to tell me about it?"

"I probably wasn't going to. I intended to tell the U.S. Secret Service first and let them tell the Carabinieri. Now I've changed my mind."

"Changed your mind about what?" she asked.

"The order in which I reveal any information. What you said back there about one of your agents being in Intensive Care and the dignitary from your country being lucky he isn't dead, resonated with me. It made sense. For me, it changed the hierarchy. The Secret Service is looking to save face, but the Carabinieri has a bigger vested interest. So, I'm down to be down as we say here in the States, but don't you hold anything from me either going forward."

"I haven't yet," she said.

"No, except for digging through the back channels on me." I said with a smirk.

When we pulled close to the police station I saw there were still a smattering of TV trucks and people milling around. It wasn't as heavy as I heard it was earlier today but the overly committed, or perhaps the bottom feeders of the networks stuck around. I parked on the street to avoid any of them filming us entering the station and we walked right through the front door. No one paid any attention to us. In the VIN office, Ileana's computer was turned off. I surmised that she'd gone home to salvage what she could of her weekend. Gary was behind his desk and visibly lit up upon seeing Cosima.

"Now we have Mr. Cade Taylor walking on the red carpet. Care to tell us what you're wearing and who is this with you?" he joked, getting up.

"Why, yes Gary. I'm wearing the new line from *none of your business* and with me is Italian Carabinieri Special Agent Cosima Verratti who just flew in from Milan, Italy" I said keeping the lightheartedness going.

Gary introduced himself as he shook Cosima's hand. "The spring line from Italy will be released in a few weeks," she said continuing the revelry.

Cosima and I settled into the moderately comfortable yet functionally necessary chairs across from Gary's desk. "Gary, before we get into the rental truck, I need to put something else on your shoulders."

"Okay. What is it?"

"It can hold until Monday, but can you find anything regarding an address in the south end of the city? The address is 11027 Girasol Avenue. The owner is Janice Gordon. She says her husband Matthew left four years ago. Whereabouts unknown but...she's lying."

"Wait! She said he is in Australia!" Cosima chimed in, eyes wide.

"She did say she thought he was in Australia, but I'm telling both of you she's lying," I said.

"What do you mean she's lying? There's an entire box of Australia papers and brochures we got from her in the trunk of your car," blurted Cosima.

I looked at Cosima.

"She's lying. Plain and simple. Building and Zoning doesn't work on Saturday. I don't know who she was talking to on the phone, but it wasn't Building and Zoning. The day Matthew left she said that she'd been at a meeting in Grove Isle all day. She recounted the entire day to us in great detail. We heard about her children being away that day at a spring break sleepaway camp. We heard about Jack Kemp, the former quarterback for the Buffalo Bills, being at her meeting. We heard about the security measures she went through at Grove Isle. We didn't hear anything else. Nothing. She didn't mention anything out of the ordinary. She adamantly said, *'I'll never forget that day'.*"

"So?" asked Cosima.

"That day was April 19, 1995."

"I still don't see the significance," she said.

It was Gary who spoke before I answered her.

"April 19, 1995, was the biggest domestic terrorist event in our nation. The Oklahoma City Bombing."

Chapter Fourteen

"I READ ABOUT THAT in Italy," said Cosima.

"168 people killed and over 650 people injured," said Gary.

"Oklahoma City is far from Miami but when you're the vice chair of the New Republicans of Miami Dade and spending the day at an event with Bob Dole, just how do you not recall the disruption to the day that the bombing must have created? How is that omitted?" I said.

Cosima had a pensive expression on her face.

"Gary, we have a fingerprint from one of the guys connected to the assassin..." I said.

"The dead guy," he filled in.

"Yes."

"The dead guy who's a dead guy because you made him a dead guy," he said with a no qualms about the iciness of his comment.

"Yes, Big G. Now can I continue?" I said.

"As I was saying, we have a matching fingerprint that was lifted from the guy I killed." I paused making sure Gary wasn't going to interrupt me again.

"Let me bring you up to speed. The same fingerprint was lifted four years ago at 11027 Girasol Avenue in a home invasion robbery. The husband, Matthew Gordon, was a high-level executive banker.

Two of the offenders held the wife, Janice, and children at the home and another two took Matthew to a bank branch in Pinecrest. They arrived at the bank before the employees arrived, forced Matthew to open the vault, and cleared it out. We think between six and seven million. Janice Gordon tells me and Cosima that months afterward Matthew went into a downward spiral and became obsessed with a new life in Australia. She believes that he's probably in Australia. Exact whereabouts unknown. She told us the last day she saw him was April 19, 1995."

"Okay, I follow you," said Gary.

"I'm interested in whatever you can find about her, him, their house...anything."

"Got it. Now let me bring *you* up to speed on this rental truck," he said using my same phrase.

"Whaddya got?" I asked him.

Gary slid a pile of papers from the edge of his desk to the center of his desk and started thumbing through the papers.

"Okay. Let's start with the paper you faxed over."

"Paper?" asked Cosima.

"The Enterprise rental truck. A resident saw three men get in it. I think the shooter may have been one of them A piece of paper fell out of the truck, and the resident found it after they drove off. She gave it to me."

"Are there any other surprises I don't know about?" she blurted.

"Cosima, you've been here only a few hours and you're seeing and learning things at the same time I am. No surprises, just revelations," I said shutting down any more consternation. "Gary, continue please."

"Ohh...kay. So back to the paper. I checked with the language lab at the University of Miami, and they directed me to an internet website that translates languages. It's the craziest thing. You type in the words, it detects the language and *translates* it to your chosen language! This will help when Ileana curses us! Anyway, in this case the writing is confirmed Albanian. The first line *Hidheni biçikletën* translates to 'Drop the bike.'"

"Drop the bike? Maybe that refers to the motorcycle. If it does than that helps link the guy I shot to the rental truck. Just a theory but it sounds logical to me. Drop the bike, as in get rid of the bike."

"The second line is *Thirrni Tazzi*. The translation on that is pretty up front. It means 'Call Tazzi.' Whoever he is," said Gary.

"Or whoever *she* is," Cosima added.

"Yes. Whomever it is. The next one is self-explanatory. *Pastroni kamionin* is 'clean up the truck.' I assume that means leave no trace and clean it for fingerprints, evidence, what have you. The fourth line also is pretty self-explanatory. *Ndërroni telefonat* is 'switch the phones.' Again, probably using throw-down phones and then dump. The last one is *Hidhni Coldstream*. 'Dump Coldstream.' Whatever that means."

"Dump Coldstream?" I said.

"What is Coldstream?" asked Cosima.

"I have no idea. We'll keep looking until it makes sense," said Gary.

"Let's table that for the moment. What about the truck?"

"They rented the truck from an Enterprise in Ojus," said Gary.

"Ojus? Where the hell is that?"

"Bro you need to brush up on your Miami history. Northwest section of the county, west of I-95 near Aventura."

I rolled my eyes. "Can you just say Northwest Dade like everyone else?"

"What? You want me to be like those dippy TV reporters that blanketly say North Dade, disregarding the demarcation lines between North Dade, Northeast Dade, and Northwest Dade? No, sir! I have principals!" said Gary.

"Go on please," I said, feeling the focus of this briefing trickling away.

"It was rented on the fourth and was to be returned on the eighth."

"Was? Today is the sixth," I said.

"Yeah well, the fellow who rented it used a phony license and a fraudulent credit card. The credit card didn't turn up as bad until three hours after he left with the truck, so they don't have any faith the truck will actually be back on the eighth. The Enterprise employee I spoke to is scattering, trying to get the truck back."

"Any good information about the guy who rented it? Anything at all?" asked Cosima.

"Enterprise is up a tree over this. The worker's name his Anthony Ichaso. He thought he was in this mess by himself but when I told him we were interested, he was relieved—soon followed by even more dread about letting the truck out of the fleet. I told him the truck was used to deliver some spoiled fish to some Coral Gables restaurants, and we were looking for it before more deliveries were made in Miami."

"Spoiled fish? Really?" I said.

"I like to see it as thinking on my feet. I'm trying to avoid tipping any willing or unwilling accomplices off, thank you very much." Gary replied with pride.

"*Pesce andato a male? È per questo che ho attraversato l'oceano?*" [Spoiled fish? This is what I crossed the ocean to hear?] Cosima said under her breath.

"This guy at Enterprise, is he gonna be there all day?" I asked.

"Anthony Ichaso? I guess so."

I looked at Cosima. "You want to take a short trip before checking into your hotel?" I asked her. "Yes. Let's be on our way," she said.

"Big G, call this guy Ichaso and tell him we're on our way to see him. Ask him if he has any surveillance footage of the guy who rented the truck, tell him to tee it up and have it ready for us. Make sure he knows not to leave until we get there," I said, quickly leaving the office.

"*Arrivederci!*" he called after us.

The drive to the Enterprise Rent-A-Car wasn't nearly as scenic but Cosima did get an eyeful of the constantly growing and rising Miami skyline. We arrived at the business which just so happens to be located across the street from Ojus Park. Once again, Big G was spot on with his information. There weren't any customers inside the rental office.

"Welcome to Enterprise. May I help you?" said the young man in a dark green polo behind the counter.

"Mr. Ichaso?" I replied.

"Yes?"

"We're detectives from Coral Gables. I believe my associate Gary Fowler called you and said we'd be coming by."

"You're the cops?" he said with a twinge of disbelief in his voice.

I showed him my badge hanging from a chain under my shirt, "I'm Detective Cade Taylor. We want to talk about your rental truck. Number 6082. We understand it was rented with a phony credit card."

"Thank God you're here. My boss is in Missouri until next week, he doesn't know yet. He's gonna vomit his lower colon if I don't get that truck back," he said, eyes pleading.

"Maybe we can help you with that. Were you able to pull up the surveillance footage from when the man came in here to rent the truck?"

"Yeah, I gathered everything up." He pulled a folder from behind the counter and handed it to Cosima.

She thumbed through it while I continued talking to him. He told us that the man who rented the truck provided a Florida driver's license and a credit card. When the card was run it had no issues and was valid. It was only a few hours after the truck was leased that the credit card company called Enterprise disputing the charge because the card was fraudulent—a Visa card issued by Republic Bank. Enterprise was now in a bind—especially Anthony Ichaso. On the copy of the driver's license was a full face picture of a dark-haired young man who resembled the man in the surveillance photos leasing the truck. The name on the credit card matched the name on the driver's license. Jordan Barzal. The address on the license was 19618 East Lake Drive, Miami.

"Do you know where that is?" asked Cosima.

"No."

"I looked the address up in our mapping system," Anthony said. "It's in the Country Club of Miami area, north of Miami Lakes. I was going to go out there after work but now that you're here, I'll leave it to the professionals."

I was feeling anything but professional. The events of the past thirty-six hours had bordered on incompetence and gross negligence. *Fiasco in flagrante.* I knew all the way deep down into my shoes that if the credit card was phony there was a very good chance the address on the license was phony too. This might be a go-nowhere proposition.

"You made a photocopy of his driver's license? Is that normal procedure?" asked Cosima.

"It is when the guy renting the truck is wearing an Irish Rolex," he said with a little laugh. Cosima looked perplexed.

I explained, "An Irish Rolex is a court-ordered ankle monitor. He's saying the guy had an ankle monitor on."

"I noticed it when I was showing him the truck and he stepped up onto the cab," Anthony said.

"Did you make duplicate copies of this folder? Can we keep these for ourselves?" I asked.

"Sure, man."

"Thank you, we'll be in touch," I said.

"Before my boss gets back from Missouri?"

"I hope so. No promises, but I hope so." Then Cosima and I left the office.

Before leaving the parking lot I called Gary, hoping to catch him before he left the office. Fortunately, he was still in the office and answered his phone.

"Cade, why are you calling me again?"

"Big G, we might have something else to look into."

"You realize you're relentless, don't you?" he said.

I let the remark slide and just continued with my reason for calling.

"The guy who rented the truck used a fraudulent credit card in the name of Jordan Barzal."

"There an address listed to this Barzal guy?" asked Gary.

"Yeah, 19618 East Lake Drive, Miami."

I could hear Gary typing on his keyboard.

"Get this. The guy who rented the truck was wearing an ankle monitor, you know, like from the court system. Can the parole board or court system check and see if there was an ankle monitor pinged here at the Enterprise truck leasing office, then pinged again near the Biltmore Hotel the day the consulate was shot?"

"And again, I say to you," Gary huffed, "you do realize it's Saturday?"

"What? These things aren't monitored on Saturday? Adjudicated criminals get to watch Saturday morning cartoons in their jammies without that bothersome ankle monitor?" I said.

"Not what I'm saying. I'm sure there's tracking software and somebody checking. It's just that it won't be as easy to find someone on a Saturday as it will be Monday through Friday. I don't need to tell you this. Never underestimate the laziness of a state employee."

"Believe me, I know," I answered.

"By the way, this Janice Gordon you spoke to today on Girasol Avenue is like, a big socialite in Miami. Lots of snippet articles and pictures of her in the Miami Herald society pages. I'm pulling them off the world wide web search engines."

"I still need to get more proficient with all that world wide web stuff. Thanks. Keep finding what you can and keep them all together. Cosima and I will be by when we can to see what you got."

"I'll put it all in a file folder and leave it in the office with your name on it. Later," he said as he hung up.

We got in the car and drove south. I wanted to get Cosima to the Biltmore so she could check in and freshen up from her very long flight. It had been a long day for her, traveling from Milan then being squired away to the southern end of Coral Gables, meeting with Gary, and now up here in the northern part of the county, or as Big G says, "Ojus."

The ride to the hotel was probably rather uninspiring for Cosima. It was a mixture of replicated single family homes, small, weathered businesses, but mostly it was a mundane vista of continual ribbons of flat poured concrete and sun-bleached aluminum light poles as we transitioned from one expressway to another. I wondered what Cosima must have thought, seeing such disparity in the South Florida landscape. Dusty, dingy dump trucks belching sooty black smoke, trucks, vans, and cars vying for the same lanes of asphalt cutting each other off and weaving through the choking traffic like the twenty-four hours of Le Mans. I glimpsed over at Cosima a few times and the hectic scenes playing in front of our windshield didn't seem to bother her at all.

"Do Miami drivers scare you?" I asked.

"This?" she said motioning, out in front of her "This is nothing compared to Italy. Driving in Italy has a very simple premise. '*Guarda il tuo fronte e lascia che tutti gli altri ti guardino le spalle*.'"

"What does that mean?"

"You watch your front and let everyone else watch your back," she said.

I wondered if she ever saw Fred Flintstone portraying the famed Italian racer Goggles Pisano.

"Seems like Miami and Milan aren't that dissimilar in driving habits," I said.

Saturday traffic was considerably lighter than the Monday to Friday freeway free-for-all that ends up being a sluggish stop-and-go exercise in commuter frustration. I made my way to the Dolphin Expressway and exited at Red Road, intending to take it almost to the front door of the Biltmore Hotel. On my way my cellphone rang.

"Hello?"

"Cade, its Tucson Lou. Are you anywhere near the Biltmore?"

I hesitated to answer. My suspicions about him switching his position with the felled Carabinieri agent and being on the inside with the shooter still caused me to be wary. Before I could answer he posed another question to me.

"Did you pick up the Carabinieri guy from the airport?"

Now my suspicion was elevated even more. How did Tucson Lou know I was supposed to pick up the Italian agent? My eyes slid over to Cosima sitting next to me. She was watching Miami in the approaching sunset whiz by her window.

"Yeah, I made that pick up. I'm on my way back to the Biltmore." I said cryptically.

"We're trying to strategize our options here. You got time to meet tonight?"

I just wanted to relax after these last couple of days, and surely Cosima needed a little rejuvenation time as well. "I'm going to swing by and drop the agent off then head home. What do you say we give it until tomorrow so we can all be rested and at our best?"

"Sounds good. I'll tell Borges. He's been asking. Let's try this again tomorrow, 10am, here at the hotel. Same thing as today at the 19th Hole Bar and Grill."

"Okay. That should work," I said.

"How far out are you?" he asked.

With a nagging reluctance, I told him we were about ten minutes away.

"Pull up to the upper level. I'll meet you outside," he said as he hung up.

We made the turn onto Anastasia Avenue from Red Road. Rapidly darkening gray shadows cast upon us as the Poinciana trees that hug the roadway passed overhead. The Seville-inspired lighted tower of the Biltmore Hotel fought with the rising moon to hold our attention.

"That's your hotel," I pointed out to Cosima.

"That's it? It's beautiful."

Twilight had settled and the professionally designed artistic lighting of the Biltmore beckoned to us. I drove up the ramp to the second level, which is actually the lobby level. Tucson Lou was waiting on the polished limestone walkway by the valet stand for us. I parked and popped open the trunk from inside the car. When Cosima stepped out of the vehicle, I could see the confusion in Tucson Lou's face. Before he could say a single word, Agent Borges walked out of the hotel towards us.

"Agents Borges and Akicita, this is Italian Carabinieri Agent Cosima Verratti," I said. "Agent Verratti, these gentlemen are United States Secret Service agents. Lou Akicita is from the Phoenix, Arizona office and Tom Borges is from the Palm Beach, Florida office."

Cosima shook both their hands. Cosima carried herself with poise, a cultured personality and the strength of femininity. The fact that she was quite attractive didn't go unnoticed by the agents. Tucson Lou stepped forward towards me and in a quiet lowered voice said, "I thought she was a he. I was expecting Julius Caeser not Miss Italy!"

"I don't know about that," I replied.

He continued talking to me in a hushed tone.

"She's gorgeous. She's our Carabinieri liaison? Holy Pope smoke. We'll brief her and have her attend the meeting tomorrow for sure. You're definitely going to be here in the morning, right? We need to make some progress or the guys in Washington will lose their minds."

"Yeah. I'll be here in the morning."

Tucson Lou darted away to be sure to retrieve Cosima's bags from the trunk of the car. "Let me show you around." he said as he led her inside the hotel. Cosima glanced back at me, and I gave her a simple hand wave as she walked inside with the exuberant Tucson Lou. Borges looked back at Lou and Cosima and chuckled.

"Guy acts like he's never seen a pretty woman before. I haven't had a chance to talk with you. You doing okay?" he said.

"Yeah. I'm okay. It's been a wild time so far."

He put both his hands on my shoulders and looked me in the eyes. "Seriously. You okay?"

"Yeah, I'm fine. We're hopefully making progress. We got a fingerprint hit off the guy with the motorcycle. We linked him to a home invasion robbery in the south end of Coral Gables. Looks like he may have been part of a gang of guys."

"No way! We finally got a good lead! Good work, Cade!" He removed his hands from my shoulders and stepped back. He looked around possibly to insure confidentiality. He then stepped forward, put his hand back on my shoulder, leaned in closer to me and said, "I think this may have been an inside job. Too much happened too soon for this to have gone the way it did."

Through the ornate framed windows of the hotel lobby, we both caught a glimpse of Tucson Lou walking with Cosima.

"I'm just saying, we need to be on our toes with this one," he said.

Tom Borges wasn't telling me anything I hadn't started thinking myself. It was good to see someone was on the same sheet of music as I was.

"I gotcha. I'm going to make tracks and get some sleep at home. I'll see you in the morning," I said.

"In the morning. Right. Let's get these puzzle pieces on the table and figure more leads. See you tomorrow," he said as he went back inside the hotel.

I walked around to the back of my car and closed the trunk, only to hear Arica Sweeten's voice.

"You have a bad habit of leaving," she said.

"Are they bad habits if I'm good at them?"

"Unfortunately, this time I'm the one leaving," she said.

"Leaving? Where to?"

"A bunch of NYPD officers shot at a guy from Guinea forty-one times, and they hit him with nineteen of those bullets. Trident

Broadcasting wants a big exposé on this one. I'm being pulled to go to New York."

"Forty-one times...wow. I'm assuming he's dead."

"Dead as a child's goldfish. As we speak, he's rigorously mortised."

"That's a serious public relation's nightmare for the NYPD," I said.

"I hate that I'm leaving palm trees and flowering hibiscus for the number four train uptown."

"Duty calls. You have to chase the story wherever it is," I said with a shrug.

"My life is a constant state of 'on-call' and 'deadline looming.'"

"Must wreak havoc on the cortisol and adrenaline levels." I said.

"So...the hotel supposedly called a taxi for me but I'm not so sure. It's been fifteen minutes already," she said, looking forlornly at my car.

Miami International Airport was diametrically opposite of my condominium at Paradise Point. I picked up on her inference. I really just wanted to go home. It had been a long day and a second trip to the airport and into the northern part of the county was not anything I wanted to do. I saw her trying to be discreet but failing to hide her pleading eyes. She looked out toward Anastasia Avenue, making an obvious point for me to see her looking for the taxi. I bit all the way in.

"I'll take you to the airport," I heard myself saying as if on autopilot.

"Oh, Cade. Really? You don't have to do that, but I'd be so grateful if you did."

"Yeah, it's no problem. Let me get your bag."

I reached into the Acura's driver-side window, pushed the trunk release, the trunk again lifted up swiftly. One of the advantages of a new car is the hydraulics are primed and eager to work. I walked to the back of the car and hefted her large suitcase into the trunk.

"You travel with a lot of stuff," I said.

"This time of year, I never know where I'll be. Winter clothes, summer attire, bathing suits, and a snazzy cocktail dress all have to be available," she answered.

I closed the trunk and held her door open for her as she smoothly sat into the passenger seat. Once I'd slid in behind the wheel and closed the door, she made her first request of me.

"Can we drive with the sunroof open? I need to soak in as much of Miami as I can before I see midtown Manhattan tonight."

I opened the sunroof for her. Then she made her second request.

"Oh, another thing. Can you stop at a pharmacy on the way? I need to get some Neosporin and Q- tips before I get to the airport."

I was already wondering if my being the airport shuttle was a bad idea on my part.

"What do you need that for?"

"An old pilot's trick. I swab the inside of my nostrils before I fly. It helps to keep me from getting sick. Airplanes are germ factories. The idea is you defend against airborne germs before they get deep into your nasal passages and make you sick."

It was logical. It was practical. But it was still an inconvenience to me. I'd planned to retrace my route to the hotel and use Red Road to take us right to the backside of the airport. I wasn't sure if we'd see any pharmacies along the way. Allen's Drugs was a five-minute drive south from the hotel. Once again out of my way and now I'd be driving south to go north, then north to go south like an errant ping pong ball. It was chafing against my sensibilities, but I had to remind myself that in the grand scheme of things in life it was really not a big deal.

"No problem," I fibbed. "There's a drug store a few blocks south of here. We'll make a quick stop and then I'll have you on your way to the airport."

I eased the car away from the curb and down the long sloping ramp. The Biltmore's large center showpiece fountain gurgled and splashed water twenty yards away. I waited for a taxi to slowly drive in front of us. It turned onto the hotel's up-ramp towards the car valets and the hotel entrance. We both inwardly knew who that taxi was meant for. Arica stiffened. She was probably wondering if I was going to take her back to the taxi, but she was already in my car. I made a commitment, I'll just see it through.

I drove west towards Alhambra Circle on our way to the pharmacy. I didn't even notice the two men in the Oldsmobile Silhouette Van across the street watching us.

Chapter Fifteen

I TURNED WEST ONTO Anastasia Avenue. The van, still unnoticed by me, began to follow us. I passed the Church of the Little Flower, still oblivious that we were being followed. The road seamlessly transitions to Sevilla Avenue for a block and then at a perfunctory traffic light I turned south on Alhambra Circle. The only thing going through my mind was wondering how I allowed myself to be roped into taking Arica to the airport when it was clearly way out of my way. It wasn't the same with Arica.

She continued to simultaneously fawn over being in beautiful Miami during the winter and lament going back to the cold weather in the northeast while I listened with as much interest as I could muster, considering it was an obvious rant about going when a job pulls you away. Not that I was not attentive, but the days had been long, and I was kind of in my own head about the case and my desire to just get home.

We were approaching the bridge that crosses the waterway at Taragona Drive. Two things snapped me of my reverie. The first thing was when Arica said that she wished she could have stayed and maybe she and I could have gotten to know each other better, and as she said: "Who knows, we could have maybe become closer than two cousins from Kentucky."

I wasn't fully expecting to hear that, and I looked over at her.

That's when we both felt a forceful jolt to the back of my car. It was such a thunderous impact that it pushed the Acura to the right side of the road. The right front end of the car collided with the right side of the bridge guardrail, slamming us to a spine-jittering stop as the ball joint on the right front tire broke, pitching the now immobile car to the right side. My seatbelt retracted and pinned me hard against the seat. The airbags didn't deploy, but the hood crumbled up backwards. Instantly, a deep crack squiggled across the top of the windshield.

"Arica, are you alright?" I said, voice high-pitched in my shock.

"Ugh! What was that?" she said with a wavering, confused voice as I struggled against the seatbelt, finally wiggling enough to unclasp it. Instead of sliding back into place the belt hung loosely against my waist and torso.

The Oldsmobile Silhouette van came to a complete stop after crashing into us, leaving about a ten-yard gap between our vehicles. His passenger air bag had deployed, blinding and disorienting his passenger. The van, marketed as a revolutionary prototype, largely had an all-plastic front end. The entire front bumper of the van had torn off, falling on the road between us. I'd seen the outline of the van in my rearview mirror, but it was as though he'd come out of nowhere and struck us. Seeing it was a van; my first thought was that a harried soccer mom trying to get home had hit us. I still wasn't processing the full extent of what had just happened.

From behind me I heard the van's driver-side door creak, and I opened my door too. The structural integrity of my door had been compromised by the rippling hood, making it creak and heave. I shoved it further open and was able to swing my right leg around, but the seatbelt still clung to my left shoulder and draped across my arm. I got both feet on the ground and turned to look back over my left shoulder. It looked like the van's driver was lighting a cigarette.

My first thought was that the driver sure was calm for a guy who just caused a bone-jangling accident. Then I quickly realized there could be spilled gasoline on the road and yelled at him, warning him to not light his cigarette. He had his right foot inside the van and his left foot firmly planted on the ground. He was intently trying to light something in his left hand. Within seconds he had whatever he was trying to light up ablaze and switched the flaming thing to his right hand. Then he leaned forward from the damaged van door threw it at us.

It was a Molotov cocktail.

A flaming rag was stuffed into the neck of a bottle, filled with some sort of combustible liquid. It tumbled awkwardly in the air. Bottles filled with liquid are not designed to be aerodynamic. The deftness of throwing this lethal concoction at us was hampered by the driver being wedged between the van and the damaged van door. The bottle bounced unbroken off of the left rear side of our car. Luckily for us it bounced once more, skittering off to my left before on its second bounce, it broke. The flammable contents in the bottle splayed out of the exploded glass in all directions, the roiling liquid's contact with the flaming rag causing a blasting inferno that rose four feet off of the ground. The flash from the Molotov cocktail was blinding. The eruption of flames, the shattering of glass, and the *whoosh* of the igniting liquid was startling, surprising, and downright scary. The flames shot out in every direction. Droplets of flaming liquid rained down upon our car and the entire left side of the bridge, each falling bead and drip searching for something to scorch and set on fire.

Arica started screaming at the hellfire around us. Her panicked shrieks filled the car. Instinctively, I pulled my feet up and fell back into the seat as the flames quickly spread under our car and outside my door. I could smell the bottle's accelerant. It smelled like gasoline.

The passenger in the van eventually got out from under the inflated airbag and stepped out of the van. He had a Mossberg Tactical 500 shotgun. He fired his first round at our car's back window. The blast from the shotgun discharging its weighted, deadly, precision-honed slug was deafening. The round burst through the rear window, disintegrating the tempered glass into little nuggets and shards that crashed down with a startingly loud crescendo. The round carried through the car, reverberating as it whizzed between us, Arica screeching. The hot lead lodged into the dashboard between our seats and burrowed into the oak veneer. Arica continued screaming but I don't think she knew it. I was stunned with sensory overload. We'd just had a van plow into us, a gasoline-fueled homemade bomb thrown at us, and now someone was shooting a shotgun at us. Arica quickly regained her wits and went into fight or flight mode.

"Fuck these fuckers!" she screamed.

Before he could fire his second loaded round at us, I had a flash of clarity and pushed the trunk release button. The trunk sprung free of its latch and rose quickly. His second round struck the underside of the car's rising trunk with a loud, clanging *twang* and changed its trajectory, ricocheting somewhere down into the trunk. We were lucky with that one, but I knew the shooter wouldn't try that again. He would be even more determined to dispense a kill shot upon both of us. The van's driver was having trouble lighting his second Molotov cocktail. In the brief respite I heard a voice:

"Çakmak i lirë! Dreq këtë!" [Cheap lighter! Fuck this!]

The shooter had joined the driver behind the van and steadied the shotgun with both hands, holding it against his hip. He fired his third round into my open car door. It spun in and demolished the interior of the door. White dust from batting behind the door's faux leather accents floated up into the dark night. In the overhead streetlight, it looked almost smoky. The slug caught the door's upper hinge, the weight of the door causing it to screech as it sagged under its own weight.

Going out through my door would be suicidal.

The soft glow of the streetlight streaming through the sunroof was the only light in the car. My mind reeled, desperately seeking any kind of tactical advantage. I raised my right leg and planted my foot on my seat, then leaned to my right, maneuvering my leg around the steering wheel. I put my hand on Arica's headrest and pushed off, propelling myself up towards the open sunroof while drawing the gun tucked at my lower back. The hanging seat belt clung to my left side like a floppy pageant sash. As I pulled myself up through the sunroof, my gun hand got tangled up in the seatbelt. I was partially out of the car, fighting to free my gun hand, and hit my elbow on the edge of the open sunroof.

The "funny bone" sensation hit me with a disabling tingling that radiated through my entire arm, shocking it, creating an involuntary opening of my hand. My gun fell back into the darkened recesses of the car—leaving me in a very precarious situation.

I was almost fully exposed on the roof. I couldn't hesitate and I couldn't duck back in the car. For the first time I got a fleeting look at our adversaries: two dark-haired men near the driver's side of the van. They both stood roof height of the van. I surprised them, emerging out of the top of the car. I clambered across the roof towards Arica's side of the car. The one holding the lighter yelled:

"*Gjuaj atë gjarpër zvarritës!*" [Shoot that crawling snake!] *Cha-Chack!*

I heard the racking of the shotgun. His next shot hit the rear quarter panel of the car. *Boom!* It tunneled a spiraling hole through the metal, rocking the car. I didn't even wait to see what would happen next. I lunged over the edge of the roof and toppled down the side of Arica's door, hitting the ground between the car and the guardrail. I reached up and flung open both Arica's door and the back door.

"Kill these assholes," she said with venom and fire in her eyes.

ARICA WAS KNEELING on the floor of the car, looking to the rear, with only the back of her seat as her only protection from the fierce barrage. I grabbed her behind the neck and pulled her outside with me, the open back door shielding us. Instinctively we both stayed low to the ground. Fighting a shotgun and Molotov cocktails without any weapons had a very low probability of survival. I grasped and grabbed at any part of her I could get my hands on, yanking her and forcibly directing her to the edge of the bridge against the three-railed barrier.

"Under now!" I shouted at her.

"*What*?" was all I heard as I shoved her under the lowest rail. She partially slid and squirmed underneath it until I heard her splash into the dark water below us. I was right behind her. I went through the middle gap in the bars, right leg first then dived across the smooth round rail to tumble into the inky black water.

I smacked into the water, flailing awkwardly. The air left my lungs from the involuntary gasp I made when I plunged into the cold brackish water. Arica was making grunting gasps, feeling the effects of the bracing water as well. I quickly swam under the bridge. Arica had the same thought because we found each other silently under the bridge in the dark water, the previously placid surface now choppy from our movements. I was struggling to stay quiet as my body heaved and shuddered. Arica sensed my struggle and control issues. She seized me by the shoulders and placed herself against my back. She wrapped her legs around me from behind and put her chin on my shoulder. She murmured in my ear.

"Relax. Breathe. Just Breathe."

Breathing was all I could think of. Relaxing was the last thing I was capable of. My eyes searched wildly around us. My fear that our assailants might try to cross the thickly shrubbed embankment and search for us was all consuming. I scanned behind us and saw the bridge pilings in the center of the murky channel. Any sign of the guys trying to kill us and I'd push Arica behind the pilings then I would move away and try to draw their fire. If they only had the one shotgun and only had rifled slugs, it would take a direct hit to one of us to be lethal. I thanked God they did not have buckshot or pellets which would spread out and cover more area.

The two men must have heard the splash of our bodies hitting the water. We could hear them frantically running about the bridge above us. We could also hear a bevy of police sirens wailing in the distance but getting closer. The footsteps above us thudded with a panicky shuffle. It sounded like they were moving back and forth between our crashed car and their own damaged van. The sirens were getting closer and from the pitch of their night piercing sirens I surmised they'd be here in less than a minute.

A very long minute.

Above us, excited voices in a language I didn't recognize carried across the water. I listened intently with just my nose and top of my head above the water. Arica continued to keep us from drifting with her limbs wrapped around me. From our secreted spot in the water, I caught a fleeting glimpse of both men running as fast as they could west on Taragona Drive. Within seconds they'd cross a miniscule hedge row at the furthest edge of Taragona Drive, and out on the busier Red Road. From there they could easily disappear under the vapor streetlights and shadowy trees.

The water was reflecting roving blue and red lights from the arriving police cars. The bouncing lights multiplied quickly as more and more police units arrived. I could imagine them trying to make sense of what they'd driven up to: two badly damaged vehicles, spent shotgun shells, bullet holes, small puddles of fire, an Acura with the driver's door nearly shorn off with a Glock handgun under the brake pedal.

I called out to one of the arriving officers, identifying myself and speaking in police code in hopes they wouldn't draw their own weapons on us. I told them to look for two white males with dark hair, last seen running west on Taragona Drive. I said that I had a civilian with me and that we'd swim to the open embankment.

"Can you swim?" Arica asked me.

"Yes, I can swim," I said partially offended she would even ask. Arica unwrapped her legs from around me.

"Based on that flubber flop you did from the bridge, I wasn't sure. If you're looking for favorable points for that thing you called a dive, I think you're seriously out of luck. Not just with me but every diving judge on the planet," she said.

"I do all my own stunts, but never intentionally," I muttered.

We started slowly swimming our way towards the embankment where three police officers were waiting, shining their light at us to be as helpful as they could while blinding us repeatedly. They helped us out of the water. Arica was placed in a police car with the heat blasting while we waited for Fire Rescue to assess our injuries. I recanted as much of the story and information as I could to the officers on the scene through still-chattering teeth. A cadre of officers drove up and down Red Road searching for the offenders as Fire Rescue arrived and both Arica and I got in the back of the truck. They wrapped us in thermal blankets.

"I was hoping to get to know you better, but I didn't think it would involve a police report," Arica said.

"I prefer a group consensus," I said, turning my head to gaze at all of the busy people outside of the truck

"You killed the guy on the motorcycle. Why didn't you kill those guys?" she asked me.

Explaining that I dropped my gun in the car was not something I wanted to do. I looked at her and shrugged.

"I met my allotment for the month."

Chapter Sixteen

IT WAS NEARLY 10pm and the crime scene was still being worked. Some lunkhead requested our dive team search the waterway that Arica and I plopped into even though I told them it wouldn't be necessary. We had accident investigation units, K-9 officers with their continuously barking partners, and enough police officers to fill the need for a backdrop shot on the TV show *Hillstreet Blues*. A dark sedan pulled up on the opposite side of the bridge. The nose of the car actually slid under the wavering crime scene tape. I was not relieved to see it was Major Brunson. He got out of his car and brushed past the two officers standing by the crime scene tape.

"Where is he?" he bellowed.

Those around him intrinsically knew he must have been talking about me. They parted the way, and he naturally followed the human corridor right towards me.

"Is that your dad?' asked Arica.

"Sort of," I said quietly.

"Taylor!" he called out as he drew close to me and Arica.

My wet hair was matted to my forehead, and the thermal blanket made an audible crinkling sound with every move I made.

"Major," I said by way of greeting.

"You look like a fucking deflated *Jiffy Pop* bag in that tinfoil. I'm glad you're okay. *Again!* Now that I got that out of the way…I can fucking add sensitivity trainer to my resume," he said.

Arica's eyebrows were raised, clearly telling me she had no idea who this was in front of her. "Who the fuck is this?" Brunson asked.

"This is Arica Sweetin. She was with me when this all went down."

"From the Italian Carabinieri?" he asked.

"No sir. I'm from Trident Broadcasting," Arica answered before I could.

I could practically feel my eyes rolling into the back of my head.

"Trident Broadcasting? The *media*?" he asked, eyes narrowed.

"Can I quote you on that probing question?" she asked him with a sarcastic lilt in her voice.

I expected the steam boiler of his personality to explode and spew out a litany of profanity. Instead, he surprised me by conducting quiet, gentle dialogue with Arica. He asked her where she was from and how she came to "be our guest in this mess." He was polite and almost congenial. Arica was feeling quite pleased with herself. It appeared she had tamed the acidic beast. He smiled jovially after talking with her and motioned for us to stand closer so he could talk to us with a measure of confidentiality. With a friendly smile across his face he began to speak. We soon learned he was just leading us on.

"Listen up my little fucking aquanauts. I got a goddamn Italian consulate in a butt-ass hospital learning to write with his non-masturbating left hand and the first thing he's going to write is a formal fucking complaint about how he got shot. Not just fucking once but fucking twice—"

"Major, all due respect, the wrist injury was a ricochet," I interjected.

"Did a piece of lead from a fucking gun fired at him penetrate his greasy political body? Huh? Well, guess the fuck what? It's fucking twice, Doctor. Not to mention a dedicated Carabinieri agent in the trauma unit. Why? I have no fucking earthly clue. But I've already looked into Miss Lois Lane here. Trouble follows her like it fucktastically fucking follows you, Cade. The two of you together are shit magnets."

"Excuse me?" she said, her voice rising.

"Were you not at Likoshane for the start of the Kosovo War last February? What about July in Richmond, South Africa? Did you forget the violence that broke out between supporters of the Inkatha Freedom Party and the ANC? Or how about the Omagh bombing in Northern Ireland last August?"

"I'm a journalist. I cover worldwide stories. What are you getting at?" she protested.

"What I'm getting at is that you've been preemptively staged every time something big has happened. You're not fucking showing up after the fact! You're in place before it fucking happens!"

"I don't need to stand for this," said Arica, shaking her head and looking for a way out.

"Yes, you fucking do. I spoke to Samantha Surman. You know? Samantha? Your assignment editor? Let me say it clearer—your fucking boss! Ms. Surman, in no uncertain terms, let it be known if you even *think* about leaving Miami Dade County before we're done with this entire shit carnival, you'll not only be out of a job, but you'll be black balled in the worldwide press corps. You will no longer be working for *Tri-fucking-dent* Broadcasting and the only thing you'll be covering is your ass from showing on goddamn QVC as you sell fucking potato peelers at 3am. She says the NYPD story has been reassigned and you're now under our...no let me rephrase that...under *my* fucking perveance. Don't believe me? Call her. You can use my unlucky *I wish I didn't have it* cellphone.

"I don't work for you," she retorted but her voice was hoarse.

"No, you don't work for me," he said, then leaned in and growled, "but you don't fucking want me working against you."

He turned his rapid-fire questioning at me. "Cade! You think these two thugs were trying to kill you?"

"I'd say obviously."

"Really? How's the fuck is that? Did they know you were going to be at the Biltmore? You checked out earlier in the day. What makes you think they'd be lingering at the Biltmore, looking for your scrawny ass? Or maybe…just maybe…they're targeting someone else." he said sliding his eyes over at Arica.

"What are you trying to say?" I asked.

"I'm saying Ms. Sweetin here was in Kosovo almost exactly a year ago when Serbians fought and killed Albanians. We know the guy you killed got his gun in Albania and by all indications, we think he was Albanian."

"Hey, you accusing windbag," Arica huffed, pacing. I told you already. It's my job—"

"What do Albanians have to do with the Italian consulate?" I interrupted.

"The Italian Consulate Baldassare Constantino was about to announce his campaign for the premier of Italy. I mentioned that in my office when I assigned you to dignitary protection. We got a confirmation from his hospital bedside that the announcement was indeed his intention."

He hadn't yelled at us when relaying that answer or used profanity. I was pleasantly relieved.

"So why the goddamn Albanians? Because they fucking control a big-as-fuck transit route for Bolivian marching dust into Italy! Do I need to spell it out for you? Co-*fucking*-caine!" he bellowed.

So much for pleasant relief.

"And…?" Arica said, drawling out the word.

"And? Constantino gets into the premiership and all the bribes and bought politicians are out. He's a vocal anti-drug advocate. He gets in he's going to squash the Albanian crime syndicate."

"And…?" Arica said, drawling out the word even longer.

"Are you daft? You were there in Kosovo. The Albanians were there. You're *here*. The Albanians are *here*. Your boss thinks you and Constanino are both targeted. So, in addition to all the fuckmotion

I got going on, I have to fucking provide around-the-fucking-clock protection for *you* now. Unless you want to climb into Constantino's hospital bed with him, I have to provide a safe location for you."

"I don't need you or anyone to protect me."

"Clearly," he said, looking Arica over as she stood in front of him wrapped in a thermal blanket.

"I'm serious," she protested.

"So am I. As a duly sworn law enforcement officer in the great state of Florida, I have the authority to employ the Baker Act and have you held for psychological evaluation for up to seventy-two hours in a state psychological facility. And believe me, I will push for all seventy- two of those hours."

"You wouldn't dare!" she cried out, voice shaking, shoulders shaking, fists clenched.

"Try me. Got an issue? Get a tissue! Unless..."

"Unless what?" she asked.

He answered her but stared at me the entire time he spoke.

"We can't have you go back to the Biltmore Hotel. It's too hot there. We can avoid all of this if we can find a place to keep you out of sight for a spell. Maybe somewhere in the southern end of the county...in a gated community...with someone who has lots of room and who can be trusted to keep you out of harm's way. Someone with dignitary protection experience..."

"Major, with all due respect—"

"Cade, I'm telling you the same thing I said to her. You got an issue? Get a tissue. She's bunking at your place."

In the background behind him our public information officer drove up in one of the seized vehicles we use for flash deals with drug traffickers. The officer parked the dark blue BMW 750 outside the crime scene tape. He walked up to Major Brunson and put the keys in his hands. Brunson, in turn, handed me the keys.

"You obviously can't drive that Acura. I'll take it up with Ramon at the rental agency. Smooth it over. It'll probably fucking cost me some goddamn courtside tickets for the fucking University of Miami Hurricanes. Don't worry about shit. I'll handle it. Now you two listen up. Public Information is going live on TV from here at 11pm. We're doing a little disinformation to protect you two. The story is straightforward: Two people, a man and a woman, were pulled from the water, unresponsive. Both are in local hospitals. No more. No less."

"Misleading the media I see," she spat.

"Like you don't mislead the public! Let's wrap this up. News trucks will be here soon. We need you both fucking gone. Cade, take Ms. Sweetin, the BMW, and get the fuck out of here."

He turned and walked away. He didn't provide any opportunity for dissention or denial. Two uniformed officers brought us Arica's suitcase, my go bag, and my gun. A quick inspection determined that the round that bounced around in the trunk missed both of our bags. We both walked with our bags to the BMW.

"This is the strangest wedding reception I've ever attended," she said.

Chapter Seventeen

WE PUT THE bags into the BMW's trunk. In the trunk were two black tactical Kevlar bulletproof vests. Major Brunson had clearly given some thought to this situation. I spent a minute refamiliarizing myself with the high-end gadgetry of the car, making a mental note to think like a German engineer and understand that not all buttons are where I'd normally expect to find them. I eventually got us under way. We stayed silent for the first mile. I think we were both trying to comprehend what had just happened, but the undeniably ferocious attack on us was incomprehensible. Assembled Molotov cocktails definitely indicated preplanning on their part. This wasn't random. Was Arica the main target? Were we both targeted? Could it have been solely me? I was concerned for how she would handle the horrors of the day, considering. she thought her night was going to be an airplane seat and cocktail peanuts. Now here she was flash bombed, shot at, shoved into the Coral Gables waterway, yelled at by a police official, and now being squired away to a relative stranger's house. I was hoping her worldly experiences would help her overcome the trauma she'd just endured. I think we were both grateful to have come out of the ordeal alive and intact.

Unlike Cosima, Arica was not concerned with any of the scenery as we drove. She stared straight ahead. It was as though she had "the thousand yard stare" often referenced concerning trauma patients by clinicians like Dr. Rangela. Many people who have endured trauma experience dissociation due to the acute stress of the event. I too was feeling the aftereffects as the adrenaline drained from my body. My mind drifted back to what I told Dr. Rangela.

"I will never lament being a dragonslayer when there are verifiable dragons amongst us."

Like I said to her as she doubted me, I don't get a time-out. *"Righteous brutality is sometimes needed against people who will use as much or more brutality to hurt me or others."*

As I drove the way I felt that tonight was a textbook example that. The good doctor may see lots of patients in the law enforcement field but until one of them has an experience like we just did, I think she might want to sit this one out before getting all psychologically "I've seen it all" hoity toity.

"You okay?" I asked the rattled reporter as she stared blankly ahead.

"Ever feel like you're no longer in control of your own life?" she said dreamily.

"Control? I don't think I get nearly enough credit for not being a raging psychopath."

"And I'm sleeping under the same roof with you tonight?"

"You get my point. What did you think about what Major Brunson said back there?"

That broke her aimless gaze. She snapped her head my way. "You mean the profanity-obsessed blowhard who may have derailed my career? That Major Brunson?"

"Yeah. He's an acquired taste. For me unfortunately he's a *required* taste."

"I think he got a few things right. The places he mentioned in the world. Yes, I've been at those places, often right when something happens. He didn't mention foresight, planning, geopolitical engagement, having trusted sources. It's called being a consummate journalist."

"I get it," I said.

"There are two things I love in life. Dogs and disasters," she said.

"Something is going on here that doesn't pass the smell test. Major Brunson doesn't always lay out his intentions in black and white like that. Your associate editor...is she the type to adhere to conditions set by someone else?"

She sighed. "I think two people getting shot, one other being killed, and now the two of us nearly being killed... At this late hour she probably caved in and will change her tune in the morning."

"Perhaps," I said.

"Cade, I was in Kosovo. It was harrowing. If Major Brunson is correct, if these guys are Albanians, then this takes on a whole new meaning."

"What do you mean 'a whole new meaning'?" I asked.

"What I'm saying is that these Albanian guys are organized and ruthless. Their whole existence is structured around loyalty, honor, and family. I'll stop short of saying arranged marriages. Both families seek lifelong bonds. Impenetrable bonds. Marriages and actual blood relations are vital to their criminal success. Don't let the idea that this is some sort of steeped-only-in-tradition kind of thing. They seek deep connections to facilitate their criminal syndicates. They aren't some local hood gang either. They Albanians have *thousands* of members in all four corners of the globe."

I mulled over what she said with wary contemplation. "Are you serious?" I asked her.

"Cade, I'm talking heroin out of Afghanistan, stolen cars out of Europe into India and Asia, collections, extortions, briberies, loan sharking, money laundering, and murder. I'm sorry, did I just say murder? How could I neglect to mention murder? They are the *kings* of whacking people. Like Major Brunson, said they control the importation of cocaine directly into Italy. They're deeply aligned with the 'Ndrangheta in Italy."

"The Endrawhata?"

"The N'drangheta. Pronounced uhn-drang-geh-tuh. My linguistically challenged canal swimmer." she said with a nearly undetectable wry smile.

"The 'Ndrangheta. We always think of Al Capone and the mafia as the pinnacle of organized crime. Italy is a whole other level. Like the Albanians, they're all about family bonds and 'don't break the trust of the family.' It's a perfect match for the 'Ndrangheta to control the inside of Italy and let the Albanians handle all the transportation and importation of drugs—notably, cocaine. The Albanians refer to themselves as clans. They're *everywhere* there's crime to be exploited and money to be made. Lots of money."

"Let me repeat what I said. *Thousands* of Albanian members! They're like a criminal ribbon of mayhem and murder that runs from the Balkans on through Western Europe, on to the United States and Canada. You go up against one of them? Be ready to fight all of them."

"Like fighting in the trailerhood." I said scanning the road in front of us.

"Hardly. I'd take junked cars, and couches in front of the double wide any day over these guys. The Albanians. They *will* come for you. They never forget. The family bond is forged on strong internal discipline, and they have zero tolerance for mistakes. Those two guys tonight might live to see another day if your public information officer can sell a convincing story that you and I are practically dead. And they *will* still be punished for not finishing the job."

I started thinking that maybe Major Brunson actually knew more than he was willing to reveal in front of Arica.

"We're doing a little disinformation to protect you two."

"Everything they do is predicated on fear," Arica went on. "The looming fear that rules over the clan guarantees blind loyalty reaches deep. Infiltrating into the Albanian crime groups is nearly impossible. And the crime clans are hierarchal. You take one out, there are layers of 'next guys' that will step right into the void."

"You learned all of this from being a correspondent in Kosovo?"

"Basically."

"What do you mean 'basically'?" I asked.

"I mean you are what you know, and you are what you are."

Her doublespeak was irritating me. "What are you saying?"

"I'm saying I am Arica Sweetin, an experienced world-traveled journalist, but my mother's full maiden name is Anna Qosja Muca. My father was from a long line of Americans, and my mother is second generation Albanian. Her family comes from the southeast region of Albania in a town called Pogradec, but I was born and raised in Pompton Lakes, New Jersey."

"You're from Jersey?"

"That's right. New Jersey. The state bird is a seagull that takes your French fries." she said. We were now further along the way and would soon be at my place.

"I did the whole growing up in an idyllic American life thing." she continued "As a kid I was always pushing to be better. I started a babysitting camp for neighbor kids when I was only twelve years old, I went to Pompton Lakes High School. I was quite bored with the whole high school thing. My dad was big on grades but by my senior year going five days a week to high school was not for me. I made a deal with him that if I kept my class ranking as a senior and could still take off every Wednesday, he wouldn't ground me. I kept my end of the bargain and so did he. I spent summers being a lifeguard—"

"So, under the bridge, wrapping of your legs around me and propping me up, that was your lifeguard training?" I asked.

"Lucky for you I didn't need to use any pressure points."

"I've been swimming my whole life. I was doing just fine." I said.

"I know, but a girl's got to get her intentions known in some way." she smiled.

"Do you speak Albanian?"

"I can hold my own and order from a menu in an Albanian restaurant."

We were nearing Paradise Point, and I made the turn towards

the complex. We went through the security manned gate at the Royal Harbour Yacht Club. I carried her suitcase up to the front door and we went inside.

"Very nice, Cade Taylor. Not at all what I was expecting." she said marveling at the condominium's interior. "I was expecting early attic, late basement for furnishings."

"It's been home for the past year. A friend owns it. I'm kind of the resident caretaker."

"I'd love to see all of it, but I really just want to take a hot shower first."

"Of course. The bedrooms are upstairs. You can take your pick of which bedroom you want."

She chose the guest bedroom with the north view of the waterway. I wouldn't go so far as to say with her travel experience that she was impressed with the place, but she was definitely pleasantly surprised to discover that I did not have a coffee table made up of milk crates and plywood. She closed the bedroom door, and I heard the water turn on in her ensuite bathroom. I went into my bathroom and stripped out of my clothes. They were still damp and with a growing pungent smell from the brackish water. I bunched them up and placed them under the faucet in the jacuzzi bathtub, letting them soak in there while I just sat on the tub's edge. I wasn't sure I ever wanted to get up, but when that was completed, I stepped into the spacious tiled shower, letting the hot water cascade down on me as I thought about how close death came to me and Arica. Everything Major Brunson said about our attackers being Albanian and about Arica being targeted by the Albanians made sense.

Still, a gnawing concept chewed inside my head.

If in fact these guys were Albanian—which after talking with Arica, I believed them to be—there could be a blood bath on the streets of Miami the likes of which we hadn't seen since the era of *Cocaine Cowboys*. Finding out her mother had Albanian heritage just complicated the scenario. Could these Albanian hitmen have been going after Arica for something she did professionally, or could this be a family issue? What was Brunson doing, forcing her protection on me? Didn't he realize that I have Cosima Verratti and the Secret Service depending on me to assist with this bundled investigation?

By the time I got out of the shower it was past 11pm. I knew in my heart I should have tried to catch the local news broadcast of our "bridge swim" but I figured I'd be seeing it for the first time just like everyone else who tuned in. I wouldn't be able to change the narrative or add and subtract from the content. It was on the broadcast airwaves and out of my control.

I felt much better showered. It went beyond being clean. I felt *cleansed*. A difference, at least to me, in so many ways. I toweled off and felt my bed calling to me. I didn't want to be a bad host, but Arica was a seasoned traveler and didn't appear to have any trouble taking care of herself. If there was something she wanted or needed in the condo, I was confident she would find it herself.

I climbed into bed. It felt good to be home and relaxed, at least in body. The moonlight was peeking through the window and casting soft, ambient light into the darkened room. I'd been in bed only a few minutes when I heard a faint knock on the bedroom door.

"Yes?" I answered. "Can I come in?"

I was in a t-shirt and boxers, the way I always sleep. I was under the covers and as decent as I was going to be.

"Come in," I said.

She quietly opened the door. Arica had found a guest robe in the closet of her bedroom. She walked to the open side of my bed. She looked at me with a moment's hesitation in her eye and then she undid the sash of the white terrycloth robe, letting it fall to the bedroom floor. She was naked and she was exquisitely beautiful. She pulled the sheets back and climbed in beside me.

"You said I could pick the bedroom I want."

Chapter Eighteen

I WOKE UP WITH the morning sun weakly streaming in and reached over feeling for Arica, only to find that she was no longer in my bed. I had a moment of confusion which quickly turned to bemusement. Within moments I heard her rummaging around downstairs. My first thought was *I hope she likes beer* since it's the practically the only thing in my refrigerator. I was lying in bed, knowing this incredibly beautiful, sexy woman was downstairs looking at bottles of Amstel Light beer in my refrigerator and probably wondering if I indeed was nothing more than an unevolved frat boy.

Clearing my head of my blissful slumber I reflected on the events of the past seventy-two hours, listing it methodically.

I killed a suspected accomplice to an Albanian hitman.

Tucson Lou and I surmised that there was inside help in the assassination attempt. I met Arica.

An alert resident, Flora Hayes, witnessed what was certainly the getaway vehicle, an Enterprise rental truck, fleet number 6082.

The hit team, in their confusion over losing the man I killed, accidentally left a piece of paper behind with some sort of checklist written in Albanian.

I teamed up with Agent Cosima Verratti from the Italian Carabinieri and together we discovered that a fingerprint from the man I killed was lifted from a home invasion robbery in Coral Gables four years ago.

We interviewed home invasion robbery victim Janice Gordon, who was less than truthful and very indifferent. Her guilt-ridden husband Matthew Gordon left the family for a new life in Australia, leaving her and their children behind.

Gary "Big G" Fowler agreed to do some comparison report work on Mrs. Gordon as well as look into the Enterprise truck lease.

Cosima and I spoke to Enterprise rental employee Anthony Ichaso, who was desperate to get the truck back before his boss returned to Miami. Ichaso informed us the truck was rented with fraudulent credit cards. He provided the name and address of the person whose cards were duplicated.

Which brought me back to Arica Sweetin. She slyly asked for a lift to the airport which turned out to be a demon's ride of doom. Two Albanians tried to kill us with Molotov cocktails and lethal spinning rounds from a shotgun.

Major Brunson chewed into us both with the anger of a banshee on fire. Brunson pointedly stated that he thought Arica was the target of the attack on us. It seemed far-fetched to me, until Arica began to chronicle intimate knowledge of the Albanian mafia. She told me she's of Albanian extraction herself, which led me to wonder if this attempt to kill us was related to her family.

Then...then...then we ended up in bed together where she did in fact leave me gasping.

I fondly basked in the memories that were created only a few hours ago. I needed to keep my burgeoning feelings for Arica in check. Her intelligence and quick wit are unmatched. I needed to keep myself grounded. She's the kind of a person that can make you fall in love hard. The kind of love that when it doesn't work out, it seems the rest of your life doesn't work out either. Arica's heart beats to the rhythm of a departing train, this world-traveled journalist always chasing the big story. A human travel visa.

I ambled out of bed and turned on the shower again. The

powerful shower jets quickly filled the bathroom with steam. In the bathroom closet was a basket filled with bars of Floris Stephanotis Luxury Soap. I'd been tapping into the provided supply of the coveted British soap for months. The bathroom soon had a lovely floral scent being carried aloft by the steam. I brushed my teeth vigorously while in the shower. The hot water felt good. Really good. Better maybe than it had after my life-or-death swim because I was so spent and exhausted. I saw the steam swirl out of the bathroom door before I heard her voice.

"Am I going to need a snorkel?" she said as she opened the shower door and stepped inside.

"How long can you hold your breath?"

"Longer than expected. I used to be a lifeguard. Remember?"

There was more than enough room in the shower for us both, yet we stayed fused to each other under one of the four showerheads. Her skin against mine, her long, deep breaths against my chest felt divine. She was beautiful like a sunrise you'd chase across continents just to see again. I'd been in the shower long before Arica got in. My skin was getting wrinkly and pruny. I was the first to leave the shower.

"Sissy," she called out to me as I closed the shower door behind me.

Minutes later she remarked as she toweled off that she was surprised I was dressed already.

"It's not my fault you shower like you're posing for a shampoo commercial," I said.

"I do it for the residuals," she quipped.

I heard my cellphone ringing in the bedroom. I waited until I'd walked out to the bedroom terrace before answering it. It was Secret Service Supervisory Agent Wayne Felton.

"Hello."

"Cade, it's Wayne Felton. Did I wake you up?"

"No. Not at all. What's up, Wayne?"

"Agent Akicita scheduled us for a meeting in an hour but we're going to put that on hold for later. I'll let you know."

"Okay. What caused the delay?" I asked.

"A few things. Before I get into all that, Cade... Are you holding out on us?" he said directly.

"Holding out on what?"

"Carabinieri Agent Verratti informed us last night that you had information that a fingerprint lifted from the guy you killed matched an offender in a cold case home invasion robbery in your city. She said that you both went and interviewed the victim." His voice was cold, accusing.

"Yeah, well, about that. Cosima and I—"

"She also mentioned an Enterprise rental truck that may have been the getaway vehicle in our shooting. She says it was rented with a bogus credit card and might still be out here in Miami somewhere."

"I hadn't seen you and was thinking—" I tried to explain.

"Let me tell you what I'm thinking. Are you keeping relative information pertaining to a Treasury investigation from us?" he said, his voice rising.

I firmly said, "I received that information when she was with me, and we decided to pay a visit to the victim of the home invasion. It was Saturday and there was a good chance the victim might be home. Fortunately for us, she was. This is a Coral Gables unsolved robbery. The truck information came late in the day, and I like I said, I hadn't had an opportunity to document everything, but an important fact is I *am* Coral Gables, and the victims from the Biltmore shooting are under the investigative governance of the Carabinieri. This isn't a Treasury case. You and I are just pulled in by proxy and by my being the trigger on the motorcyclist."

"I beg to differ, but I'll table that for now. We got a positive identification on the dead motorcyclist last night. Guy's name was Erjon Dren."

"Erjon Dren?" I repeated.

"The guy was in the enforcement side of things for Albanian mobs. Somehow, he stayed out of jail, but we have a source that confirmed he was a real tough one. The kind of guy who'd punch a storm and win. I mean, a serious, bad, *mean* thug. You did us all a favor. It would have just been a matter of time until he'd cross paths with one of us in law enforcement."

The first thought that crossed my mind was how had Lieutenant Maddalone and Miami Dade Homicide make a fingerprint match but didn't discover Erjon Dren's name?

"How did you make a positive identification on Erjon Dren?" I asked Felton. "We got it from Miami Dade Homicide," he said.

So much for Lieutenant Maddalone being a reliable conduit of information. I guess his competency in relaying information didn't function on his Sunday day off. I also took note that Agent Felton didn't ask anything about our near-death ordeal last night. Either he was very callous, didn't see the local news, or had no idea what happened. If you asked me based on him being a federal agent, he is probably a callous no news watching guy who has no idea what is happening. I'll ring the bell on all three. Major Brunson was absolutely playing this one close to the vest and holding the information cards at the bottom of the deck. With what I learned about Albanian mobs from Arica and the ferocity of Brunson's ire last night, it was logical for me to not mention it, even though Agent Felton already thought I was holding back information. This secrecy put me in an odd spot. I decided to keep my faith in Brunson and let it sit for the moment.

"Agents Akicita and Borges are following a developing Treasury Department lead with a prolific Albanian credit card ring. The ring's been busting us up all over the eastern seaboard. Both of my agents have intel that might lead to a connection. We want to go at them when we have it all worked out. Cosima Verratti's on board with our decision as well. We're going to bring you in when we start hammering it down. Maybe later today, might be tomorrow."

"Okay," was all I could muster to say.

"Cade, now that you have a name with the motorcyclist...I don't want you to get sideways about it. You did a good job the other day. You may have saved someone, maybe even one of us from being killed. I'll call you later today, we'll set up a pow-wow amongst us."

I hung up and sat on the chaise lounge with the morning sun warming my body. I looked at my phone, contemplating the conversation with Agent Felton.

This case was getting murkier by the hour.

There's no way he knows about what happened to Arica and me. Just no way. He would have said something.

Major Brunson must have had a serious vice grip on the dissemination of information related to us. We hadn't been very far from the hotel when the Albanians rammed our car. Even if Felton had an upper floor southside room he would have seen the police lights last night. Yet he never mentioned it at all. There was something else he didn't mention—that Cosima and I were tracking the Enterprise truck. The very truck the Albanian crew used to spirit away the would-be assassin. Cosima must have not told him. But why not? I knew I'd have to see Cosima sometime that day, and I would find out why she was holding that information back.

"Anything important?" Arica asked me.

"The usual usual," I said.

"Do you always double-speak?"

"Not really, maybe, sometimes." I said, confusing her even more.

"I thought I'd be eating a bagel on Madison Avenue this morning. Any ideas for breakfast?" she asked.

Within minutes we were pulling into the shopping complex right in front of the Muffin Tin restaurant. The quaint little bistro was full of Sunday morning diners, many of them experiencing the first Sunday of the year without an NFL game to watch or talk about. The mood was very gentile in the restaurant, and we were fortunate to get a table for two by the front windows looking out over the parking lot. I didn't feel exposed by the window and quite frankly thought it would afford us the best protection to see an adversary, should there be any out there. Arica settled into her chair across from me and looked approvingly at the menu.

"This place reminds me of a little café I would go to as a child visiting my grandmother. She always got hot tea and a grilled blueberry muffin," Arica said.

Arica ordered the country morning skillet, and I decided on the Havana Melt...and a grilled blueberry muffin for us to share.

"Last night..." she said, starting the conversation.

"Last night?" I replied.

"Not *last night*, last night..."

"Do you always double-speak?" I said.

"I mean I'm not talking about last night; I'm talking about *before* last night. The night before the last part of last night," she said.

"Does sex make you confused?" I teased her.

"Hardly. I'm talking about our unplanned late-night swim." she said gesturing with her arms as she tried to explain herself.

I waded into the conversation relieving her of her momentary exasperation.

"I don't know everything, but I know that it might not be the same men from last night, but there will be others. If what you said about Albanian crime groups is true, this isn't over. If the disinformation Major Brunson put out about us being in a local hospital holds up, I'd guess they're using their network to find out what hospital you and I are in."

"That doesn't sound very optimistic." she said.

"Two Balkan desperados throw a Molotov cocktail at us before firing four shotgun rounds at us? Optimism is not high on the response board."

"That's as disturbing to hear now as it was last night. So, what now? I mean, we can't stay underground forever."

"Major Brunson pegged you as the sole target in the attack last night. Aside from your inner team at Trident Broadcasting, did anybody else know about your plans to travel to New York?"

"No. I got the call. No different than any other time. Gotta move and be somewhere practically before I even hang up. I'm the queen of packing and leaving…" She paused for a beat. "Anyway, nothing out of the ordinary I was working my cellphone, calling the concierge to get a taxi, checking flights, asking for my hotel bill to be sent to corporate accounting…all the stuff I've done from Karachi to Kansas City. I was on the elevator and in the lobby within fifteen minutes."

I was running the timeline of what she just said in my head. I have conducted enough interviews in my life to detect certain cues of untruthfulness. Her eyes. Her body language. The way she held her hands…nothing foretold me of any deception.

"That quick?" I asked.

"That quick," she replied with a snap of her fingers.

"Could someone on your team have set you up? About this New York story? How important was it for you to be the one covering it?"

"I'm stateside and experienced. That's all they need to set me in motion."

"There just isn't a whole lot of time to get an Albanian hit team in place unless they were positioned outside the hotel and planning to go after you somewhere in the hotel…" I pondered out loud.

"That's a scary thought. They clearly didn't care about killing innocent people. If they'd tried it at the hotel, it would have been a blood bath…and you can forget about tourism. No one will ever stay at the Biltmore Hotel for years after all the carnage in the past few days," she said.

"I think tourism is the last of our concerns. Let's take it in stages. You slept away from the hotel last night, you're in a different car, and we're away from the general area they might be looking for you. We have some good precautions in place. I'd caution you not to reveal anything to Trident Broadcasting about where you are."

Arica took it all in and pensively looked out the window at the full parking lot of cars. The conversation trailed off, and she went even deeper into her thoughts. She took in my cautionary advice and with a nod of her head acknowledged what I had just said.

"I get it. I get it," she said softly.

"Still talking double-speak. I see" I teased. "No, it's not the sex!"

"Uh huh." I said sarcastically.

"Although I'm sure your neighbors probably think we were filming an action movie."

The waitress placed our inviting meals in front of us. The grilled blueberry muffin had a wafting aroma of sizzling butter and heated blueberries. Arica's lips twitched in anticipation at the large muffin cut in half on the plate.

"Just like I remember with my grandmother."

We enjoyed our breakfast and upon leaving the restaurant I scanned the parking lot. Being sure to go out the door before her. Nothing seemed out of place or potentially harmful.

"Is there somewhere I could go to pick up a few things? I'd like to get a few shorts or shirts that are more geared for an unexpected longer stay in South Florida, if you get my drift," she said.

We drove the short distance to the Falls Shopping Center. The Falls is an upscale, open-air plaza designed around a lushly landscaped, man-made lagoon featuring numerous tributaries, waterfalls and accented bridges crossing the crystal-clear running water. There are curated and specifically chosen art pieces and sculptures placed amongst the selected tropical landscaping. A three-story Bloomingdale's department store anchors the east side of the property and a Macy's replicates that on the west side of the mall. A six-screen Regal Cinema is a mainstay in the pleasant shopping center.

"Oh, this is nice. It reminds me of shopping in Bangkok," she remarked as we walked near the center lagoon.

Shopping was not my forte. Especially shopping in Bangkok. It was obvious from my talks with Arica that while I was here in Miami dipping and diving all about Dade County, she was busy seeing a larger portion of the world. The yin and yang of international stories and international commerce. She was chasing the next big story in the world, and I was trying to not *be* the next big story in the world. I was rooted in Miami, and she had no roots.

She noticed the Mel Gibson movie "Payback" was playing at the Regal Cinema as we walked by. "Mel Gibson is so perfectly imperfect. I like imperfect," she said, grinning at me.

"What's that supposed to mean?"

"It means we should see a movie and sit in comfy seats and eat our weight in popcorn. I adore popcorn."

Spending the afternoon tucked away in a darkened movie theater was a very good way to keep Arica safe and the both of us cloistered and out of sight. I bought a two-ticket package that had unlimited popcorn refills. Her love of popcorn was not an exaggeration, and the unlimited refills were a bargain. When the movie ended, we walked amongst the late afternoon crowd of shoppers and Arica went into multiple stores browsing merchandise and buying a few things. I grew anxious and wanted to get her back to my place where I felt she would be better protected. It was now mid to late afternoon and barely touching the dinner hour. Satiated by the mountains of popcorn, I still suggested dinner so that I can get the approaching evening secured, and in turn get her ensconced back home.

"Dinner? Did you not see me horking down all that popcorn?" she said.

"Let's get something we can take home and eat later. How do you feel about Italian?"

"*Il Cortile* on Mulberry Street in Little Italy is a favorite of mine. Do you think we can make it there tonight?" she teased.

"Hardly. Your chance to go to Little Italy in New York City came and went last night. There's a great little place practically across U.S.1 from here. I order from them all the time."

"Antipasto with a side order of garlic rolls?" she said with upturned lips.

I called Papa Ricco's Italian Restaurant and put in a to-go order for an antipasto salad with a side order of garlic rolls, linguine with meatballs, and a medium pizza with mushrooms, green peppers, and Italian sausage.

"You got pizza too?" Arica asked me as I finished the call.

"Pizza is for much later. You ever have pizza in the bathtub?"

"Does it have to be the bathtub?"

I just looked down shaking my head and smiled.

"Come on. By the time we get to Papa Ricco's our order should be ready."

We picked up our order and went back to my place in Paradise Point. We'd just settled in, and Arica went directly upstairs. That's when my cellphone rang. It was Major Brunson. The ringing of the phone punctured the idyllic normalcy of my day and reaffirmed just as I had told Dr. Rangela that in VIN *"It's a never-ending cycle."*

"Cade, the damn sunglass syndicate at the fucking Secret Service is still fucking buzzing about this whole thing."

"Isn't this more of an Italian Carabinieri situation?"

"Of course it is, but this goddamn Felton guy is taking it fucking personally that a dignitary got winged on his fucking watch. This asshole requested—and got approval—to keep him and whatever semblance of a team he has to stay on-site at the splendidly fucking expensive Biltmore until there's fucking suitable traction on this case."

"Okay?" I replied.

"They developed information on some Albanian counterfeiters—"

"Yeah, Felton called me and said something about that."

"Then why the fuck am I retelling you this shit when I could be watching Morley Safer fuck over some dimwit on *60 Minutes*?"

"Felton didn't say too much when he called this morning."

"That must be before Gary Fowler put a few things together. The stolen credit card used to rent the truck was taken from a man named Jordan Barzal. Mr. Barzal's address is 19618 East Lake Drive, Miami."

"Yes, I'm aware of that," I said.

"Cade, can you close your fucking yapper and just listen for once? Barzal told Miami Dade cops that he thinks his credit card was stolen in the mail. Gary did a little neighborhood search and discovered that there's a Coldstream Drive practically around the corner. Didn't one of the notations written in Albanian say something like 'Dump Coldstream'?" he asked.

Hidhni Coldstream.

"It was torn sheet of paper with notations on it..." I said.

"Right so what are the chances the Secret Service is looking for these Albanian fucklards and the address from the truck rental is right around the damn corner?"

"Do you think they got that careless or lazy?" I asked him.

"They're criminals. Gary says you told him that one of these ironheads had on a court-mandated ankle monitor. How fucking brilliant do you think they are that one of them got pinched? Nonetheless, don't underestimate these violent fuckers. They fucking shot two people and tried to kill that goddamn TV reporter you got sitting on your couch."

I reflexively looked towards the couch. Arica was still upstairs.

"Okay, so what does Agent Felton want to do?"

"He and that wahoo from Phoenix—"

"Tucson," I corrected him. "Agent Akicita. Tucson Lou."

"Does it really fucking matter, Cade? I don't give a Miami fuck if he's from Scottsdale, Flagstaff, or standing on a fucking corner in Winslow, Arizona. The two of them and that other agent from Palm Beach want to hit the streets at the crack-ass of dawn and start looking for these damn Albanians. Be fucking geared up and hot-shit ready at the parking lot of the Venetian Pool. Festivities start at 5am. They want to be moving towards North Dade before sunrise. Reach out and make sure that agent from the Carabinieri is included."

"Got it. What about protection for Arica Sweetin?"

"I arranged for Detective Johan Williamson to step in on that. He'll be at your place at 4:30 am. Make sure to put him on your fancy-dancy guest list. If you don't want him going through your underwear drawer, he can stay outside in the car. I don't really fucking care as long as we got eyes on her in some capacity."

"Understood."

"What?"

"I mean I understand," I replied.

"Keep me appraised," he said before hanging up.

I called the complex's front gate and had Detective Johan Williamson added to the guest list. I left a voice message on Cosima Verratti's cellphone informing her of the plans—that we'd be gathering up two blocks away from the hotel by the city's Venetian Pool. She texted me back a minute later and said she knew the plan and would prefer me to be the one she rides with, rather than any of the Secret Service agents. I texted back that I would pick her up at 4:45 am by the hotel's upper-level valet stand. Ironically, the same location where all my recent monstrous mayhem originated.

"The sunsets here are astounding!" Arica called down to me.

I could hear the master bath's large marble bathtub filling with water. Arica came down the stairs with a floral-print beach towel cinched tightly around her. She had a seductive strength about her that made her sexuality mesmerizing. I was speechless as she comfortably eased down the stairs with an irresistible sexy presence. She smiled that radiant smile of hers as I watched her pick up the pizza box from the kitchen counter across the condo. She plucked the pizza cutting wheel from the utensil carafe. Wordlessly she turned away with the pizza, and the pizza cutting wheel and started back up the stairs.

"You know that the pizza comes already cut," I called out to her.

"Who said it's for the pizza?" she said as she continued up the stairs.

Chapter Nineteen

I TOLD ARICA THAT I'd be leaving early in the morning and that Johan would be stationed outside but she suggested I let him come inside and rather than sit in his car all day. The next morning as quietly as I could, I slipped out of bed and out of the condominium. I relayed Arica's message to Johan Williamson who was parked out front, and he went inside. The digital clock on my car's dashboard said 4:33 am as I passed through the Royal Harbour Yacht Club. Traffic was nonexistent, and I was right on time to pick up Cosima at the Biltmore Hotel. She was outside and got into my car. The early hour rendered us both sleepily quiet.

"Good morning."

"Good morning, Cade. Have you been keeping busy?"

"Somewhat. How about you?"

"I'll tell you later," she said, returning to a peacefully hushed morning.

Her peacefulness was short lived. Within two minutes we were pulling into the parking lot of the Venetian Pool. Agents Felton, Borges, and Akicita were standing outside of two parked dark sedans. Cosima and I joined them.

"Too early for you, Cade?" said Borges with that smug smile of his. "Not exactly doper time is it?"

"Time is a foreign concept in the drug world," I said.

"Okay, we're all here," said Felton by way of greeting, and pointed at me. "Cade, you'll drive the lead. Cosima, you'll be with Cade. The goal is to get up to Coldstream Drive, see if we can find any of our Albanian friends up there. On the map Coldstream Drive is just a short little strip with houses on a golf course. Borges is taking his car and has opted to take the west side of Coldstream. Me and Tucson Lou will be in the middle. Cade, you and Cosima will be on the east side. We should have a good visual on all parts of the street. We're looking for anyone that matches our shooter or anything that looks fishy."

Felton handed me a Secret Service radio for me and Cosima to have in our car. "It's got a full charge. Make sure I get it back."

We all went to our cars: Felton and Tucson Lou in one car, Borges solo, and me and Cosima in mine. It seemed like an ungodly hour to start this stakeout, but we beat so much of the dreaded South Florida traffic. I put both tactical vests on the backseat of my car. I didn't see a need to don the vest at 5:00 in the morning but I wanted to have them handy.

The Palmetto Expressway was unclogged, and we went right into the "big bend" north of Miami Lakes, then continued west from Miami Gardens Drive to the Country Club of Miami. The ride north was quiet both in my car and on the radio. As we neared Coldstream Drive the silence was punctured by a transmission from Borges on the radio:

"I got the west side."

Felton and Akicita took the middle of the street, and we fell into place on the east side. The sun was barely rising when Cosima finally began to perk up.

"I got hardly any sleep last night," she said.

"Me too," I said as I wondered if the pizza box was still in the bathroom.

"Ever since you dropped me off Lou has been all up in my business."

"In your business?"

"*Si! Lui è più vicino a me di un'ombra!*" [Yes! He is closer to me than a shadow!]

"I don't know what that means but it sounds like maybe he's been crowding you," I said.

"Exactly! I'm here to work, not work *out* with him, meet him in the lounge for dinner, and hear his stories about being in Naples with President Clinton. He keeps trying to talk Italian to me and he isn't very good."

"I get it. My boss and I feel this is more of a Carabinieri case than a Secret Service case. Were you able to spend time with your agent in the hospital?"

"He's going to survive. I don't know what the quality of his life will be, but he is going to live. I don't foresee him coming back to the Carabinieri. They had to do a lot of surgical work on him—a bowel resection and anastomosis, and a ton of other things. I met with the consulate as well. He was in good spirits. He vowed this would not keep him from continuing his campaign. Italy could use a man of his caliber; he seems very nice. Very authentic. Committed to his country. I didn't meet her, but he told me that his lovely fiancé has been at his bedside nearly the entire time."

"Agent Felton accused me of holding back information. Truth is, I didn't really have much time to brief him or the Secret Service about the rental truck." I said.

"Its all okay. I briefed them last night about a lot of it. Borges seems really interested, and I think Felton wants a win. Then again, we all want a win on this one or I'll have some explaining to do when I get back to Milan. Lou is hard to read. He's a little spacey" she commented as she adjusted the air conditioning vent away from her.

"Did you know that Lou was originally stationed on the hotel terrace where the consulate was going to speak? But your Carabinieri Agent came down from New York and wanted to feel the sunshine, so they switched positions," I told her.

She whipped her head around towards me, eyes narrowed. "They switched on their own, without any approval?" she asked.

"Far as I know," I said. "Tucson Lou might be fighting a little survivor guilt. That could have easily been him on the terrace. He was really struggling with the failure of the event; he told me it would be his own Clint Hill moment."

"Who is Clint Hill?" she asked.

"A long retired Secret Service Agent who was assigned to President Kennedy's protection detail that fateful November day in Dallas. He's known for being the agent who jumped onto the back of Kennedy's limousine, trying to shield the President and Mrs. Kennedy. For the exceptional agent he was, Hill is always historically linked to that moment. Tucson Lou thinks this will be his own linkage to a failed event."

"I see," she said.

"Did Lou mention the melted ice to you?"

"No. What melted ice?"

"We think the shooter was inside dressed as a hotel worker—"

"Yes, I know," she said.

"Well, the bank of doors behind the consulate that led out to the terrace were locked. Except one. The exact one the shooter made his escape through. He knew that one particular door that was intentionally unlocked. On either side of the door frame, we discovered puddles of very cold water on the carpet. We theorized that ice was placed on each side of the door frame as a marker. The shooter could see the ice on his escape run and know what door to go through. By the time the investigation started the ice would have melted and no one would've been the wiser."

Cosima silently assessed what I was telling her. I remembered what Lou had told me when we were in the ballroom while the investigation of the shooting was taking place.

"Borges had the east side of the room by the windows. Felton was near the front. The Carabinieri wanted to be front and center."

"All three of the agents were in the ballroom when this went down. I think they want some redemption." I sad.

The next three hours went by with mind-numbing dullness. An occasional resident walking a dog, a child and his backpack being ushered into a minivan for the daily commute to school, but predominantly it was just another quiet suburb street in Miami whose residents were waking up to the routine of their lives. The radio was silent. Everyone was placidly subdued by the demand to be on Coldstream Drive so early. It was after 8am when the silence was broken by a very calm-sounding Tom Borges on the radio. "Just had a garage door open at 7437. Stand by, I'll advise."

"You think that is anything?" Cosima asked me.

"Sometimes you get on surveillance, and a homeowner will come out and ask who you are or why you're parked in front of their house. Most people just flash their badge and try and make the encounter as short and uninformed as they can."

"In Italy we just tell them *smamma*. Which literally means 'beat it.'"

"Smamma? I'll have to remember that." I said making a mental note to myself

It was at that moment that we heard a breathless Borges transmit, "I got a shake!"

I straightened up and slammed the car into drive. "He's running!" I said to the now-alert Cosima before she could ask me what a shake was.

The BMW roared like a lion as I pushed down hard on the gas, the torque shoving Cosima towards her door. There wasn't anything more to be said between us. She knew the dynamic of our morning had just shifted. As I turned the wheel to the left, we both got a view of Felton pulling out from the grassy swale in the middle of the street. Tucson Lou's passenger door was open and as Felton peeled away, Lou leaped out of the car and ran west towards Borge's car.

I spotted Borges' car as we raced towards his location. It was empty, the driver's door hung open. Still screaming down Coldstream Drive, we both startled at the sound of a gunshot.

Bam!

Lou flinched at the sound, but he kept on running. Felton pulled up at a house, its open garage door revealing the yawning interior. My focus wasn't on the contents of the garage but on locating Borges. Lou arrived on foot just as we pulled up. He kept running past the open garage door and turned the corner around the front side of the house.

Bam. Bam.

Two more gunshots rang out. I locked up the brakes and before we came to a complete stop the passenger door was open and Cosima jumped out, yelling back to me: "Inside!"

She ran full- speed into the garage following Felton. I slammed the car into park and burst out of the car. I was drawing my weapon as I crossed in front of the house, sprinting to the corner to follow Lou. I slammed hard against the stucco exterior, the rough concrete gouging into my right elbow. I barely registered the neighbors coming out of their homes upon hearing the gunshots. I did a very quick Israeli peek around the corner. No sign of the Secret Service agents or anyone else. I dashed around the corner and kept running towards the golf course behind the house. Lou and Borges still weren't in view. The radio was in my car, leaving me cut off from everyone. I could hear my own breathing as I tried to maintain my composure. The house was at an angle, causing the grassy pathway between the two to narrow. I swung my gun across my torso and aimed to my left. I assumed...actually, I hoped...that Cosima and Felton had gone straight from the front of the house clear through and out the back door. That would put them somewhere on my right, leading me to put trust that my right side was more secure than my left.

Already sweat was rolling down the back of my neck and my pulse was racing as I drew rapidly closer to the pinch point between the two houses. I kept my running momentum and never stopped, ducking low and using the neighbor's pool pump and sand filter as a best as I could for cover. Dipping behind the pool machinery, I saw Borges on the ground with Lou hovering over him. Off to their right was a man on his back at the fringe of the golf course. The man wore sweatpants and a gray t-shirt, quickly being covered in a fast-spreading blood stain. I kept running towards Lou and Borges. Lou saw me coming towards them. Lou's gun was holstered. Borges' gun was lying in the grass next to him.

"Cade! Press on his shoulder!" Lou yelled at me.

Borges was on his back, blankly looking up at the sky. Blood soaked his left shoulder. His eyes were glassy, and spittle bubbled at the corner of his mouth. I practically slid onto the ground beside him and without hesitation pressed my hands firmly on his shirt over the largest, deepest blood pool. He jolted upright, and his eyes widened. He screamed in pain.

I looked over at the other unknown man lying in the grass. Lou said, "Don't worry about him. He's dead."

Cosima and Felton came bounding out the rear glass doors of the house with guns drawn. Their expressions were a morphing mixture of concern and confusion as they ran to us. I maintained direct pressure on Borge's shoulder.

"Felton! You got your phone? Call 911!" I barked at him.

He stumbled through the call trying to tell the emergency dispatcher who he was, that he was a U.S. Secret Service agent, then he fumbled even more on the address.

"Put it on speaker! Put it near me!" I commanded him and he held the phone near my face.

I yelled towards the phone in Miami Dade police code to the dispatcher:

"Three-fifteen! Officer down! Officer down! Coldstream Drive, north of Miami Lakes. Coldstream Drive on the west end of the street. Three-fifteen! I need units! Start rescue on a three. Start Air Rescue One for an airlift from the Country Club of Miami directly behind my QTH! Subject is forty-five. 341 is a federal agent. This is

Gables, 923!" I screamed into the small void between my face and the phone.

Felton kept the line open. In less than two minutes we started hearing sirens. Felton laid the phone in the grass and lifted Borges' legs, elevating them above his heart, trying to thwart Borges from going into shock. Cosima checked the pulse on the dead guy, then used her cellphone to take a picture of his face. There was no gun with the dead guy. Uniformed Miami Dade officers arrived in droves. One of the first responding officers had a trauma bandage that quickly clots gaping wounds. I released my pressure grip on Borges' shoulder, seeing a distinctive powder burn from the bullet churning into his flesh. The officer dutifully applied the bandage over the fresh wound. Miami Dade Fire Rescue arrived within minutes, and with the assembling police units the crime scene began to transform into a Miami Dade P.D. investigation. A yellow tarp was placed over the deceased unknown male.

A contingency of officers formed a wide circle on the adjacent golf course. Using roadside flares and occasional short bursts from hand-held fire extinguishers, they created a landing zone for the Air Rescue One medical transport helicopter for Borges. I couldn't help but see the irony of a second landing zone on yet another second golf course for yet another second agent shot. Lou volunteered to take the life flight with Borges to Jackson Memorial Hospital Trauma Center. Before he left with the stretcher to the landing zone, I asked Lou what happened.

"I don't know! I got around the house and Tom was down, and the other guy was down. I could tell right away that the other guy was dead. I mean graveyard dead. Gone. No chance. It made helping Tom easier because I didn't have to deal with the other guy. Then you showed up."

"One gun?" I asked as he started to roll with the hurrying officers and paramedics holding I.V.s, oxygen tanks, and an EKG machine as they wheeled Borges over the golf course to the awaiting helicopter.

"One gun! Unless the dead guy's laying on one. One gun!" he shouted over the increasing roar of the helicopter blades.

I stopped moving and stood back as they rolled the stretcher up to the open doors of the helicopter. The morning golfers understood the need for an interruption to their early tee times. There will always be the one or two guys who selfishly pout about the disruption, but they stayed silent. The golfers gathered on the fairway a safe distance from all the activity in front of them. One of the golfers in a blue Izod shirt was closest to the scene, leaning on his nine-iron. I walked over to him and the rest of his group and asked if they saw or heard anything. The golfer in the blue shirt spoke first.

"It was like a *bang*, then a moment later two more bangs. I thought it was firecrackers—"

"I thought it was car backfiring," interrupted one of his partners.

"It's about context, you know? You're not expecting this type of thing, so your mind is trying to make sense of it all," said the blue shirt golfer.

I looked at him and let him think about what he was saying. "I mean *my* mind. My mind wasn't expecting it." he clarified. "So, you heard the gunshots but did any of you see anything?"

The quartet of golfers closest to where Tom Borges was when the situation unfolded all told me that they didn't see anything. At this point two Miami Dade officers joined me to take over getting information and statements from the golfers. Before walking away, I asked the golfers once again if they recalled seeing or hearing anything. One of the golfers who'd been quiet spoke up.

"Before the gunshots I heard one of them say something."

"What did you hear?" I asked.

"I'm not sure it was weird. It sounded like '*Ndalo! Jam unë!*'"

"What?"

"*Ndalo! Jam unë!*" the golfer repeated. "I heard it twice."

"Twice?" I asked him.

"Yeah. Twice."

"What the heck is that?" the golfer in the blue Izod said to him.

"I'm telling you what I heard. I thought it was someone calling a dog or something. *Ndalo! Jam unë. Ndalo! Jam unë.*"

Chapter Twenty

Twenty minutes later Agent Felton enlisted the help of three Miami Dade officers in securing the residence.

"We got a lot of stuff in there," he said to me. "What stuff?" I asked.

"You'll see." He turned his attention to Cosima. "Come with us and let's lock down the inside of the house."

We entered through the rear glass doors. The house had all the markings of a stash house. Minimum furniture, nothing on the walls, lots of used take-away food containers, pizza boxes, a stinky, overflowing garbage can, a large-screen TV with loose cables and plugs connecting to bare wall outlets. In the center of what I guess was designed to be the living room were three heat press-type machines. Multicolored slivers of plastic littered the floor all around them. On top of a wobbly, scratched table that looked like it had been pulled from a trash pile were stacks and bundles of mail. I leaned over the pile of mail and saw that one of the open envelopes was a mortgage solicitation to an address in Hallandale Beach, Florida.

"What's all this?" asked Cosima.

"This looks like the motherlode of phony credit cards from our Albanian friends," Felton said. "I'm sorry, what?" I asked.

"They've been stealing mail," he said, pointing at the stacks of envelopes, "looking for addresses, names, birth dates, anything that they can find to create phony cards. There are racks of sheets of mylar and plastic in the garage and enough kid stickers from Toys 'R' Us to fill a kindergarten class."

"What's with the kid stickers?" I asked.

"They want the holograms from the stickers. Reflective holograms from all the ponies, unicorns, dancing seals, whatever the stickers are. They cut tiny little squares out of the stickers and affix them to the cards, make them look like a legitimate hologram to waiters, salesclerks, service attendees..."

"For real?" I exclaimed.

"When did you last check the hologram on your credit cards?"

"I've never checked the hologram on my cards," I said.

"Exactly. These guys have been churning out hundreds of these bogus credit cards, committing identity theft, and fleecing businesses all around the globe. The internet hasn't caught up to them yet and every day more businesses are creating websites with no safeguards against fraud." he said.

"Except for the mail there aren't any stolen goods in this house," noticed Cosima.

"This is where they were making the phony cards. Cutting the plastic and mylar from the sheets in the garage and heat pressure printing the cards in here. The things they're buying are probably being shipped and fenced in Albanian stronghold cities like Detroit, Jacksonville, and of course their biggest area of concentration, the Bronx," said Felton.

"So, what do we know about the dead guy?" I asked him.

"Him? He was probably the house sitter. Looks like they were wrapping things up here and moving on. Thank God Tom knew what to look for—when the guy opened the garage Tom saw all the plastic and mylar. Looks like the guy ran and then there was a struggle in the back. This is a win for the Secret Service."

"A win? How is this a win? You just had an agent shot," I said, incredulous.

"As far as Washington is concerned this will be chocked up as a big win." said Felton looking around before directing his attention back at me. "This is a major credit card fraud ring that has been operating all up and down the east coast. They've been three steps in front of us in every way. No matter what we tried, they seemed to always be out of reach. We'd get close and they'd move on only to come back bigger and more sophisticated than the last time. True professionals these guys are. So yes, this is a win—for Washington. It's not a win for Tom and doesn't look like a win for us...right now. But if Tom recovers, which I think he will, I can see unit citations and agency awards for him, Lou and myself."

"As disturbing as that mindset is, how does a credit card ring figure in the attempted assassination of potentially the next premier of Italy?" asked Cosima.

"Disturbing?" Felton exclaimed testily, turning on her with cold eyes and the most emotion I'd ever seen from him.

She fixed her eyes right back on him. "Yes. Disturbing. Recovering machinery and a pallet of plastic sheets is not equal to my agent being shot, our political candidate being shot, and now your own agent being shot. It's disturbing!"

"Agent Verratti, you may not understand the politics and achievements of American law enforcement, but we need to take our victories when we can." he said sternly addressing her. "The United States Secret Service is the only...I mean *only* law enforcement agency that realistically drills and trains for the inevitable time that one of our agents may be shot. We don't seek or welcome it but recognize that the proverbial 'taking a bullet' is part of our job description. This is who we are, and this is what we do," snapped Felton.

More investigators were filtering into the house.

"Wayne, this is something you know more about than we do," I said gently to ease the tension. "Cosima and I will go out back and see what we can learn about the dead guy." I motioned for her to leave with me.

When we were outside Cosima let loose with a barrage of Italian angst.

"*È una vittoria che gli agenti siano quasi morti? Che razza di stronzate sono queste? Porca miseria!*"

[Is it a victory that the agents almost died? What kind of bullshit is this? Holy crap!]

Miami Dade Homicide was now on the scene. Three of them were with the dead body. We introduced ourselves. They weren't too interested in us, but they did show enough professional courtesy to tell us what they knew so far. They pulled back the tarp. Fierce powder burns circled the ugly, raw, gaping bullet wounds with coagulated and dried blood packed inside.

Two bullet wounds: one into his chest and the other in his upper abdomen.

"See those powder burns? That's up close. The gun was about an inch from the first round in the chest and pressed directly on the abdomen on the second shot," the investigator said.

"How do you know which shot was first and which shot was second? asked Cosima.

"A couple of things. Like here, we have a decent presence of powder stippling," he said.

"Stippling?" she asked.

"Unburnt powder particles that are embedded in the skin around the wound. See these black particle spots?" he said, pointing at the chest wound. "This indicates a close-up shot. This is how we get a good idea about which shot was fired at different ranges. It's a good indication of the shot sequence. With our guy here, he was shot in the chest and then in the abdomen."

"You're certain?" I asked.

"More certain than taxes and traffic in Miami," he said looking up at me. "There are soot deposits right her at the wound. It's a lot like stippling, this black soot around his abdomen wound tells us for sure this was a close range bullet entry point."

"If the deceased didn't have a gun how the Secret Service agent get shot?" I asked, hoping any of the three assembled investigators would answer.

"My guess? They struggled and fought over the agent's gun. The agent took one in the shoulder but was able to retain his gun and shot our guy here twice," said another investigator without looking up as he wrote notes into a black binder.

"Any idea who he is?"

The second agent made a *hmmph* and raised an eyebrow with annoyance. "Place is full of phony I.D.s and credit cards, he was wearing sweatpants and had nothing on him. I'd say unless finger-prints and dental match, we won't know for a while."

I saw Felton standing out by the back patio talking on his cellphone. I thanked the Miami Dade homicide investigators and with Cosima, walked over to Felton as he was finishing up his call.

"That was Tucson Lou," he said as he hung up. "Tom is in surgery for the removal of the bullet. The doctors are optimistic that he'll be okay. There are a ton of people here and I have at least six guys coming from the Miami field office. You two don't need to be here. Miami Dade has your information. This will be a slog of a day for the Secret Service. I mean a whole day of investigating and confiscating. We're just looking at the tip of the iceberg. It's one of the biggest credit card identity theft rings we've ever seen. Seriously, get going before you get drafted into doing stuff."

I didn't need to be told twice. Felton turned back to the buzzing activity at the house as Cosima and I got back into my car. I had two missed calls, one was from Brunson, the other from Gary. I called Major Brunson first.

"Cade the Special Agent in charge of the Secret Service's Miami field office has been fucking calling me all morning. He said it's a fucking shit zoo of a crime scene, but he did say that you and that agent from the Carabinieri did a great job out there today. Actually, he praised all of you. He says he thinks the Palm Beach agent who was shot is going to recover."

"That's what we're hearing, too."

"Gary's making big fucking progress on whatever that damn thing is you asked him to fucking look into with that woman Janice Gordon. Give him a call, call me later and we will after action this fucking shooting."

"Okay," I barely muttered before he abruptly hung up.

Cosima and I were now blocks away from the shooting and the routine of a sunny day in Miami started to take hold. I planned on taking the Palmetto Expressway south and take the rest of the day to myself. I planned to drop Cosima off at the Biltmore Hotel and hopefully get home in time to pick up Arica. I needed to decompress. Grinding my hand into a gushing bullet wound was not something I'd woken up expecting to do today. Days like these bring on a rapid case of Keys Disease. I could send Detective Johan Williamson on his way and Arica, and I could head down to Snooks in Key Largo for the afternoon. Sunset with frosty libations in hand, overlooking Buttonwood Sound and the Gulf of Mexico...sounded like just what the doctor would order including Dr. Rangela. My mind wistfully drifted to the idea of being many miles away from Coldstream Drive and the mayhem I just went through. I wanted to get Gary out of the way and focus on getting to points south, so I called Gary on speaker phone.

"Veen."

"Hello Illeana, is Gary in?"

"*Pero ¿por qué tu* call like each time I'm busy? [But why do you call like each time I'm busy?]

"My timing can be questionable," I proffered.

"Questionable? No. Its *siempre!*" [always]

The line went silent and then Gary's voice came on.

"Big G. The Major says you're looking for me. You're on speaker with me and Cosima."

I could almost sense a straightening of his body and a more authoritative tone in his voice when he heard that Cosima was listening in. From the onset I could tell he was trying to impress Cosima.

"Cade *we* really need you to come in and look at this file on Janice Gordon. *We* keep finding more information on her, especially with her work related to the New Republicans of Miami Dade."

"Wait. Hold on. Who is this *we* you keep referring to?"

"Well, I mean..." he stammered.

"Big G, Cosima and I just had one heck of a morning. We had a shooting up off that Coldstream Drive location. One of the agents took a bullet in the shoulder, he's in surgery at Jackson Memorial. We got a bad guy dead. The house is a virtual production factory for phony credit cards and I.D.s So, taking that all into consideration I need you to just give me the intel straight." I said holding back the weary exasperation I was feeling.

"You guys okay?" he asked.

"Yeah. We really weren't fully involved but it's still a calamity. Cops everywhere. Secret Service agents, forensic crime scene technicians, and a huge amount of people cataloging all the machinery, bogus credit cards and I.D.s. We're glad to be heading out of there. Can you check that internet translation website and put an Albanian phrase in it?"

"Now?"

"Yes, now! We got a dead Albanian who said something before he was killed."

"Hang on a second. Let me open the website."

"How long will that take?"

"You know nothing about computers, do you? Let it boot up... Okay, I got it open, what did he say?"

"*Ndalo Jam unë.*"

"What? How do you spell that?" he asked.

"How should I know? I don't even know if I'm saying it correctly."

"Give it to me again slowly."

"Nah...day... jam...oo" I said trying to mimic the golfer's speech as best as I could.

I heard him typing slowly as he said, "You aren't Albanian so I can only try and guess phonetically what you're saying. It might be 'Stop. It's me.' I can't be sure because your pronunciation might be totally out of whack."

"Stop. It's me," I repeated.

"Yeah. I mean maybe," he said in a very Miami way. "Now can we get back to Janice Gordon?" Tell me more about Janice Gordon."

"Actually, there isn't really anything earth-shattering, she just found a way to get her picture taken a lot. A real socialite she is. *The Miami Herald, The Palm Beach Post, Ocean Drive Magazine...* She finds a way to get to all the galas and balls. A lot of fundraising nonprofit stuff too. She's on a lot of boards and trustee positions like the Friends of Miami Zoo, Fairchild Tropical Gardens, Founders Club of Baptist Hospital...the list goes on."

"Big G. Aside from all this philanthropic work and society news is there any word on her husband Matthew Gordon? Anything we can tangibly bite into?"

"No. He isn't with her in any of the photos or mentioned in the articles. One guy keeps popping up in the background, but he isn't identified."

"Any hits on the ankle monitor?" I asked him.

"Nothing yet. I'm still waiting to hear from the guy at the courthouse. I've left three messages for him to call me. So, about this file... Will Cosima and you be coming by?" he said with thinly disguised hopefulness in his voice.

"I'm southbound on the Palmetto Expressway. I need to take Cosima by the hotel so if we can, we'll come by."

"Sounds good," he said as he hung up.

"I don't see the connection," said Cosima.

"I think I know what you're going to say. You mean the connection to the Italian Consulate Baldassare Constantino."

"*Esattamente!*" [Exactly!]

"If these guys are making millions in credit card fraud, why would they want to assassinate the consulate? He might still be the next premier of Italy. What are these Albanian grifting, scummy thieves and thugs doing trying to kill a potential international world leader?" she asked.

"It makes no sense to me either. Let's look at it objectively. Does this have any political ramifications?" I asked her.

"No."

"Does it align with any geopolitical agenda?"

"No."

"Have any radical faction groups come forward and taken responsibility for the shooting?"

"No."

"Did the consulate make any declarations against credit card fraud in Italy?"

"No."

"So how is it that your consulate is targeted by the Albanians? It makes no sense at all."

"None of this makes any sense," she said staring out at the very urban landscape.

We bypassed the industrial areas of the town of Medley as we zipped along at sixty miles an hour. We were approaching Miami International Airport when my cellphone rang.

"Cade. Are you still on the Palmetto?" Gary said on speaker-phone, excitement in his voice.

"Yeah. I just passed Northwest 58th Street."

"Take the next exit!" he shouted.

Chapter Twenty-One

"EXIT AT 36TH and go east, the guy just called from the courthouse, they got a positive signal on the ankle monitor a few blocks from the Palmetto Expressway," he said, all one sentence with his heightened urgency.

The Northwest 36th Street exit was approaching quickly. I barely glanced at my rearview mirror and did a "Miami slide," sharply crossing three lanes of traffic without slowing down, squealing off the exit, Gary still talking on speaker.

"My guy says he has active signaling from the ankle monitor around Milam Dairy Road. Guy's name is Luvas Dren."

"Dren? The guy with the motorcycle I killed was Erjon Dren!" I exclaimed.

"My guess is it's his brother. The INS had an immigration hold on him. He got a stay extension from a judge, so the INS put the monitor on him. You're not going to believe this—they wanted to be sure he didn't leave the country before they deported him themselves."

"That's crazy," said Cosima.

"I know, right? INS picked him up when he overstayed at the Mayfair Hotel by six days and spent 9,100 dollars on fake credit cards. When Miami police went to arrest him for fraud in the hotel room they found two phony drivers' licenses and three stolen handguns," said Gary.

"Let me guess, the three handguns were from a shipment that went to a trade show in Europe last March," I said.

"The guy at the courthouse said the guns were stolen from a firearm show in a place called Tiranë in Albania."

"Bingo!" I exclaimed. "The same trade show that his brother got his gun from."

"Where are you now?" asked Gary expectantly.

"East on 36th Street, just passing a Chevron gas station. Lots of trucks and traffic. We've slowed down a lot."

"Stand by, I just lost our guy. I have to call him back. I'll call you back too."

"You believe this?" I said, looking at Cosima, whose mouth hung open.

She shook her head, muttering what Agent Felton laid on her back on Coldstream Drive. "You may not understand the politics and achievements of American law enforcement."

"Funny. I'm a little concerned this may be a wild goose chase..."

"What's a goose chase?" she asked me.

"It's an expression, like an exercise in futility. It isn't going to lead anything."

"Okay. Why do you think that?"

"You see that large, angled, whitish building up ahead on the left?" I asked her.

"Yes."

"That's the Turner Guilford Knight Correctional Center. It's called TGK. It's one of our two county jails, right there... right in front of us on Milam Dairy Road. The same road that Gary said the signal was coming from. I don't have a lot of faith in government employees. If this guy at the courthouse is saying the signal's coming from the area of Milam Dairy Road and where we are now, there's a very good chance that ankle monitor is sitting in a bin wearing down its battery in the jail somewhere. It's probably a false reading. A wild goose chase."

We were creeping along in the dense, slow-moving traffic. I wasn't very optimistic that this ankle monitor signal was going to lead to anything. In my mind I was already plotting my way out of the traffic and using the back way around the airport to get Cosima back to the Biltmore Hotel. This little false hope deviation we were taking was severely hindering my ability to get to Snooks in Key Largo at my desired time. My Keys Disease was possibly going to need to go into remission for a while. Gary called back.

"We have a good signal now. Turn north on Milam Dairy Road, then make your first right."

"Big G. That first right is the entrance to TGK. I think we're chasing a phantom signal," I said feeling the exasperation starting to take hold.

"Cade, I came here to work. Let's just give it a try," said Cosima.

I quickly remembered the pointed conversation I had with Cosima when we left Janice Gordon's house.

"...although you came here to work, I didn't come here to work for you."

I saw this was going nowhere. I didn't want to get into it with Cosima. As much as it chafed me in the absolute worst ways, if I made a quick attempt at placating both Big G and Cosima, I could maybe salvage my afternoon. Gary normally handled the financing and operational budget of our task force; Cosima is not from Miami, let alone even the United States. All I could think was how could I have let these two completely separate people hijack my day? I silently kicked myself for not being assertive with both of them when I made the connection about the signal pinging from the largest jail in Miami Dade County. This was fishing in a dry pond. It would lead to nothing and just topple my afternoon plans of darting down to Key Largo.

"Big G, we're directly in front of TGK. Right by the flagpoles. Are you sure about this? I think this is a big zero," I said into the phone.

"The guy says keep going east, it's on the right."

"Gary, I can't go any further east and to the right is the overpass for 36th Street that goes over the Florida East Coast railyard. This isn't working, man."

Ahead of us the paved road terminated into a lot surrounded by a fifteen-foot fence. The fence was topped with large, coiled concertina barbed wire running the entire length. That's when Cosima spoke up again:

"Take the dirt path on the right."

A single lane of crushed white gravel ran between the fence and the rising shoulder of the overpass. I maneuvered the BMW slowly between the fence post and the weed-choked berm until the path opened a few feet—for a moment. With the narrowness of the path, the seemingly endless fence on our left, and a formidable concrete retaining wall on the right, taller than the BMW, it felt like the world was closing in on us. I took minor comfort in the residual tire tracks on the road—other vehicles drove this lane fairly often.

The gravel continuously crunched under the tires as more strategically placed rows of fencing and barbed wire cropped up on the other side of the fence. Beyond that were concrete modules laid in straight rows. I could only assume they housed inmates. The sound of cars and trucks passing on the other side of the wall and above us grew as we continued to drive. After about 100 yards the road turned to the right and went under the overpass. On our left was a murky brown canal with saw grass and Florida holly berry bushes interspersed along the bank.

Banded utility pipes arched over the canal like man-made drab gray rainbows of metal and plastic. Sharp metal four-foot-high brackets were on each side of the piping, deterring anybody from trying to cross the thirty-yard-wide canals by walking or shimmying across the pipes. Seventy-foot Australian pine trees flanked the other side of the canal, their roots dug ferociously into the rocky bank, syphoning water from the canal. Beyond the trees was an eyesore industrial landscape of buildings, railroad tracks, trains, barrels, and dumpsters. The overpass dominated the sky above with its poured concrete pillars, and forty foot long interlocking bridge abutment pieces. Movies and songs glamorize being under a bridge as romantic and serene. There was nothing aesthetically appealing about being under the overpass. It was also loud. As if the bridge above us was screaming in fury. The sound of the cars and trucks rumbling overhead not only echoed down to us but reverberated continuously. In certain rushing moments, a heavy truck shook the bridge.

"Are you on the south side of Northwest 36th Street? Our guy wants to know," Gary said. "Does it really matter? This is a wasteland, Big G." I said barely containing my frustration.

"He says the signal cut out. Something about a satellite moving, earth rotation, and all that. He says it will be back up in eighteen minutes."

"Eighteen minutes? Not twenty. Eighteen?" I said, exasperated.

"It's what he does, Cade. He knows his business. He must know something we don't. He says the signal is on the south side of Northwest 36th. That's all I can tell you."

"Alright. Call me back," I said.

I parked directly under the bridge, letting it shield us from the sun. Cosima and I sat silently in the car for a moment, listening to the symphonic beat of the rumbling traffic above. I think we were both pondering what would be the next course of action. So far, Gary's urgency and ardent tone said this was valid information. Everything I was seeing and thinking told me it wasn't. The property in front of us was surrounded by a poorly maintained chain link fence, topped with dense kudzu vines. The minimal barbed wire strands across the top of the fencing provided an ample growing environment for the thick, green, clinging vine. The fence gate hung awkwardly off dented aluminum fence posts, probably from vehicles nicking them as they drove in and out of the property. The gravel road continued into the property. I noticed the fence line extended all the way to the water's edge, rendering the property fully vulnerable on one side. The barbed wire on the side fencing was surely more posturing than protection. I could discern a few aluminum sheds and small concrete block buildings no bigger than a Little League dugout. I turned off the car.

"We can sit here and wait for eighteen minutes for Gary to call, or we can go see what's on the other side of the fence," I said to Cosima.

She looked at me with a smirk.

"I already know what you're going to say," I said.

"I'm here to work and I'm in Miami. I shouldn't have to explain?" she said as she opened the door.

I left my cellphone on the floor of the car. I didn't want an inadvertent call from Gary alerting anybody of our presence. I gently closed the car door, being as quiet as possible—a pointless gesture due to the traffic overhead. I looked across the car at Cosima. She was studying the parcel of land in front of us. I assume she saw the junked and barren acreage the same as I was.

"Cade. After what happened to Tom Borges today let's put on the vests in the backseat," she said, still looking ahead. "You never know. Besides it will help us identify ourselves sooner. You don't exactly look like Officer Friendly with that hair of yours."

I hadn't seen a reason to put on the heavy vests at 4:30 that morning and I didn't see the need to wear them for a jaunt through high grass, weeds, and enough rusty sheds, piping, and discarded material to warrant a Tetanus shot just for stepping through the gate. Cosima looked at me and then opened the back door. She pulled both vests out and laid them across the trunk of the car.

"Are they both the same size?" she asked.

Placate.

Appease.

Mollify.

Pacify.

Choose whatever term you like. As for me the word of the day was obviously *placate*. Either way I didn't want to go against her on this, especially after Borges' unfortunate morning. She was right.

It was logical and safe to put on the ballistic vest, if even for a few minutes. I kept the car unlocked and put the car keys on the front left tire. I didn't want to be fumbling for keys and with door locks if I had to make a "tactical retreat."

"I think they're the same size." I said.

She pushed one my way. "You take this one. It has a Glock magazine in the front flap. That magazine won't fit my Beretta."

Someone had left a .40 caliber, fully loaded Glock magazine in the vest. The Carabinieri carried Beretta 92FS handguns. It made sense for me to take the vest with a loaded magazine that fits my handgun. She quickly had the vest over her head, pulled it down, and snugly wrapped it around her torso with the thick Velcro straps. Across her chest in bold white letters were the words:

CGPD VIN POLICE.

"You look like one of us," I said.

"Get a picture with your phone when it's over," she said, smiling.

The BMW was parked far enough back that it was concealed from the property. Once we were properly geared up, we started walking towards the open gate twenty yards in front of us. The closer we got to the gate the more we saw that the property was a much larger track of land than we initially thought. The gravel road went through the gate and ran the length of the east side of the property along the canal. Another canal was on the south side and the road curved west and appeared to continue all the way back to Milam Dairy Road. We stayed rooted in the opening of the gate, looking around at the assembled hodge podge of buildings, aluminum sheds, large shipping containers, dilapidated carts, broken down trucks, and cannibalized construction equipment. There was no semblance of order.

"Let's spread out a little, but not too far from each other," I said to her.

It was a tactical decision. Standing beside each other would make us easy targets for an assault weapon or a shotgun blast. We walked west through the veritable wasteland of machinery and aluminum sheds. The ground was uneven and riddled with shallow potholes in the gravel. Rainfall had collected in the large potholes and was now fetid and stagnant. Mud, grime, corrosion, and neglect vied to be the prevalent reason for the wretched conditions. The backseat of a Ford pickup truck rested outside the door to one of the larger sheds. An air conditioner jutted, sagging out of a window, green algae spreading across the shed underneath it. A plastic McArthur Dairy milk crate was nailed high above the frayed door of another shed. A sun-bleached, deflated basketball sat in a mud puddle.

My initial thought was where should we start? Was there any chance someone actually spent time here?

"We can check a few of these sheds but I don't think we'll find anybody here," I said.

I went to the nearest shed. Cosima held back in an observation position with her weapon holstered. I pulled open the rickety door.

Inside, blueprint plans and multiple rolled sheets of paper covered two wooden tables. A few chairs; a bone-dry five-gallon plastic water bottle atop an unplugged, moldy water dispenser; the stench of mildew and rotted wooden floorboards permeated the place. I didn't want to stay inside the hot, musty shed too long. The stench of its decay would only need a few minutes to seep into my clothes.

"How about you take the next one and *I* get to wait outside?" I joked with Cosima.

"What? Spider webs and dust are too much for you?" she joked back. "The one on the end is twice the size of this one. I'll go in with you. *Non essere un codardo, affronta la situazione!*"

"What does that mean?" I asked her with a curios chuckle.

"Don't be a coward and confront the situation," she said, laughing.

There was a large, milky white mud puddle in front of the shed stairs. The Miami Dade School Board put these types of buildings on my middle school campus when I was an adolescent. They called them "portables." If they had dividing walls separating them into six small classrooms, we called them "six packs." They were meant to be self-contained with their own power hook-ups and air conditioning systems. This one had seen better days. Much better days.

The portable was raised about three feet off the ground on concrete block pilings. Termite- infested stairs led to the door, the railing long ago broken away and laying in the weedy grass below. The roof was visibly compromised with rotting fascia. A fiber-glass-rippled exterior panel had pulled away from its rusty rivets and leaned precariously like a piece of misaligned shiplap. Time had warped the door, and it was bowing out from the frame. I didn't even bother trying to use the dented aluminum doorknob. I slipped my foot in between the door and the door jamb and just by turning my ankle caused the decrepit door to swing open.

I looked behind me at Cosima.

"This is like our own Miami version of the ruins of Pompei." I said.

I stepped into the messy structure. It was reminiscent of the six packs that I remembered from my middle school years. The only light coming in was from rows of small windows along the external walls. I tried the light switch just inside the door, and an overhead fluorescent light flickered before fizzling out. The portable was still connected to an electrical source. More than likely a temporary junction box outside on a two-by-six board driven into the ground near a live power line. Sunlight streamed in through a gaping hole in the ceiling. The putrid carpet was in patches, and most of the wood-slatted floor was exposed and rotting. When I looked down through the holes I could see sparse clumps of grass. The interior dividing wall was a sooty mess. Someone must have been squatting in here, using gathered leaves and paper to light a fire. It was a miracle there was no dead body, poisoned by carbon monoxide.

I took it all in as quickly as I could: three shopping carts filled with red clay barrel roofing tiles; about sixteen rolls of black roofing paper, frayed and brittle with decay; a metal flagpole with a tattered Miami Dade Couty flag leaning against one of the shopping carts. Probably a holdover from when the county must have used this as an onsite building. There was a dusty portable welding machine plugged into an outlet just inside the open door. We stepped inside the ramshackle structure and walked to the back, side-stepping the holes.

"Have you seen enough?" I asked Cosima.

"How do you account for the ankle monitor signaling here?" she said as she looked around at the squalor.

Before I could answer her, we both stiffened up wide eyed at the distinctive, ominous sound of a shotgun being racked.

Chapter Twenty-Two

RAINING AND INSTINCTS kicked in.

Cosima dropped to the floor. I dove to my right, crashing into a shopping cart filled with roofing tiles, toppling it over and spilling tiles onto the floor. I scampered behind the pile just as the first shot rang out. The 00 buckshot from the twelve-gauge round and the spray spread out about four feet above the floor. The rounds carried over Cosima who was now crawling to the other side of the portable, looking for cover behind two dented filing cabinets. Two rounds hit the roofing tiles I was cowering behind.

The spewing lead coming in at four feet above the ground signified to me the shooter was still outside and hadn't fully climbed the stairs yet. I needed to keep him from entering and picking us both off like sitting ducks. I quickly popped my head up, extended my shooting arm across the quaking heap of tiles, and fired a two-round burst at the open doorway.

Our adversary's retreating footsteps pounded down the dilapidated stairs. But to my dismay, the shooter wasn't retreating but simply adjusting himself away from return fire as he discharged two more blasts. The pellets penetrated the cheap corrugated exterior wall easily and scattered all around me. My barricade of tiles stopped five of the pellets from hitting me. The tiles were exploding from the rounds, and terracotta dust and fragments flew in the air.

"Cosima! You good?" I yelled across what was now a veritable shooting range.

"Good!" she yelled back.

Hearing our voices, the shooter scatter-shot the rounds at the exterior walls and through the open door. Shotgun pellets caromed and sliced through everything that was four feet or higher. Cosima dug in even lower into the cruddy carpet and bare wood flooring. I did the same, my face pressed against the dingy floor when I spied one of the holes in the floor about five feet away. The wood slats had given way to a neglected overhead roof leak. I grabbed the flagpole. I yanked on the flag. Its rusty grommets were no match for my aggressive tug, and the faded, tattered flag fell away. The next rounds whistled in high, tearing into the drop ceiling, sending a rectangular fluorescent light fixture crashing down. The long-dormant bulbs shattered into thousands of glass particles, adding to the dust cloud of glass, plastic, and wood in the air. I lay prone on my stomach and used the flagpole to root around the hole in the floor, jabbing and poking the edges. The wood was pliable. Spongy and weak. I made a decision.

"Cosima! Cover me!" I yelled at her.

I stayed as low as I could to the floor and with the flagpole in my hand, I dove to the hole. I caught Cosima peeked around from her secreted position, letting a three-round burst go from her Berretta. I landed nearly on top of the hole. Using the pole like a crowbar, forcefully thrusting, I expanded the hole's opening. The wood gave way easily. I plopped down into the hole and fell onto the soggy ground below the portable. I poked my head up into the hole in the weakened floor above me, my eyes level with the floor. I saw Cosima's wide eyes looking at me.

"On three, come to me!" I said. "One..."

She was already crawling on her hand and knees to me before I finished the count. I raised my Glock up and fired three rounds towards the door to give her cover. Within seconds she was headfirst in the hole. I dropped down as I simultaneously raised up my arm and grabbed behind her neck, yanking her by the head down with me.

I fell on my back, and she was right with me as she slithered down the hole head-first. She landed on me. We were a tangled mess of arms and legs under the portable, in the pungent, dirty, sun-deprived space. She pushed off of me and I rolled onto my stomach. I could see the shooter's feet near the northeast corner of the portable.

A court monitor was wrapped around his left ankle.

He dropped to one knee and turned the pump-action shotgun, revealing the open port of the smoking gun. I could tell by the way he took a knee that he tactically knew what he was doing. My assertation was confirmed when he rapidly reloaded the weapon by inserting the first new shell with his right hand over the top of the open chamber. He racked the shotgun and then with the loaded gun ready, he deftly fed the chamber from below with four more shells. He readied the gun in his right arm with his left index finger on the trigger. I remembered what Tucson Lou had said to me in the Biltmore Hotel ballroom.

"He's left handed."

"Left handed?" I repeated.

"Yeah. He fired with his left hand. He ran up to the podium from the right side of the room. Like it was planned…"

Cosima and I could not stay together. The shooter would just need to lean down and shoot a three-round burst under the portable to kill us instantly. Gun in her right hand, Cosima started crawling through the mucky underside of the building towards the shooter. I figured that he'd go to the open door again. I barrel-rolled to the east side where the door and staircase were. The space was tight, but I cleared the underside of the building by mere inches with each rotation, rolling over discarded pieces of paper, crushed beer cans, and twigs, protected by the tactical vest. I held my gun close to my chest with both hands.

The shooter must have sensed something or heard me. He

started running to the corner of the building. He stopped short and appeared to be doing a quick peek around the corner.

He expected to see us coming out of the door.

I was nearing the edge of the building. Sunlight and shadow made a clear demarcation line. He was running towards me, still unaware that I was on the ground under the building. It would be faster to roll out from underneath the portable but the noise and the disorientation of where I'd be as compared to the shooter made that option dicey at best. I took a moment to decide the best course of action. Cosima made that decision for me. From under the building and lying on her stomach, she fired three rounds from her Berretta. Two of them struck the shooter. One tore into his right calf, the other struck him on the top of his foot, obliterating his dorsal pedal artery. Blood erupted out of his foot like a geyser. He screamed in pain.

My final body roll put me at the edge of the building. I leaned out and got my first glimpse of the shooter.

He had short dark hair and a good three-day stubble. He was wincing in pain, teeth gritted and his eyes closed. He opened his eyes and immediately saw me, half out from under the building, still on my right side. I held my Glock with both hands in front of me, pointed directly at him. His eyes widened. It was either him or me. If he moved the gun any closer or if I hesitated, I was going to be dead.

He swung the shotgun towards me and shouted, *"T'a hangert dreqi shpirtin!"* [May the devil eat your soul!]

I fired two rounds. Both rounds tore right through his chest. They spun him away from me, his body awkwardly turning as his body contorted. He died with his body splayed at the bottom of the stairs in one of the unpleasant, stagnant mud puddles.

Cosima came around the corner behind him with her gun ready. Dirt streaked her face. Her pants were torn at the knee. The CGPD tactical vest was muddy and caked with white dirt. By the look in her eyes, I'm sure I looked the same way. My shoulder was scraped and bleeding from when I first leaped behind the roof tiles. For a moment we just stared at each other. Finally, I spoke.

"You good?"

"Good," she said as she holstered her gun.

I tried my best to avoid the mud puddle he was lying in, but it was unavoidable. I knelt in the stinky water and got a better look at the shooter. I wedged my hand under his wet leg and felt the ankle monitor on his leg.

"I'm willing to bet this is Luvas Dren, the brother of Erjon Dren," I said, drying my hand on my pants.

Cosima said, "I heard you tell Gary that Erjon Dren is from the motorcycle. If this is his brother, which I'm pretty sure he is, we may have an Albanian crime war about to be waged on us."

I remembered what Arica told me. There were thousands of Albanian members, a "criminal ribbon of mayhem and murder." To go up against one of them was to fight them all. They never stop and they never forget.

"There's no we here. I killed him," I said looking past her and gathering my thoughts.

"Semantics. We both shot him. The Carabinieri can handle this and anything the Albanians want to try," she insisted causing me to focus my eyes on her.

"There will be a ton of investigating going on here in the next ninety minutes. More than what we saw at Coldstream Drive this morning. Stay either with me or away from anybody asking questions. That stuff can wait. Keep the Coral Gables vest on, let them assume you're Coral Gables. We don't need international press snooping around." I said preemptively preparing for the immediate inquiry this shooting was going to cause.

She nodded, looking down at the corpse of Luvas Dren. "Do you think he's the one who shot my agent?" she asked me.

"I don't know. It kind of makes sense that the shooter of the consulate and your agent would rely on his brother to pick him up."

I reached for my cellphone. I didn't have it. I looked around at the ground and realized that maybe I'd dropped it inside the portable.

"I need to find my cellphone," I said.

"I think you left it in the car," she said.

Right. I was feeling stupid about leaving my phone in the car now.

"Stay here. I'm going to walk back and get my phone," I said to her.

I started walking back towards the BMW. The warm breeze from the canal helped me to momentarily keep my composure. My shoulder hurt and I was beyond overly fatigued. A dragonfly buzzed by looking for something to gather from the wild milkweed growing near a long-forgotten Waste Management dumpster. I shook my head, still taken aback by this pigsty of decommissioned Miami Dade sheds, containers, portables and any other marginalized thing that a financial bean counter from the county felt was an asset to keep on the financial ledgers rather than haul away to the county dump. In many ways this was a bit of a Miami Dade dump in its own creation.

I zig-zagged on the gravel road, sidestepping the mud puddles when I heard a vehicle engine that sounded close. I glanced at the rising overpass but the sound grew louder. Closer. I turned to look back at where I'd just come from and saw a right-out-of-the-showroom shiny black Ford F350 Lariat pickup truck cresting the turn around the south side of the property. I ducked behind a small wooden utility shed, praying they hadn't seen me. The truck pulled up in front of a two- story concrete building. It was the only decent structure on the property. They parked between two picnic tables under a lone Ficus tree. I was torn about going to get my phone and going back to alert Cosima. I ejected my magazine from my gun and inserted the full magazine that had been in my vest. I slipped the half-empty magazine back into the pouch of the vest. You never can know how many bullets you will need.

Common sense and my training told me to run as fast as I could, get my cellphone and call for immediate back up. More people would help Cosima and myself. But in that sprint for the phone, Cosima would be alone and unaware of the new threat. If I didn't get the phone at least she would have me with her.

Foregoing the phone, I ran back to where Cosima was. When I got to the spot where I'd killed Luvas Dren, she was nowhere to be seen. Then I heard the voices.

Chapter Twenty-Three

Two men were yelling in English with thick European accents, excited and angry, asking questions so fast that whoever they were talking to would be challenged to answer.

"Who are you? What are you doing here?"

"Tell us now or I swear I'll cut you like a fucking boar."

"Where is Luvas?"

"Luvas?"

"Luvas!"

They both began yelling Luvas Dren's name loudly. Calling for him. I deduced because of their concern for Luvas Dren they were Albanian. It sounded like they were very close to me. I slowly peeked around the shed. The two men were holding onto Cosima. They had disarmed her and one of them had her gun tucked into the waistband of his jeans. The other one was roughly grasping her by the shoulder with one hand and using his other hand to pull hard on her hair, yanking her head far back. She was in between the two of them, squirming. The one with her gun slapped her in the face hard. She recoiled and scrunched her face with her eyes closed tightly, trying to bravely endure the attack.

It was a one in a million shot to take one of them out without hitting her. To shoot both would be a two million to one shot. They both had Heckler & Koch P7M8 nine-millimeter handguns. The one who had Cosima's gun in his waistband carried his own gun in a holster on his hip. The one gripping Cosima wore his in a thigh holster, but he pulled out a Rambo-sized knife instead and screamed in her face:

"Kurvë e mallkuar, do t'i pres sytë dhe do t'ua jap qenve të mi."

[Damned whore, I'll cut out your eyes and feed them to my dogs.]

I figured I had probably less than a minute before they drastically hurt Cosima—or even worse, killed her. If they were focused on Luvas I had a chance to help her. Once they discovered him dead it would be all over for Cosima. I had to think fast.

I hurriedly backtracked to where Luvas' dead body lay in the filthy puddle. I jumped over his body and landed on the decrepit wooden stairs at the open doorway of the portable. I rubbed and scraped my shoes on the dingy carpet, attempting to make my shoes as dry as I could. I hoped and prayed my idea would work. One of those prayers was that the plugged-in welder inside would work when I turned it on. Breath held, I threw the switch on and surprisingly the welder fired up. I uncoiled its long welding cables, making sure not to let the positive and negative clamps touch. Wood is a poor conductor of electricity. Standing on the wooden steps I dropped the cables over the edge of the stairs into the puddle where Luvas' body was. Bright flashes sparked, and his lifeless body jolted once from the electrical current coursing through the puddle.

I jumped off the stairs as far as I could away from his twitching body. When I hit the ground, I made sure I was as far as I could be from the puddle, but the electrified ground still tingled from the surging current. I shuffled my feet keeping as much contact as I could with the ground as I moved further away from Luvas. If I lifted my feet and a rogue arch rose from the puddle, I would become the connecting point for the current.

The shouting and threats to Cosima were becoming more ardent, interspersed with slaps. I needed to get them away from her as fast as I could. Every second counted. Divide and conquer. If I could just get a little space between them and her I might be able to take them out. They yelled even louder for Luvas.

"Luvas! *Ku je*?" [Luvas! Where are you?]

Over and over, the call for Luvas was louder and more panicked. I decided to try, as they say in football, to call an audible. Literally. Remembering Gary's definition of what the golfer heard at Coldstream Drive, I tried my best to sound Albanian. Hoping that their fear, agitation, and anger would cloud their thinking I tilted my head down towards the tactical vest to muffle my voice and shouted, "*Jam unë.*"

[It's me.]

It wasn't the best articulated response, but it was all I had. One of them immediately called for Luvas again, but his tone was more suspicious than searching.

I had to get them to come to Luvas' body any way I could. Using a discarded two-by-four, I banged on the side of an aluminum shed and yelled, "*Jam unë*" three times. I kept banging on the shed, hoping to hide my inability to speak Albanian fluently and to distort what I thought Luvas Dren may have sounded like. I heard them getting closer and it sounded as though they were dragging Cosima with them. I pulled back and stood behind the shed with my gun raised and ready to fire. If they tried to bring Cosima towards Dren's body, I was prepared to start shooting to keep Cosima from being electrocuted. The first one I saw was the one with the gun on his hip. He stepped into view, and he immediately saw Luvas down on the ground.

"*Luvas! Zoti im! Luvas!*" [Luvas! My God! Luvas!]

He ran towards the corpse while the one holding Cosima held back, maintaining a hard grip around Cosima's neck. He still had the knife in his hand. The other one continued running to Luvas calling his name. He approached Luvas in full stride and before he even realized Luvas was dead, he stepped in a small wet spot near the puddle.

The wet spot had enough current in it to knock him off his feet.

His body flew back about three feet, and he landed flat on his back. His legs went straight up in the air, and I saw the thick rubber-soled boots on his feet. Those thick soles probably kept him from being electrocuted, but he definitely got juiced. He was on his back, eyes closed, and out cold. When he stepped into the wet spot, I heard the welder cut off and knew that he'd inadvertently short-circuited the power. The other guy and Cosima were about twenty feet behind him.

They weren't sure what caused him to be thrown back. They saw him running towards Luvas and then he was airborne and unconscious before he even hit the ground. Confused and angry, the other guy was yelling now at both of his downed comrades. He was coming unglued and had wildfire in his eyes. Cosima struggled to break free of his grasp and he lashed at her with the huge, serrated knife.

I stepped out from behind the shed.

His first swipe at her missed but the next one didn't. This time the blade sliced across the tactical vest, splitting the cover open. The grooved, bullet-resistant Kevlar underneath thwarted the knife from penetrating and cutting her.

He was aggressively fast, and Cosima fell back onto the dirty ground, leaving him towering over her. She reached up and yanked hard on the pistol in his thigh holster. I was advancing fast on him with my gun in the firing position. He saw me and he felt Cosima tugging on his gun, and for a fraction of a second, he was frozen with indecision. He must have known he needed his gun to fight me, and he had to dispatch Cosima quickly to do that. He raised the knife up to stab her right through her upturned face. I fired a three-round burst, aiming high to avoid Cosima.

My bullets found their target.

He had his arm raised to slash Cosima. My first round would have gone right through his temple, but it struck his raised arm and shredded through the triceps. The next round struck him in his upper chest; the third round smashed him in the lower part of his jaw. Bone fragments from his jaw, an eruption of blood, cartilage from his sinus, and four of his teeth rained down on Cosima. Blood continued to stream out of his face, and he dropped to the ground, landing face first partially on top of Cosima. She pushed him back and then used her legs to kick him off of her. His gun was partially out of his holster. I don't know if it was instinct or anger, but Cosima continued wiggling and yanking it from the thigh holster. I went straight towards him, gun still at the ready, my eyes locked on him. Honestly, I don't know if it was instinct or anger on my part either.

Cosima had extracted his gun, and she held him in her sights with it, scooting backwards away and wearing one of the most contemptuous looks I've ever seen.

"Cosima. Cosima! He's dead. It's over. He's dead. Put the gun down," I said softly as I holstered my gun.

She transfixed an icy glare on his ragged, dead body. His face was obliterated. He didn't even look human anymore. The entire lower part of his face was a bloody pulpy misshaped mess. I was now standing over him. Cosima still stared at him intently, holding his gun. She didn't say anything, and she didn't acknowledge me. Luvas and the other unconscious thug were on the ground behind me. I knelt and tried to roll the dead man over. I rummaged through his pockets for identification, almost head-to-head with Cosima as I leaned forward to inspect the body more.

Suddenly Cosima sprang up and dove at me. She leaped across his dead body and crashed into me hard with both hands against my shoulders. The dead guy's gun was in her right hand, and I saw it come up at my face. I was knocked off balance, and she used all the strength in her legs to drive right through me. I fell back. She was still pushing, was now up against me as she rode me down to the ground. I landed on my back, the wind knocked out of me, with her body pressed on top of me. Her face was inches from mine. The gun in her hand was aimed at my head.

I was stunned by the loud discharge of the gun so near to my ear. The heat from the bullet's discharge blew across the side of my face. Muzzle flash and particles of cordite and gunpowder blackened the side of my face. Arm extended, she fired three quick rounds, leaving a faint zinging whine ring in my ears. The expelled shell casings arched in the air before dropping to the ground. She stopped shooting. She just laid on top of me with her gun hand fully extended past my head.

I had gotten careless.

In all the adrenaline-fueled action I assumed the other criminal was still unconscious. Unbeknownst to me he had revived and was lucid enough to get up and draw his gun and take a bead on me—but Cosima's rounds found their mark. He stumbled a step backwards and then toppled over, dead, a few feet from Luvas.

Off in the distance Cosima and I both heard sirens. She inhaled deeply, then let out a long exhale. Except for the approaching sirens there was a surreal quiet to the aftermath. I swallowed hard a few times, collecting my emotions. I do believe she did the same. She eventually spoke.

"You saved my life."

"You saved my life too," I said.

Her eyes roved around at the silent carnage around us. She then looked me in the eyes. "I'm here to work and I'm in Miami. I shouldn't have to explain," she said.

Chapter Twenty-Four

I HAVE ABSOLUTELY NO idea what it must be like to be in a disturbed beehive but if what unfolded in the next four hours was any indication I can tell you I wouldn't last a few minutes in that life. The number of police, investigators, federal agencies, crime scene technicians, tow trucks, assembled tents, industrial fans, portable lights, was incomprehensible. There was enough crime scene tape to lasso the moon but not enough to fence in my bad decisions. I was presently getting an earful about my bad decisions from Major Brunson.

"Cade, you need to thank your ever fucking lasting stars that Gary called in the fucking cavalry when he couldn't reach you on your cellphone. Why the fuck didn't you bring your damn phone with you?"

He jutted his finger at me as he admonished me. "I was trying to be tactical."

"*Tactical*? Does this look like the result of a good fucking tactical decisions?" he said, motioning at all of the activity around us.

"Maybe the optimum word is 'stealthy,'" I replied, the fatigue obvious in my voice.

"Stealthy? That's what going with? Cade, my patience is like one of those department store gift cards. I got no idea how much is left on it but let's give it a real good fucking try. Why don't we? It's just you, me and every goddamn cop in Miami Dade County out here in this glowing shit- beacon of mayhem. I mean holy shit fuck; do you *see* all the resources out here? Nut crusher alert! The overtime salaries alone will bury the fucking county finance director."

I was scraped up and bloody. I felt haggard and depleted. Today a U.S. Secret Service agent had been shot in the shoulder. Four men died today in two different locations. Three of those men tried to kill me and an Italian National Police agent. Cosima was bruised and bashed about and nearly stabbed with a knife bigger than the chef's ego at a Michelin five-star restaurant. Cosima had already been transported to Jackson Memorial Hospital for observation. I was empty. Major Brunson chewing my ear off about what went wrong and avoiding the conversation about what went right was irksome and I was not in the mood to hear any more.

"Not everything went as planned but overall, I think it fell well within industry standards," I said, voice soaked with sarcasm.

"Cade, over the years I have become fucktose intolerant. I'm not drinking this." He stormed off.

I sat there in a pensive mood, fighting the fogginess I was feeling. Adrenaline had worn down and now my thoughts were my only nagging companion. I needed to focus on the fact that I was here, and the three Albanians were not. Nothing more to add. I remembered what I thought to myself when I was sitting in Dr. Rangela's office.

My mind could be like a bad section of town. Don't venture in there alone. If you do, keep the windows up and the doors locked.

I followed the same edict I had in her office. I steadied myself internally.

I intentionally worked on focusing my mind on what was and not what could have been. I tried to be in the moment, feeling and listening to myself breathe as I sat on the bumper of a Miami Dade Police Crime Scene van. About thirty feet away, Major Brunson's back was to me, his hands on his hips surveying all the activity around us.

He was joined by Wayne Felton. He and the Secret Service agent spoke at length. I saw Brunson motion towards me and the two men walked towards me. I resigned myself to the idea there would be more talking. Felton looked like a crumpled paper bag. Still functional but less than ideal.

"Twice in one day," Felton said. "I think this is a record for me, personally. How ya holding up, Cade?"

"Good. I'm good. Thank you."

"The Secret Service owes you a big debt of gratitude. I think collectively, we all owe you a tremendous thank you. These guys could have attacked anybody in law enforcement, and it might have had a tragic outcome." His eyes followed the activity around us. "What went down here today is a first for us. Thank you, Cade. This Albanian crew had been eluding us for well over five years. You and Agent Verratti did some great work today, not just for us but for the Carabinieri too. I can't extend the congratulations and gratitude enough to you. Thank you."

"You're welcome...I guess," I said, a little perplexed.

"Did you hear the news?" he asked me.

"What news?"

He glanced at Brunson who shrugged. "No one talked to you about the two-story building by the Ficus trees and picnic tables? The one where they parked the pickup truck?"

"No," I muttered.

"They're still tabulating everything. Looks like we got even more stolen mail and material linking them to the Coldstream Drive address. Rolls of plastic, boxes of fraudulent credit cards, heat presses, more guns, a lot more guns many from that H&K batch stolen in Albania. And get this... a rough estimate of about two million in cash," said Felton.

"That should pay for the overtime," I assured Brunson.

"And then some. They also had about 80,000 in cash under the driver's seat in the truck. An emergency stash to get out of town if they ever had to."

"Lots of toll roads, no less," I said with a smirk.

"Miami Dade thinks the one dead in the mud puddle—"

"Luvas Dren," I interjected.

"Yeah. They think that Luvas Dren's fingerprints are a match to the prints lifted at the Biltmore Hotel shooting. Looks like he was our shooter. To me, he looked like the guy in the back of the ballroom. They'll have a confirmation in a few hours."

"So, if these pieces are filling the puzzle, we can deduce that the Albanians were in a large scale credit card fraud and identity theft ring that was making what? How much do you think?" I asked.

"We at the Secret Service think about thirty million a year," he said.

My fatigue gave way to curiosity. "Thirty million. Nearly 600,000 a week. Why in this dump of a place? Why here?" I asked.

Felton pondered it for a moment. "If I had to guess, I'd say a few things. They probably had real headaches with Luvas Dren's ankle monitor. If anybody from Federal Probation or INS were to look for him they'd see the extreme proximity to the jail and think it was a false echo. That he or the ankle monitor were in the jail."

The same theory I had told Gary, thinking that it was the entrance to TGK. *"I think we're chasing a phantom signal."*

Felton turned to Brunson, saying, "This place is an overlooked tract of land. I mean who even knew this place was here?"

Major Brunson scoffed. "Do either of you know what's just a block or two south of us here on Milam Dairy Road?"

Agent Felton and I shook our heads.

"The Miami U.S. fucking Mail Center! You think these ass clowns were stealing mail in small batches? These fuckers were grabbing bags of it and high-tailing it right fucking back here. That damn Coldstream Drive address was nothing more than a little satellite office for them. The real fucking stuff was taking place right here under our very noses," said Brunson.

Felton cleared his throat and said, "Cade, we also recovered the Enterprise rental truck. It was parked on the western edge of the property near a bunch of old electrical transformers."

"Sounds like it's a one-stop shop for all. Where do we go from here?" I said.

"The Special Agent in Charge of the Miami field office and I will be doing a press conference with local law enforcement in three hours at the Biltmore Hotel. Major Brunson will be there as well as members of the Miami Dade PD."

"You said you wanted to thank me. I can think of one way you can thank me," I said.

"What's that, Cade?" asked Felton.

"Do you recall Arica Sweetin?" I said.

"Yes. How could I not? She was with you at the bar in the Biltmore. Beautiful and sharp as a tack. I remember her very well, she was in the 19th Hole restaurant when you got called away."

"Yes, that's her. She works for Trident Broadcasting. It seems the Albanians were targeting her. Major Brunson made a great decision putting her in our protective custody. So..." I paused for emphasis and to gauge Major Brunson's reaction. "Since she's been put in time-out and will be behind her media contemporaries on this story, how about granting her an exclusive a half hour before your actual press conference?"

"I can't speak for the Special Agent in Charge but have her meet me in the 19th Hole restaurant at 5:30pm. I'll give her a scoop, and a half hour jump on the press conference," he said.

Major Brunson didn't show any reaction in either way. "Thanks, I appreciate that," I said.

"Cade, we'll do an even deeper debrief on this in a few days. Tom Borges should be out of the hospital tomorrow. After all we've been through, Lou and I are staying a few extra days in Miami for the debrief. Plan on being at the Biltmore Hotel in about two days and we'll all sit down and put a cap on this."

"Sounds good."

"Okay. I'm going to wrap it up here and then head to the Biltmore. Major Brunson I'll see you there. Cade, we'll circle back in two days." He turned away and was soon swallowed up by the swarming activity around us.

Major Brunson and I watched him saunter off.

"He has a bit of a fucking lift in his step, doesn't he? Having your whole damn career made and whatever fucking accolades come to you in the future because of local South Florida cops will do that for you," said Brunson as he watched Felton walk away.

I kept quiet, still processing the day.

"I'm going to call Johan Williamson and tell him to drive Ms. Sweetin to the hotel. When they're finished with you here you can pick her up. Take a few days off until you debrief," he said.

"Sounds good," I said again.

After Major Brunson walked away. I used my cellphone which had been retrieved for me and called Arica.

"You know that I woke up this morning and went downstairs and there was a guy sitting on your couch eating Fritos," she said.

"I told you someone would be there while I was gone."

"I know, but Fritos? They smell like snack food with B.O! The guy has the culinary choices of a toddler."

"I hear you, but he's a good guy," I said, knowing my eating habits were no better.

"He's currently out on the terrace on the phone. I think he's talking to Major Foul Mouth."

"Yeah, they're talking about you probably," I said.

"Me? Why me?" she said, startled.

"Big developments in the case today. The Albanians are dead, and Agent Borges caught one in the shoulder. Major Brunson should be telling Johan to take you to the Biltmore Hotel. There's going to be a press conference."

"What? They're dead?" she gasped.

"Yeah, it's been a very convoluted day to say the least."

"You said Borges caught one in the shoulder. Do you mean that Tom was shot?" she asked.

"Yes. Major Brunson wanted you to have an exclusive," I partially fibbed. "So, Agent Felton from the Secret Service will be meeting with you at the 19th Hole restaurant a half hour before the press conference. He said be there at 5:30pm."

"What?" she said again.

"It's been a big day. I hope to be there to pick you up after the press conference."

"I'll need to make some calls and get a stringer crew on site. I'm going to have to move fast. I'll call you when I'm wrapped up at the Biltmore," she said.

Fifteen minutes later Lieutenant Charlie Maddalone arrived to once again take possession of my gun and provide me with yet another replacement firearm.

"Haven't we done these enough times already?" he said.

"I like to look at it as consistency," I replied.

"Consistency? That's what you call this?" he said looking at all the humming activity around us.

"Consistency is just stubbornness with a better PR team," I said.

"Uh huh." he said as he jotted information on a form.

"Hey, I thought you were going to tell us when we figured out the identity of Erjon Dren?" I said.

"Er what who?" he said, still writing.

"Erjon Dren. The motorcyclist. You said both us and Miami Dade Homicide would get notified when the results came back. We'd obtain what homicide receives at the same time."

"Well, I never heard anything. I guess they didn't either," he said.

I remembered my conversation with Felton on the phone. I asked him how he made a positive identification on Erjon Dren.

"We got it from Miami Dade Homicide," he said.

Lieutenant Maddalone wrapped up his part of the investigation and left with the Glock I used in today's shooting.

The investigation was in full "get it done" mode. Everyone on the scene seemed to know exactly they needed to do. Equipment was rolled in, and equipment was rolled out. Measurements and photographs were being taken. There was a lot of writing on legal yellow pads and a lot of small clusters of investigators conferring and comparing. I stayed on the scene another two hours, answering whatever questions that were asked of me and explaining whatever nuance of the events that were needed to be clarified. I eventually was able to get to my car. I was thankful I had parked under the overpass and the shaded car was kept out of the bright sunshine. I decided to take the gravel road around the property and use it to go west, out to Milam Dairy Road. I drove home and endured the clogged roads and traffic. Johan Willaimson and Arica had already left.

I was a mess. Muddy, dirty, sweaty, and bloody. I trudged upstairs. I turned on the shower and absentmindedly watched the water flow out of the shower head. I was tired. I was *exhausted*. I thought it would be just easier to step into the shower and remove my wet clothes, but I didn't think I had the energy or patience to wrestle and wrangle the wet clothes off my body. I stripped off my clothes and threw them into a Hefty bag. I knew I'd never be wearing any of them ever again. I wanted a drink.

Badly.

But at some point, I'd be driving back to the Biltmore, and I needed to withhold my desire for a nerve-steadying drink. Nerve-steadying drinks often led to steady nervous drinking. I had to stay in the moment, do what I needed to do, starting with this shower. For the first time the quietness of the condominium was unsettling to me. The events of the day were playing in my head on a continual loop. The sun was behind the building, and the shady third-floor terrace was inviting. I laid back in one of the chaise lounges and watched the billowy clouds drift by. I dozed off for about twenty minutes, and whether anybody ever believes in "power naps" or not, the twenty-minute slumber gave me a boost in energy that was sorely needed.

On my drive to the Biltmore, I was thinking about a few of the things that transpired. One thing that stuck in my mind was what Major Brunson said to Arica after we jumped into the waterway to avoid the Albanians.

"What I'm getting at is that you've been preemptively staged every time something big has happened."

"You were there in Kosovo. The Albanians were there. You're here. The Albanians are here."

I thought about what Arica told me in the car as we drove home from the near murder hit on us at the bridge.

"I think that he had a few things correct. The places he mentioned in the world. Yes, I've been at those places, often right when something happens. He didn't mention foresight, planning, geopolitical engagement, having trusted sources."

What sparked this train of thought was her reaction to Borges getting shot in the arm.

"You said Borges caught one in the shoulder. Do you mean that Tom was shot?"

She didn't call him Borges, or Agent Borges. She called him Tom.

"...He didn't mention foresight, planning, geopolitical engagement, having trusted sources."

Trusted sources.

Chapter Twenty-Five

I WAS IN THE vicinity of the Biltmore when I got the phone call from Arica.

"Okay it's a wrap," she said.

"How'd it go?" I asked her.

"It went well. I can't wait to tell you all about it. From what I heard you have stories to tell as well."

"I figured you'd want to hear it from the official authorities and not from a slimy detective like me."

"I never said slimy. You said slimy. I just didn't disagree with you," she said, chuckling. "We both know you're not slimy. Trident Broadcasting has me booked at the Biltmore for the next two days. With the latest developments, my assignment editor thinks it's safe for me to leave *Chez Cade*."

"The perks of your job amaze me," I said.

"It's not always like that. I slept in a rat trap of a hotel in Reno once. It was so disgusting. The bed sheets were so rough I thought they were made in a sawmill. I slept in my clothes."

"Take the good with the bad I guess," I said.

"I'm starved. Are you hungry?" she asked me.

"Yeah, I'm pretty hungry but I don't want to eat at the Biltmore,"

I said, already imagining the repeat of a media circus that must be there.

"Well, think of a place and get here soon. Trident Broadcasting is buying. I'm so famished I'm eyeing the couch cushions for crumbs here. Call me when you're close and I'll meet you at the valet stand."

Like clockwork I called Arica, and she was waiting at the valet stand. I couldn't help but recall the plight we both endured two nights ago and how it all started right there at the valet stand. She greeted me with a kiss and remarked that the side of my face was red and looked like a sunburn. The muzzle flash from Cosima's gun had left a little temporary low-grade scorch on my face. I opened the car door for her, and she slid into the seat, holding a very full leather tote bag.

I selected a restaurant not far away that was quaint and quiet on the nights they weren't hosting live jazz acts. I like jazz, but tonight I just wanted to eat my way through the menu and bend an elbow at the bar. I found a parking spot on Alhambra Circle directly in front of the place. The Globe restaurant bar opened two years ago in the Lorraine Travel building. Its décor was eclectic, and the menu was inspired by culinary entrees from around the world. Hence the name. We decided to sit inside and were seated at one of the tables with a view of the ornate staircase and the inviting bar. The bar is appointed in deep resonated wood and adorned with multiple small globes displayed across a transom-like shelf above the carefully curated liquor selections. Our waiter was very prompt, and I think he could guess we were famished.

We started off with an appetizer of Bahamian conch fritters and split the South African lobster club sandwich. Arica ordered the pear ravioli, and I selected the grilled Argentine churrasco.

"We're really hungry," she explained to the waiter.

Before he turned away, she placed the same drink order she had at the Biltmore.

"I'll have a MacAllan 12 Year Double Cask. Separate ice in a chilled glass."

He looked at me expectantly.

Before I answered I looked past him through the window at the BMW parked outside. I turned my gaze back to him.

"I'll have a werewolf Jameson neat."

"Werewolf?" he asked, confused.

"Yes. A werewolf. Like how in the movies, they always chain the guy up before he turns into a werewolf. No matter what I tell you, no matter what I say, do not allow me to have more than one," I stressed to him.

He smiled and turned away to the bar. He returned a few minutes with both of our drinks on a circular burnished wooden tray. He carefully put our drinks on the table in front of us. He reached into the front of his apron and put a can of Coors Light in front of Arica.

"Here's a silver bullet for Lon Chaney Jr. here," he said with a big smile.

We all had a great laugh. It was the first time I'd laughed in days. We toasted with our respective liquor choices.

"Cade, Agent Felton said that you and a Carabinieri agent killed three of the Albanians today."

"True."

"Care to elaborate?" she asked.

"Were you able to get your exclusive filmed and out into the world?" I asked her subconsciously leaning back away from her and the probing question.

"Yes."

"Then I don't care to elaborate."

"Cade, you don't play fair. Ever. At all."

"If you've already filed your story and it's as you say in your business, 'in the can' then what's the point of elaborating about it?"

"Because I care about you. Hello? I've seen you naked...like, a lot!" she said smiling.

Overhearing her comment, the bemused waiter placed the conch fritters and the indulgent lobster club sandwich on the table.

We tucked in on the food like it was going to be our last meal. The sandwich was divine, and the fritters were reminiscent of a little place I knew in Great Guana Cay in the Abaco's.

"Have you ever been to the Abaco's in the Bahamas?" I asked her.

"Is that an invite?" she asked crinkling her eyes with a slight smile and tilt of her head.

"Always," I replied.

We talked a little bit more and then the conversation turned back to the shooting of the three Albanians today.

"Are you asking as a journalist or out of concern for me?" I asked.

"Well, since there's a little blood seeping through your shirt at your shoulder, I'll flip all the cards and say *you* for 500," she said.

"Okay. I'm not much of an initiated talker. Ask away and I'll see if I can answer," I said.

She was obviously very good at interviewing and asking the right questions without appearing to be probing or ghoulish. She was very intrigued that most of the investigation was conducted by tracking Luvas Dren's ankle monitor. Our entrées arrived, and although we'd torn through the sandwich and fritters, we both ate our meals while she continued to gather what backstory she could. The assistance of the Carabinieri was essential to the solving of this case and if their New York-based agent didn't swap his assignment with Tucson Lou, the full input from the Carabinieri may have been different. Vastly different. Arica was very impressed to find out that the Carabinieri agent was a woman.

"She sounds like a total badass," she said.

"Badass with a Berretta handgun and a Fendi bag," I said.

Arica looked across the table at me and the corners of her eyes moistened a little.

"How do you do it?" she asked me.

"Do what?"

"Pack all this in. Put all this carnage away and get up the next day and read the sports page in the *Miami Herald* as if it's just another day?"

Her question caught me off guard and I sat there momentarily twirling my fork on the tablecloth trying to find the best way to answer her. I'd given it a lot of thought recently, thanks to Dr. Rangela.

"I don't think the phrase 'packing it in' really applies. When you pack something in you just condense it into a tight compartment. You know what psychologists say about compartments. Eventually you have to go back in and squeeze more in or you have to empty it. I try and recognize that these are all separate events. The common denominator is that they involve me, but they actually involve the police department. I'm just an extension of that."

I will never lament being a dragonslayer when there are verifiable dragons amongst us.

"An extension? You may not be the television Cade, but without an extension cord plugged into an outlet, the TV isn't coming on. I think it goes beyond being an extension of the agency. *You* are the energy and the viability of the process."

"Interesting analogy," I said hoping to hurry the conversation into a different corner of my psyche.

My life is a smoking crater. That's all.

I opted to open up a little about the case and steer the conversation from me, specifically to the Albanians. Dr. Rangela would call this "deferring and deflecting." I call it trying to enjoy dinner.

"What we and the Carabinieri can't seem to figure is how the assassination attempt on the Italian consulate factors into all of this. These guys were credit card and identity thieves. They were from Albanian crime syndicates, and yes, they were more than the sum of their crimes but to assassinate a viable political candidate in a secured press conference? That seems way out of their league. Way out of their league."

"Cade, I told you, the Albanian crime groups are ruthless. I'm going to remind you that fraudulent credit cards aren't all they do."

She did tell me after our little dip in the waterway. They were into everything and everywhere. Asia, Europe, Afghanistan. Loan sharking, money laundering, murder...

"They are the kings *of whacking people."*

"I remember what you said about their ruthlessness..."

"Ruthlessness? That adjective doesn't even begin to explain how they are. How about aggressive brutality? Relentless vengeance? Savagery unparalleled? The viciousness of these criminals is unrivaled. Need I remind you that *you* have three...no, technically four, as in F-O-U-R Albanian notches on your gun? Cade, if they find out you were the killer of four of their brethren...it's not something that will just go away," she said.

"I know," I said exhaling and looking at my plate.

"I'm not saying you'll need to look over your shoulder for the entirety of your life, but I need to advise you that the sword of Albania is sharp and has a long reach."

"With that said can I hope that there won't be a follow-up new stories from anything you learned at this table tonight?" I asked.

"Today's newspaper is tomorrow's birdcage liner. Keeping up with the headlines is like playing Whac-A-Mole with a blindfold. The news moves and the news moves on. Its moving as we sit here right now." she said with a dismissive wave of her hand.

"With regards to packing and unpacking the emotional carnage... Can't I say the same about you? Considering all the hot spots in the world you've been to," I said.

She stiffened. "It's different," she said. "How so?"

"I often arrive in those hotspots when the deed's already been done. The skirmish, war, conflict, whatever you want to call it, it's already started. I'm not one of the combatants. I'm not a participant. I'm an observer." she said putting her own perspective out to be heard.

That's not what Major Brunson thought. He hadn't said observer. He said "preemptively staged."

"Arica, Major Brunson was very emphatic that he felt you were in a lot of those locations earlier than your competition. That maybe you'd been tipped off about some of these events."

"Really? Brunson? That gasbag who has a swear word for every occasion? The guy's a profanity Swiss Army knife and you're going to let his flagrant and abusive comments shape your thinking?"

"The coincidence is eyebrow raising. Wouldn't you agree?" I said ignoring her question.

"Agree? I agree to none of that nonsense. Brunson's not a sooth-sayer with magical potions and amulets that define the universe. Especially a universe outside of bluster and profanity."

"No, he's not, but in both of our fields of work we *do* rely on information and people. We like to pretend they're super-secret. In law enforcement, we say they're confidential informants. In the media? They're 'sources.'" I said.

"Yes. So?"

"You obviously have sources. We're just trying to gather an under-standing of why the consulate was targeted. You were here. You were in place. A new media organization like Triad Broadcasting felt that this quickly assembled press conference was newsworthy enough to send you down here on the fly. Last minute. I just question if Trident Broadcasting had a reliable *source* and sold you on coming down— or did you have the reliable source and sold *them* on coming down?"

The conversation was becoming heavy.

"Cade, if you're asking me about sources here or elsewhere, I don't need to remind you that I cannot comment, even in the slightest on that."

"I know. You don't need to comment. I have a good idea how this assignment came together already."

Chapter Twenty-Six

DIGGING IN TO see if Tom Borges was a source for Arica was immaterial. She's a global correspondent and knows people at all levels in the world. That's how she maintains and excels in her career. The media has come to many members of the Coral Gables Police Department and sought an angle, an edge, an exclusionary portal into a story. It's part of the landscape. We in law enforcement have used the media to our advantage, too.

Major Brunson had deftly used the media to our advantage the other night.

"We're doing a little disinformation to protect you two."

We finished dinner and respected the professional confidentiality line between us. As we stepped outside, we took in the balmy night air. South Florida in February can be one of the most desirable places to be in the United States.

"I'm already going to miss this," she said.

"Me?" I said as I opened her car door for her.

"Well, I meant the weather, but sure, why not you too?" She giggled as she kissed me.

I started the car and remembered that Gary had a file about Janice Gordon waiting for me in the office. The police department was only a few short blocks away.

'You okay if we swing by my office and pick something up real quick?"

"Is it handcuffs, tear gas, or one of those weird club things you macho machos carry?"

"No, it's just a file."

"I guess so, but don't think for a second I'm not the least bit disappointed," she teased.

Walking into the police department, Arica said, "This building's vibe is abandoned warehouse meets existential crisis."

"I know. I think if the walls could talk, they'd just sigh and mumble, 'We tried.'" I said echoing her opinion.

The VIN office was partially tidy. Illena's desk was front and center with piles of papers on one corner of the desk. On the credenza behind her chair was a Moka pot for making Café Cubano, the caffeine rocket fuel we eagerly slurped down every afternoon. On the edge of Gary's desk was a manila folder and my name on a post-it smack in the middle of it. I picked it up and started to open it.

"Cade, haven't we had enough of this today? Let's just get it and go. Put it aside and get out of here."

She was right. Enough was enough, at least for today. I tucked the file under my arm, and we left the building. I laid the file on the back seat of the car, and we drove down the vibrating parking ramps of the building.

"Are these ramps supposed to jiggle under the weight of our car?" she asked.

"The engineers said it's supposed to do that. Something about weight distribution," I said.

"Uh huh," she replied obviously not buying any of that engineering theory. "Cade, the Biltmore is nice. Very nice. The pool is a wonderment unto itself. But I'd rather be back at your place than at the hotel. Is it too forward to suggest we go there?"

"Not at all. I'd prefer it. Less chance of a noise complaint," I said.

"A noise complaint? You are ambitious."

"You're right. Let's make noises only dogs can hear," I said, and she laughed. "Do you need to go back to the hotel to get anything?"

She lifted up the large leather tote and dropped it heavily into her lap showing me its heftiness. She put it back on the car's floorboard. "World traveler here, Cade! I'm always prepared. I hope the weather is nice tomorrow, it would be nice to sit by the pool."

"Arica, would you rather be at my pool or go back to the Biltmore and its luxurious pool?"

"Your pool. I like to know who's peeing in the pool that I'm in," she said.

We arrived at the condominium at the Royal Harbour Yacht Club. The feather like breezes from Biscayne Bay welcomed us as we exited the car. The soft *twang* of a sailboat's bell chimed in the night somewhere from the marina. Miami's skyline, miles away, cast a white glow in the eastern night sky. Once inside we moved closer, hands brushing, eyes locked, until our closeness melted into a slow, sultry kiss that promised more. The world outside faded, leaving just us, wrapped in the heat of the moment, the condo our private sanctuary. The night unfolded like a dream you wish you could repeat over and over, luxuriating in the soft sheets of my bed, the peek-a-boo moon revealing itself from behind the clouds at will, casting a soft glow over our skin, amplifying every sensation. Laughter mingled with whispers, and time paused as we lost ourselves in the rhythm of our connection. The condominium, with its cozy corners, moon basked terraces, plush furniture, and intentional décor details felt like it was built precisely for us for this specific night—every surface a canvas for our passion. By the time we collapsed, breathless and grinning, the stars outside seemed to wink in approval, as if the entire universe had been in on our perfect, sexy night. As we settled in to finally sleep Arica curled up close to me.

"Get right," she said as she sought the best way to rest her head on my shoulder.

"What do you mean 'get right'?"

"I don't know. Lower your shoulder or something. But get right," she playfully protested as she snuggled against me.

The morning sun streamed through the window valances. After I'd finally appeased her desire for me to "get right" she eventually fell asleep with her head on my shoulder, where she still was. Although the bed was overrun with pillows I was flattered that she'd choose my shoulder to lay her head upon. Careful not to disturb her slumber, I slipped out from under her and toddled off to the shower. My filthy clothes from yesterday were still in the trash bag against the jacuzzi bathtub. After my shower I toweled off and put on the plush terrycloth robe that came with the condo. I stepped back into the bedroom. Arica was now awake.

"I think I'm going to take a bath. The other night the tub was magnificent. A girl remembers things like that," she said.

I returned to the bathroom, turned on the gold-plated faucet, and the opulent marble tub began filling with hot water. As I got dressed and gathered up the bag of my discarded clothes, Arica got out of bed. She was naked, and stunningly beautiful. She had a sublime attractiveness that was intoxicating. She gave me a kiss, and I couldn't help but gawk at her as she sauntered into the bathroom, closing the door behind her. I was transfixed, staring at the closed door for a moment.

After gaining my composure I said through the door, "I was thinking something for breakfast."

"Surprise me, but do it with pastry," she said as I heard the water turn off.

Pastry in southern Miami Dade County, I thought to myself as I left the complex. I drove north to Joanna's Marketplace. There was still an ample supply of fresh baked goods in the display case, and I selected an assortment of croissants, muffins, Danish, and coffee. When I got back Arica was dressed in a bathing suit and a floral cover-up.

"Was I incorrect to assume there was a swimming pool here somewhere?" she asked.

"There's a really nice one across the parking lot by the center tennis court," I said.

"Center tennis court? Is there more than one tennis court.?"

"Yes, there's one by the main gate with a walking trail out to the beach."

"Beach?" she said excitedly.

"Beach with a high potential for saltwater crocodiles...just saying."

"Hard pass," she said.

We enjoyed the goodies from Joanna's, then went down to the pool. The water was warmed by a solar heater and the languid gurgle of the circulating water was very relaxing. We'd been there for an hour and a half when Arica's cellphone rang. She took the call poolside. When she hung up she said:

"That was work. Looks like I'm being pulled out of here on a late flight tonight to Amman Jordan."

"Wait. What?"

"That was my assignment editor, Samantha Surman. King Hussein passed away a few days ago and they think there's going to be some rising factions that may disrupt the transfer of the kingdom to his son. The news waits for nothing and nobody Cade. There's a Lufthansa flight at 10pm to Berlin. From there I connect to Amman. The ticket's been purchased and will be waiting for me at the counter at Miami International Airport," she rattled off, with a practiced detached, and routine voice.

I felt crestfallen. I wasn't expecting our time to end so quickly. I also was a little upset at myself for not seeing that this was a very real potential outcome, if not today than any day after today. I had locked my emotions and heart in a cast iron vault for so long...These feelings were my own fault. The very minute I spoke with her in the Biltmore bar I should have stayed clear of any traveling romance. Too many staticky late-night long-distance phone calls, too many questions of 'where are you now', too many 'not much to say on my part' lines, as the routine of my life in Miami could be either yawn-inducing or full-on sheer terror—neither of which would I feel like talking about over the phone to Copenhagen, Istanbul, or Mauritius. Letting people into my life was not something I was accustomed to. People can cloud judgement, create tentative hesitations in my life. Hesitations that could get me or someone else killed.

This dropping of my guard, as wonderful as it felt, was a delayed gut punch. A take-the-wind- out-of-my-lungs gut punch. But who did I have to blame other than myself? She told me up front who she was and what her career demanded of her. I should have adhered to my initial assessment of Arica: her heart beats to the rhythm of a departing train. A human travel visa.

I am Miami. That's what I am. She is the world. That's what she is.

Her passport has stamps that bleed over and overlap each other. Her ATM card works in 1900 machines around the world and the numbers on her American Express are worn flat. Me? My passport has a couple of stamps to the Bahamas and back. I have a Burdines credit card and a Bank of Coral Gables Visa that rarely sees daylight from the confines of my wallet. Arica was on a whole different level than me. Every road she hasn't walked down whispers her name, beckoning her to get up and go. It was silly of me to think there could be any future between us. My life was late-hour shots of Jameson, beers in a beach chair, and too many despots and scuzzy cretins cycling through the criminal justice system. With Arica, I was swinging for a fence that was way out of my strike zone.

"Cade, I don't like this anymore than you do," she said, trying to soften the news.

"No. It's okay. I get it. It was an inevitable phone call," I said, trying to tamp down my disappointment. "I was hoping we could get down to Key Largo for dinner tonight."

"I'm sorry. Can I have a raincheck?"

"Anytime," I said, forcing a slight smile.

"Kind of like the song, huh Cade? *'We had it all just like Bogey and Bacall...'*" she sang, trying to put a loving spin on the fact she'd be leaving in less than eight hours.

"Eight hours. I guess we can make the most of it. Right?" I said.

"Any ideas?" she said.

"We can start by getting out of the pool and going back to my place," I suggested.

Chapter Twenty-Seven

B Y LATE AFTERNOON we knew we had to go to the Biltmore Hotel to get the rest of Arica's things. It was logical to have dinner at the Biltmore. After all, Trident Broadcasting was picking up the tab.

Just before we were set to leave my cellphone rang. "Cade. It's Wayne Felton."

"Hey, Wayne. Nothing but mayhem lately, huh?"

"It's been crazy, but a good crazy. Really good actually. The bullet grazed Borges more than penetrated. Don't get me wrong, I'm sure it hurt like a bitch but thankfully it kind of burrowed on the outer part of his shoulder and went out without a lot of significant damage. They're releasing him in a few hours. He's going to come here to the Biltmore and then we're hoping to have a final go-over meeting in the morning. I have to catch a flight back to Memphis in the afternoon, and Lou's going back to Tucson."

"Show's over, I guess," I said.

"Show's over. But what a show it was! Right? I mean talk about heck in a handbasket. I thought for sure we were going to get reamed by Washington. Typical, right? We bust our butts to keep tens of thousands safe at the Super Bowl and then some guy dressed like a waiter shoots an unknown Italian politician and *we* get hammered.

Now Washington is singing our praises because we finally hit that Albanian crime group hard. This job... I tell ya. It's hell on every aspect of my life."

"What about Cosima?" I asked.

"I haven't seen her. I've tried to reach her. I think she's here at the hotel. I'll leave a message for her at the front desk. Let's count on meeting at 8am at the 19th Hole for breakfast. Lou and I can properly say goodbye and we can congratulate Tom on his recovery."

"Sounds like a plan. I'll see you in the morning," I said as I hung up.

I didn't want to tell him we were going to be at the Biltmore in a half hour. I wanted to maximize my time with Arica and not be dragged into a whole guns and criminals gab fest. Back slapping and handshakes could wait until the morning. As I hung up, I turned to Arica.

"That was Wayne Felton from the Secret Service. He wants to meet tomorrow morning at the Biltmore at 8am."

"Eight in the morning? What is he, crazy? Who does anything at 8am?"

"Actually, we did something at 8am," I said with a devilish grin.

"I mean something that doesn't involve messy hair and a shower afterwards."

"I think you're describing working out in a gym," I said.

"Really Cade? When have you ever gotten up at 8am to sweat with a bunch of strangers in a gym? Seriously? You're used to coming home from a night out at 8am."

"Well...maybe...I mean, sometimes."

"The lovely bean counters at Trident Broadcasting are paying for my unused hotel room through tomorrow. Let's go to dinner, you take my room card and stay at the Biltmore tonight. That will save you a ton of aggravation in the morning," she said.

"Wow. Thank you. That will make it much easier indeed."

We had dinner at the hotel's Fontana restaurant, sitting outside by the fountain in the courtyard. The sun was setting. The blushing pink, ethereal lavender, and zesty tangerine colors blazed across the sandstone-colored walls of the hotel. It was a beautiful time to have dinner. We shared an appetizer of *melanzane*. I ordered the *taglierini con vongole* and Arica had the *branzino*. Arica wasn't drinking.

"It throws off the bio rhythms when I fly," she said.

Dinner was a sumptuous affair and a proper send-off before Arica boarded her flight for Amman. She gave me her room card and jokingly admonished me to "behave myself." I had my car brought up by the valet. Arica almost verbatim repeated the same words from the last time I offered to take her to the airport.

"Can you drive with the sunroof open? I need to take in as much of Miami as I can before I leave for Jordan."

We drove to Miami International Airport. This time Arica had her Neosporin and there was no need to make any stops along the way. Although it wasn't said, I do think we both felt the irony of returning to the airport considering the near-death experience we dodged on our last jaunt there. Those kind of events bond people for life. It certainly did for us. The drive went very quickly. Hanging onto newfound moments will hasten the perception of time.

I learned a little hack years ago that if I parked in the airport's rarely used south parking lot, I could practically walk a mere thirty yards right into the south terminal. I retrieved Arica's bag from the car, and we walked into the terminal. I watched her go to the Lufthansa counter, her every move captured in my mind. Within a few minutes she had her ticket to Berlin and the ticket for her connecting flight to Amman.

"Business class. Not bad," she said perusing the tickets. There was a moment of awkwardness as we stood in the terminal. "Can you use that tiny badge of yours and go out to the concourse with me?"

"It's not tiny," I said.

"Said every man ever," she joked. "Actually, I'm getting really pressed for time. I won't be able to access my Blackberry once I'm on the plane. I don't know if it will even work across the Atlantic, let alone overseas. I'll need to read some of these messages from the office and get everything lined up for Amman."

"Blackberry? What is that?" I asked.

She pulled out a newfangled beeper-looking thing out of her bag "It just came out last month. Trident bought a bunch of them for us. I'm still getting used to it. It's like a pager on steroids. It does a ton more. It can be very addictive. One of my colleagues calls it a 'crackberry'. I don't know how we managed before without it. You should get one."

"No, I shouldn't," I said.

"Yes, you should. I know things, Cade Taylor."

"Okay, Miss Frequent Flier Miles, what do you know?" I teased.

"I know that you're going to have a big Missing Arica hole in your heart that even pizza can't fill."

"I can see you don't understand the binding and filling properties of cheesy goodness," I said.

"Cade Taylor! Did you just say that a pizza can fill the void of me being gone?"

"I'm kidding. How about you? Are you going to miss me? Yes or yes?"

"Given my choices I'll say yes."

"I knew that before I asked you," I said.

It was then we both heard the PA announcement that her flight would be boarding in thirty minutes.

"That's me," she said wistfully. "I need to get on my Blackberry and catch up on things before I board."

"I know," I said as I moved closer to her.

We held a long embrace and fell into deep, passionate kisses. I felt her start to ease away from me. She stepped back and looked into my eyes.

"It's Miami. I'm sure some big story will lead you back here in the future. Right?" I said.

"If not a big story maybe I'll just come back for Cuban food, sunsets, and another chance to convince you that not everything that leaves you gasping is bad for you," she said.

"Next time I'll have a pocket inhaler," I said stoically.

We said a final goodbye, and she turned away, going to her airport gate. She turned back and said to me, "If you're thinking of going Christmas shopping for me, I'm a size window seat in plane tickets."

With that she joined the traveling passengers as they funneled down a hallway and out of sight.

She was gone.

I wanted out of that airport. I didn't want to be around anybody. I was thankful I'd been able to park close to the airport and would be able to be in the quiet confines of my car soon. I walked towards the exit. I refused to even entertain the idea of looking back.

Not now. Not this time.

I know that inside of me...down in the dormant depths of me...I felt a subtle change in myself after being with Arica. My sardonic edges had slightly curled, letting light in under the eaves of my heart. Rather than keep hammering the past shut I should start prying up the nails holding down my future. Try giving in to the rest of the world. A world that isn't running on cocaine, murder, and money laundering. Embrace the normalcy of living for a purpose other than righting wrongs and strenuously holding the rough, frayed rope that keeps the dark humanity beast from devouring everything before it. The universe moves in ways we can never even attempt to understand. It's been said that some people come into our lives as a reason, a season, or a lesson. What if Arica was none of those things, or an amalgamation of all of them? How could I know? Arica was gone. At least for now. At the very least she was gone until the crazy rotational spin of our lives puts us back in the same longitude and latitude. Maybe different situations or different fate could help that happen.

We can always hope, right?

Although said in a different context but still applicable, my mind went back to what Dr. Rangela said about hope.

"Hope is not a strategy."

I needed to remind myself that passports are proof that people are allowed to leave, but not a guarantee that they will come back. I'd like to think her life will be more sedate without my continual chaos—then again, she seemed to always be on her way to chaos somewhere in the world. I pondered what my immediate future would be, how I'd cope. Would every airplane in the sky remind me of how those gravity-defying big birds kept taking Arica away? Would I be telling every bartender to turn up the volume when the news comes on? Would I lament every missed call from an unknown number? What would the next steps of my life be like now that I'd experienced Arica?

I drove back to the Biltmore Hotel, and I left my car with the valet. I grabbed my go bag and the file that Gary had set aside for me. Being back in the hotel I suddenly really felt alone. I went up to the hotel room that Trident Broadcasting had booked for Arica. There was nary a trace that she had even been there. I settled into the room and was eager to get tomorrow's little send-off breakfast behind me. Way behind me. I still had Keys Disease and even without Arica, a few libations in the sunny vibrations somewhere between the island of Key West and the island of "I Know What is Best" might be what any doctor would order. Even Dr. Rangela.

As I looked north out of the hotel window, Miami International Airport was six miles away in almost a straight line from where I was standing. Little flickering white lights with small red dots moved from west to east in the sky at almost three-minute intervals, leaving Miami for points unknown. At least unknown by me. I looked at my watch. 10:21pm. Any one of those departing airplanes could be Arica.

I moved away from the window and sat on the edge of the king-sized bed. I contemplated calling room service and having a bucket of Heinekens brought up. I was weighing the benefits of numbing my soul versus drinking alone in a hotel room when my cellphone rang.

It was Cosima.

"Well, hello there," I said trying to sound cheery.

"Cade, it's good to hear your voice. *Dio mio!* What a few days we've had," she said.

"I'm still just trying to process it all—" I started to say before she interrupted me.

"Cade, I have something to tell you!"

"Well, before you do that, tell me first how you're doing," I said, partially cutting her off.

She was momentarily taken off guard, like she'd had a running dialogue of our conversation playing in her head and I threw her off with my interruption. "I am good. Nothing broken, just bruising on my face. The doctor says it will clear up in a few days. I may have an eye black—"

"Black eye," I interjected.

"Yes, a black eye for a week or more. Teeth are good. Hearing good. Everything is good," she said.

I could sense her anxiousness to tell me something in her unusual brevity. I wasn't in the mood to see anybody and intentionally didn't tell her I was staying at the Biltmore Hotel. We had been to the hottest basement in hell together, but I was just not in the mood to commiserate, celebrate, castigate, or contemplate with anyone.

"Will you be at the 19th Hole at eight in the morning for the Secret Service meeting?" I asked.

"Yes. I thought I was going to be leaving for Milan tomorrow night, but I am waiting to hear from the Carabinieri. I may be staying a little longer."

Curiosity got the better of me. "Why is that?" I asked her.

"They sent me to the hospital for observation. The medical care was very good. Everyone was very professional. I have no complaints. I realized that I was in the same hospital as our agent and Consulate Baldassare Constantino. I recognized it from when I went to see both of them. Our agent is making progress but there's still a big hill to climb."

"We're all thinking of him," I said.

"Thank you, but it's not him I am calling about. I'm calling about Baldassare Constantino."

"Is he okay?"

"Oh, he is more than okay. He's getting the best care imaginable and should be home at the consulate residence either tomorrow or the next day. I'm calling because when I was there, he was having lunch in his room with his fiancée. The Carabinieri agent we have stationed outside his hospital suite let me in. The door to the main area of the suite was partially open. I got to the door, and I had to stop. I couldn't go in."

"Why?" I asked.

"Because his fiancée is Janice Gordon!"

Chapter Twenty-Eight

INCOMPREHENSIBLE. THIS ADDED a huge wrinkle in the pattern. A complete high and tight curveball.

"She's his *fiancée*? For real? Are you sure?"

"Remember how tired she was when she let us in the house? She said she'd been up all night with a health crisis here with a dear friend. Well, guess what? That health crisis was Baldassare Constanino being shot!" she said her voice slightly rising in the phone's earpiece.

The memory of her saying that came back to me.

"I'm sorry, I'm a little loopy about remembering everything. I didn't sleep well last night. We have a health crisis here with a dear friend and it's taking a lot out of me.

"Wait a minute. Wait a damn minute! Are you saying that the gangsters who invaded Janice Gordon's house, who we now know are the same guys that tried to kill the consulate, the very same consulate who just happens to be her fiancée?"

"Exactly!" she said.

"There's no way that this is coincidental."

"Cade! Seriously! Are you looking for a silver lining here? Of course it isn't coincidental. The question is how does it all come together? Do you remember how she was when we went to talk to her?"

"Yes of course."

"She was congenial until we got ready to leave. She thought I was a Coral Gables detective. Then you informed her I was Carabinieri. Remember?"

"I do."

"She turned three shades of white and practically closed the door on us," she said. *"On loan? What does that mean? Why the Italian police? This is a surprise."*

"Come to think of it, that was a pretty abrupt end to our visit," I said.

"It most certainly was. What about when you told her the police found Erjon Dren's fingerprints at her home robbery and how it was of *'high importance to the Italian authorities'* and she didn't mention anything...*niente*...about her fiancée, the potential next premier of Italy. *Che odore orribile si sta rivelando!*"

"What does that mean?"

"It means it stinks. This whole thing is a stinking mess," she said.

My wheels were turning. "We knew nothing about her husband Matthew. Nothing. How do you say that again?"

"*Niente.*"

"Niente. Nothing. Yet when we were leaving and she learned you were from the Carabinieri she didn't ask about her fiancé, or the home invasion robbery. She asked us about Matthew. Looking back, that was odd," I said.

"But how is Matthew connected to this Italian concern?" she asked.

"Exactly! She called it an Italian concern. What does that mean?" Cosima said.

"A *concern*? Her fiancée nearly got whacked in front of a delegation of Italian and American attendees. That's more than just an 'Italian concern'. An Italian concern is when there are no orange peel garnishes for a Negroni. Maybe losing one husband in some convoluted crazy Australian situation isn't enough. She has to have her fiancée break two ribs backstopping an assassin's bullet." I said.

Cosima's voice was raised when she said, "Let's not forget that one of my agents suffered a severe and life-altering bullet wound on that day, too. If Janice Gordon had anything to do with this, I will take one of her precious Bobby Varga scarfs and hang her upside down from the nearest palm tree."

"Believe me I know. I know all too well," I said, trying to calm her down. "Hang on a second. I need to check something."

I put the phone down and walked across the room. I picked up the Janice Gordon file and started looking through it as I returned to the phone.

"I'm going to need to call you back."

Chapter Twenty-Niine.

9:45 AM THE next morning, I was sitting in the opulent lobby of the Biltmore Hotel. People were milling about. I kept my eye on the front doors. Detective Johan Williamson and Lieutenant Charlie Maddalone walked in.

"Cade, you know I don't need to tell you how bad this will be for all of us if you and Cosima are wrong," said Maddalone.

"Noted," I said, looking past them trying to figure out where Cosima was.

When I was starting to get nervous, the elevator doors opened, and Cosima stepped out. She was wearing dark sunglasses to try and hide her black eye. Her cheek was still swollen from the violent encounter she had with the Albanian thug in the Miami Dade utility yard.

"Do you think two will be enough?" she said, looking between Charlie and Johan.

"Technically four with me and you," I said.

As per requested by Major Brunson, both Lieutenant Maddalone and Detective Williamson were wearing police uniforms rather than their normal training supervisor and detective attire. They both seemed to be feeling uncomfortable in the uniforms. Comprised of a blend of cotton and polyester, the uniforms can be shiny, stifling, donut crumb catchers. Some genius decided that polyester was ideal for police uniforms. It's an industry synthetic fabric that screams, "I'm cheap, but I'll outlive you all."

"Okay. Give Cosima and me a fifteen-minute lead then come join us in the 19th Hole. I don't think the uniforms are going to scare anybody, but no one can say they didn't know who you were," I said to both men. "You ready?" I said turning to Cosima.

"I am here—"

"I know. I know. You're here to work. You're in Miami. You shouldn't have to explain," I finished for her.

"You two are like some Italian American version of a sitcom marriage," said Charlie.

"She's got a Luciano Pavarotti opera soul; I've got a Jimmy Buffett Caribbean Soul. Go figure," I said as she and I started making our way towards the restaurant.

We walked in relative silence through the hotel and went through the French doors out towards the pathway to the restaurant. We passed by two greenskeepers tending to the pétanque court.

"I don't know what that is, but it isn't bocce," she said.

When we arrived at the restaurant it was prearranged that I would go in first. Cosima would follow about forty-five seconds after and sit further down, away from me. I walked into the restaurant. There were a few golfers in the main dining area of the restaurant. Through the floor to ceiling windows, I saw Felton, Tucson Lou and Tom Borges standing outside on the covered lanai, talking. I joined them outside.

Felton and Lou were dressed in golfing attire. Lou was wearing a russet-colored Bermuda shorts, an Arizona State University white polo shirt, and a white pair of multi-cleated Footjoy golf shoes. Felton wore a green striped Munsingwear shirt and light green shorts. He was also wearing golf shoes, more traditional than Lou's with metal spikes on the soles. Comparatively, Borges was not in golf attire. He looked better than the last time I saw him. For a man who was shot days ago he looked remarkably well. As I approached them it seemed that all three men brightened up and were happy to see me.

"There he is! Man of the hour!" exalted Tucson Lou as I approached and shook hands with all three of them.

"Tom, how are you doing?" I asked Borges.

"Better. Much better. Doctors said it wasn't nearly as bad as I thought. I thought I was going to lose my arm. Cade, thank you. I mean seriously, thank you. You were right in there with the blood and everything. I'm very grateful."

"Don't think twice about it. I'm sure you'd have done the same for me." The mood was one of enduring a storm and victory.

"So, what's with you two? Hitting the links?" I asked Wayne and Lou.

"That was always the plan. Do the Super Bowl and get in a few rounds here at the Biltmore. I have a late afternoon flight to Memphis and Lou here is going back to Tucson early tomorrow morning. I hope we can get in at least nine holes. But before we get on the course, how about a little celebratory beverage?" he said as he motioned to the waiter to bring over a prearranged chilled bottle of Veuve Clicquot Brut Champagne.

Cosima walked out onto the lanai and the three men broke into applause and cheers. Borges clapped with slight difficulty but still managed. There were big smiles and big congratulatory smiles, words, and hugs. The waiter arrived with the bottle of champagne in a silver bucket. Ice was spilling out over the top of it. The waiter popped the cork and filled four flutes, giving the first one to Cosima. Felton proposed a toast to the great work we all did. I sat down at the long table across from Borges, and as planned, Cosima sat a few seats down. Tucson Lou still smitten by her and was very quick to sit at her side. Fenton sat next to Borges.

Conversation centered around all of the events of the past few days. The irony of how our Biltmore shooter, Luvas Dren's, court-issued ankle monitor led to the downfall of the Albanian gang was the crux of the conversation. I decided to take the lead in the conversation.

"You know I'm just the local guy in Miami, but the international aspects of your jobs must be exciting. We have a European agent here and you three from the Secret Service. I'm sure you all have great stories you could tell."

In the eyes of the Secret Service Agents, I could see the brief replay of careers in motion.

I pushed more. "I've always wondered about something. Especially with the Secret Service. How do you do it, how do you stay composed when you're surrounded by such political power, affluence, high-end events, sumptuous dinners, lavish affairs... All this wonderment around you and you're being held in check, standing in front of an elevator, standing by the motorcade, or watching a guest complain about the lobster thermidor while your own stomach grumbles. Do you ever think that you're on the outside looking in constantly?"

Lou said, "It's not about us Cade. It's about maintaining the safety of the principals and the events."

"Of course, but all that exposure has to create a feeling that maybe you got in the wrong line on career day. An uncontested local politician in a small-town winds up being a governor or senator and next thing you know they're on Air Force One demanding cracked crab on every flight to France. You must think sometimes, 'that could have been me' instead of some duplicitous dolt whose daddy started junior's path to the White House with a campaign donation to some frat buddy."

"Jealousy doesn't suit you well, Cade," said Borges.

"I'm just saying that you know not every hotel on the road is the Biltmore. How many times did you hope a sandwich that had sat out in the communications center for three hours was still available when you pushed off detail? Meanwhile the primary and everyone else are leaving with three-tier Godiva chocolate ballotin boxes and so many swag bags an aide has to carry them."

Cosima stood up and held her filled champagne glass up in front of her. "*La dolce vita!*"

"*La dolce vita!*" each of us toasted.

"May the only pain in our lives be champagne!" she said, putting an even brighter cap on the toast.

Even with her sunglasses on I could feel her intentional gaze on me. I swallowed the remnants of the bubbly French champagne and slightly tilted my flute back and forth in my hand as I looked into the curved depth of the handblown glass. I set the flute in front of me and looked across the table at Felton and Borges.

"Did it ever cross anybody's mind that the reason the Albanians were so successful for so long is because they had inside help?"

"Inside help? That's insane," said Felton

"They avoided detection for a long time. A long time to the tune of thirty million a year. You have to ask yourself..." I said letting my voice trail off as I raised my eyebrows at the thought.

"I still don't believe that. They were lucky, that's all," Felton said.

"Even Tom thought there might be inside doings. Ain't that right, Tom?" I said putting my eyes solely on Borges.

"Well, I said... I mean..."

"Didn't you tell me at the valet stand that too much had happened too soon for the shooting of the consulate to have gone the way it did?"

"Well yeah I mean, right, yes," Tom stammered.

"See? Even Tom here thinks there was inside help in keeping the Albanians from being discovered. Thirty million dollars...a *year*! Thirty million simoleans! Think about that. If someone on the inside was making just three percent of that take...what would that be?"

"900,000 dollars a year," answered Cosima.

"Wow. $900,000 a year! Wayne, I believe it was you who said the Albanians had been eluding you for at least five years. Right?

"*This crew had been eluding us for well over five years.*"

"That sounds about right," said Felton.

"Five years and a measly three percent...is how much again?"

"Four point five million," answered Cosima.

"Four point five million dollars...wow Sounds like a lot of money. But then again if you're making 150 million over five years it's a small price to pay to ensure that the Feds don't find you."

Tucson Lou glanced at his watch. "We have a tee time. Make it quick. What are you getting at, Taylor?" he said with a flavor of agitation in his words.

"Nothing, Lou. Should I be getting at something?"

"I don't like the attitude," said Lou with a hardened look.

"What exactly did *you* do after the consulate was shot?" I asked him.

"The Carabinieri were all over him. I thought their agent was dead. I tried to help him as best as I could. Within seconds there were a bunch of us helping him. I got up and started searching for the gunman on the golf course. Why?"

"How about you, Wayne? What did you do?" I asked Felton.

"My operation. I held the room," he said sternly.

"How about you, Tom? What did you do?"

"What do you mean what did I do? I went to the east side and checked on *you*. Remember? I was the first one to get to you!"

"It's odd you were the only one to go immediately to the east side post. The dumpster-watching post. The nothing should happen here post. Especially since the assassin clearly went straight out the back—"

Lou interrupted with, "Me and Wayne were looking to get in a few rounds after a nice send-off and you seem to have a wild hare up your butt about something. It sounds to me that you're about to cross a very delicate line."

"Oh, I have every intention of crossing that line," I said.

"Taylor, I think we've heard enough," said Felton.

"Heard enough? Really? Since you've heard enough have you ever heard about the bad shepherd?" I asked him pointedly.

"The bad shepherd? No, but okay Cade, against my better judgment and leveraged against our golf tee time, I'll bite. What's the bad shepherd?" asked Felton.

"The shepherd has a responsibility to protect his flock of sheep from the wolf. The sheep feel safe with the shepherd. He's entrusted to protect the sheep, and he's learned to be a good shepherd. His presence alone instills a feeling of comfort in the flock. They can graze the verdant grass, sleep in the shade of trees, drink from the spring-fed pond, all knowing the shepherd will protect them from the wolf. Except," I said turning my gaze to Tucson Lou, "what the sheep don't realize is that they will spend their entire existence fearing the wolf, only to eventually be eaten by the shepherd."

"And? What makes him a bad shepherd?" asked Felton.

"The bad shepherd is the shepherd who lets the wolf in purposefully to kill members of the flock that he finds troublesome, or not to his liking. He isolates those sheep from the flock and creates a way for the wolf to get in."

Silence among us and I suspect held breath by Cosima.

Lieutenant Maddalone and Johan Willaimson entered the lanai. Maddalone put the Janice Gordon file on the table in front of me. They didn't acknowledge anyone and stayed quiet. I made no effort to welcome them to the gathering. Maddalone stood off to the side closer to me. Johan was nearer to Lou and Cosima.

"Cosima. Do you remember what the Miami Dade Homicide detective said about what an up- close gunshot wound looks like?"

"Yes, yes...he talked about stippling. Unburnt powder particles embedded in the skin," she said conversationally.

I remembered every word. *"Unburnt powder particles that are embedded in the skin around the wound. See these black particle spots? This indicates a close-up shot. This is how we get a good idea about which shot was fired at different ranges. It's a good indication of the shot sequence. With our guy here, he was shot in the chest and then in the abdomen."*

"Meaning what?" I asked her.

"Meaning that if a gun was placed against you, it would leave stippling," she said.

"Tom, your gunshot wound didn't have any stippling. I know, I was there looking at it," I said to Borges.

"Fuck you Taylor, I took a bullet in the line of duty."

"Yes, you did. You sure did, Tom."

Felton, Borges, and Lou had clear agitation on their faces. Tucson Lou glared at me. His eyes darted, I could read that he was unsure whom the conversation was directed at, but he could sense that whoever it was carried a U.S. Secret Service badge. I slid the Janice Gordon file across the table to Felton. In the file were numerous pictures from multiple media sources of Gordon attending New Republicans of Miami Dade social events. As Gordon and her fellow members met with various key Republican politicians Tom Borges could be seen clearly in the background in a few of the pictures working in his official Secret Service capacities. Although he was never identified, in the more recent articles and blurbs, Borges can be seen sitting next to her, as an attendee. An invitee enjoying the same lavishness everyone else was. His suits had a customized style to them and in a few he was in black-tie tuxedos. With Janice Gordon. As a paramour.

As Felton perused the file, I waited for that tell-tale sign of him understanding the implication. When his eyes would shift up to look at Borges. As expected, he lifted his eyes from the pages and looked at Borges.

I quietly filled in the blanks. "Wayne, the woman in the pictures with Agent Borges is Janice Gordon. Her husband disappeared a few years ago. She is the current fiancée of the Italian consulate. She's also the same woman whose home was invaded years ago by the very same Albanian thugs who shot her fiancée, the consulate."

"And who shot my agent," said Cosima coldly.

I could see Borges shift in his seat. His eyes darted between the uniform presence of Maddalone and Willamson. He was thinking. Wondering exactly what was in the file in Felton's hands.

Borges found out Cosima and I had been out to see Janice that morning. Janice Gordon said she was on the phone with Building and Zoning when we arrived at her house. I found deception there easily. So, who was she on the phone with? I believed it was Borges.

"Did you send the police here? Well, they're here. Yup. Standing right in front of me. You're not scaring me."

Then it hit me full-on.

Major Brunson said it was *Arica* the Albanians were trying to kill. Arica was just collateral damage. I was who they wanted!

Borges sold me out!

Felton knew I'd be coming back to the hotel to drop off Cosima. He told Tucson Lou, who informed Borges. I was suspicious of Lou at the time and was wary when he called me inquiring about my expected arrival at the Biltmore with Cosima. It was actually Borges who had told him to call me.

"Sounds good. I'll tell Borges. He's been asking."

Both Secret Service agents were awaiting my arrival with Cosima. It was Borges who signaled the waiting Albanians from the valet stand. He identified me to the Albanians. He set me up. He was the bad shepherd. He let the wolves, these filthy Albanian wolves into the flock more than once.

Flashes of him putting his hands on my shoulders. *"Seriously. You okay?"* He handed me up. Not once, but twice.

I remembered him stepping back, looking around, I assumed to insure confidentiality before leaning in closer to me...

Failing to keep my composure and my anger in check, I lost it.

"Borges, you fucking stinking pig. We all heard the two shots followed by a single shot. Homicide said the dead Albanian had two shots to the abdomen and chest. Both fatal. Witnesses on the golf course heard him say 'It's me. It's me.' Does that sound like the pleadings of a stranger to any of you here?" I said, raising my voice, my fists clenched until they ached.

Borges sat there seething. Staring at me with scorching anger in his eyes.

"No answer? Okay, well let me tell you then. Fuck you, Borges! You shot *yourself* and killed the Albanian to cover your ass! You set me up, and you set up the consulate."

The entire outdoor seating area of the 19th Hole restaurant got eerily quiet...but only for a moment. Then Borges did something I don't think any of us were expecting.

Chapter Thirty

Borges quickly raised a 9-millimeter handgun from somewhere under the table. He was very fast. Before any of us could react, he slammed the side of the gun against Felton's head. Felton let out a loud shriek of pain and reeled back, dazed and stunned. He wavered in his seat, clutching the side of his head. Blood trickled through his fingers. The impact of the gun cut a three-inch gash above his left ear. Borges reoriented the gun in his right hand. It was as if I saw it all unfolding in slow motion. Johan Williamson scattered low to the ground looking for protection behind a two top table. I could hear Lieutenant Maddalone moving loudly somewhere behind me. An unseen tray of glasses crashed to the floor. It was Cosima who caught my attention. She was very quick to act, swiftly drawing her own Berretta. Borges didn't hesitate for a moment. He leveled the gun right at Cosima.

"Gun!" yelled Lou.

Lou pushed forcefully off the top of the table with his right hand and dove to his left. He extended himself and twirled his body, partially exposing as much of himself as he could to face Borge's gun.

Aiming directly at Cosima, Borges pulled the trigger.

Lou had propelled himself across the table, shielding Cosima from the gun. Unspent, crinkly charged particles and hot expended gasses from the barrel bathed Borges' gun in a bluish smoky haze. The smell of gunpowder and cordite was immediate, the roaring blast deafening. The round hit Lou at his ribs under his shoulder. Lou screamed wildly in pain. Blood was already gushing out of his left side before he'd stopped diving in front of Cosima. He fell back hard against Cosima and knocked her backwards out of her seat. He tumbled over the side of the table on top of her, and they both disappeared from my view as they crashed heavily to the floor.

Johan Williamson was still somewhere low out of my sight. That entire side of the meeting was down low to the ground. The only two still upright were me and Charlie Maddalone. Felton was stupefied. He was groggy and dry heaving from the head blow. In one big step, Borges was out of his chair and was upon Felton in a flash. He wrapped one arm around the senior agent's neck tightly, and yanked Felton up out of his chair. Borges was using Felton as a human shield to protect himself from me and Lieutenant Maddalone. Felton was now not only suffering from the violent blow to the head, but in obvious distress from the tight hold across his throat. He used both his hands to try and pull Borges' arm away from his neck, leaving Felton no other way to strike out at or fight Borges. His plight caused him to fall back into Borges making it even easier for Borges to control him. With his other hand Borges pressed the gun hard up against Felton's temple. Borges was in complete control.

I'd started reaching for my gun when I saw Borges pull his up from under the table. I had confidence that Charlie Maddalone was somewhere behind me and also had his gun unholstered. Now with Borges on his feet, I side-stepped away from Borges and Felton and sought the partial protection of a plaster pillar. Borges was waddling backwards dragging Felton along in front of him.

"Drop your weapon!" Charlie yelled from behind me.

It was purely a rote in and rote out repetitive command ingrained in Maddalone's head from years of being the department's training commander. It was clear that Borges had just assaulted a senior Secret Service agent, attempted to shoot a Carabinieri agent, inadvertently shot a fellow Secret Service agent and now had a hostage. Dropping weapons did not seem like something he'd be inclined to do. My first concern was to retain some type of protective cover while focusing the sights of my weapon on Borges. I was already fully mentally committed that if the opportunity to save Felton and shoot Borges arose, I was going to take it. The air was filled with Lou's wailing, painful moans and the clinky clanky shuffle of Felton's golf shoes on the tile floor while he fought to maintain traction as he was being pulled away by Borges.

Borges tugged and yanked on Felton, keeping him upright as they moved backward like a lumbering Chinese parade dragon. I never took my aim off them. Borges was deftly keeping his exposure minimal as he crouched behind Felton, both moving back towards the doors that led outside.

"Johan, call it in! You and Cosima stay with Lou!" yelled Maddalone.

Felton and Borges moved. I moved.

I kept the same distance between myself and the two of them. I fought the urge to get closer or to bum rush the two of them. One miscalculation on my part could cost Felton his life or get myself and Maddalone shot. As Borges dragged Felton back towards the outside area I kept as much cover as I could, but I moved continually towards them with my gun drawn.

"Drop it, Borges! It's over!" I yelled at him.

Borges didn't respond. He kept yanking Felton backwards with him, hiding behind the nearly incapacitated hostage. Felton looked sickly. His eyes had a pleading, unsteady gaze and his shuffling back with Borges was more like a stagger. The duo arrived at the door that led outside. The door clanged and vibrated from the weight of both of their bodies pushing against it.

I could still hear Maddalone moving off to my left. I couldn't see him but I'm sure he was careful to avoid crossfire and was moving in a triangle with me off of Felton and Borges.

"Give it up, Borges," I commanded again.

This time Borges gave me a furtive glance, his anger like a coiled serpent showing in his eyes, ready to strike at the slightest provocation. Then he spoke.

"Taylor, you fucked everything!" he shouted. "No, Tom. You did," I said.

Borges briefly moved the gun away from the side of Felton's head. He cranked a single round somewhere off to my left, firing where I thought Maddalone was. The whopping percussion from the round made me clench my teeth until I could feel my back molars grinding. Then I heard Maddalone's voice call out to me.

"QRU!"

Maddalone was using the police term by Miami Dade County agencies for "all okay." The term and the brevity of its message was foreign to Borges. I could see his eyes dart back and forth for a split second. He shook his head, confused, but continued pulling Felton out into the morning sunshine. Borges looked as if the strenuous task of lugging Felton was wearing heavily on him. They were moving slower. Much slower. Borges was looking around more frequently. He was searching for an exit out of this hellscape he'd put himself in.

"This is not going to end well for you. Give it up Borges," I yelled again.

"End well? How do you think it's going to end? You asshole!" he hollered at me. "You think you and your buddy there are gonna take me in? A federal agent in a federal penitentiary? Like a sitting duck in the prison yard with cutthroat criminals who'll kill me the first chance they get. Sweeping the shitty chapel after a mass every Sunday. Beans and rice and Jesus Christ! No way. I'd rather kill all of you before that."

"You have no chance. Drop the gun," yelled Maddalone.

Although slowed considerably, they continued to shuffle back towards the edge of the veranda. They were approaching a large outdoor carved coral and oolite staircase that led down to the grass below. If Borges made it to the stairs he could shove Felton forward and make a run for it. Or he could simply kill Felton and then shoot it out with us. Borges was getting desperate. The fire in his eyes was now clouded by confusion and fear. He was probably wondering how his life had caromed so quickly into this quagmire. They were feet from the edge of the staircase, and I could sense Borges contemplating what to do next. I wanted to keep talking to him. Try and overload his sensibilities.

"Did she ever love you, Tom? Or did she just use you?"

"Shut up!" he railed back at me.

"How'd that work? You kept seeing Janice at events. Eventually you two had an affair and then her husband Matthew was in the way?"

"Shut up, Taylor!" he screamed shrilly.

"Big money. You can't compete. Call the Albanian shitbirds. Hatch a plan to embezzle from the bank, do the home invasion. Still not enough money, huh Tom? Easy solution—Matthew Gordon's life insurance. Too bad he was never officially declared dead. You fucked up, Tom." I said keeping my words as short as possible.

From my peripheral vision I got a glimpse of Maddalone moving stealthily away off to my left. I started to do the same. Widen the triangle. Now Borges had to turn his head repeatedly to be able to see us both. Felton was struggling more slowly, trying to free himself from the tight clutch around his windpipe. He was beet-red in the face, and his eyes were brimming with tears.

"What happened, Tom? She leave you for Constantino? Fuck up your plans?" I called to him. His face was as red as Wayne's, but with anger broiling over.

I could sense we were reaching a point where something had to give. Borges couldn't keep holding his hostage up.

Wayne Felton couldn't take much more.

Anguish was creeping across Borges' face. He was looking in a frantic, scattered way all about the veranda, back and forth between Charlie and me, his head on a swivel. Maddalone and I were too far apart for him to shoot one of us and still have an easy shot at the other.

My guess was he'd want to shoot me first. I was the one who brought his house of cards down around him.

I locked eyes with the slow-blinking Felton for the briefest of seconds. It snapped him back for a second, and he must have taken that as a go signal. Felton raised his left knee up and then slammed the bottom of his spiked golf shoe against Borges' shin. He aggressively raked the sharp spikes down the length of Borges' leg. Borges yelped in pain and loosened his grip around Felton's neck. He dropped his shoulder momentarily as he reflexively raised his serrated shin up and Felton collapsed in a heap, pulling Borges forward with him as he fought to keep control over Felton.

That was all Maddalone needed.

Charlie fired two rounds that struck Borges. One tunneled into his right rib cage on the right, causing Borges to side stutter step to his left. The other bullet skimmed across his chest and grazed his sternum. Borges still had his gun in his hand. He had a look on his face that was mixture of incredulous disbelief, searing pain, and determination to take at least one of us with him.

I fired two rounds. What shooting instructors laud as a "double tap."

My first round hit him center mass and his gun hand flopped as his legs gave out from under him. The second round was just a few inches lower and tore into his abdomen. He sunk into the ground as if defeated by the weight of everything he had done. Like the life and any tangible component of energy fled his body at exactly the same time. His lifeless form fell on top of Felton.

I finally looked fully to my left and saw Maddalone. He was sweating and he still held a Viking tiller's grip on his gun. Veins pulsed in his hands and forearms as he gripped it, staring at Borges. Charlie had never been in a police-involved shooting, least not one that was fatal. He habitually upbraided me with scorn each and every time he had to appear on one of my shootings. He was the one who implored Major Brunson to have me pay a visit to Dr. Rangela.

Now he was experiencing this police shooting from a whole different perspective.

He holstered his gun but continued staring at the bloody body of Borges. Felton had wiggled out from under Borges and was off to the side on his hands and knees, trying to take in as much oxygen as he could through his compromised windpipe. Once again, I could hear approaching sirens, getting louder and closer.

I looked at Maddalone. He looked at me. I took the lead.

"Don't say anything. Investigators will have plenty of time to get your version of what happened. We all know what happened here and we have Felton to collaborate as well. You and I are going to be the subject of the investigation. We don't write reports. We don't go on or off record about anything," I said to him. Charlie nodded once.

The seeping blood was forming crimson viscous pools under Borges. Within a few seconds gravity asserted itself and Borge's contorted corpse slumped fully over onto its side.

Maddalone finally regained his ability to speak. "I've been on a bunch of these shootings before, mostly yours, Cade. It sure feels and looks different from this side. I'm not really sure what I'm feeling."

I looked over at Felton who seemed to be finally breathing normally. "I'm sure he's feeling relief. I'm sure he's thankful that you and I did what we did," I said.

"You think so?" he asked me, seeking some sort of absolution. I saw his need for acceptance and for someone to understand that lethal measures were needed for what we had just been through.

"Definitely," I said. "Charlie, never lament being a dragonslayer when there are verifiable dragons amongst us. Welcome to the shadows, where we all lurk."

Chapter Thrity-One

THREE WEEKS HAD gone by. The aftermath of everything that had occurred was still a buzzing topic in law enforcement circles. It was buzzing in other circles of life as well—especially here in South Florida. I was sitting in Major Brunson's office as he chose to remind me of the consuming interest and enormity of it all.

"My contact at the Carabinieri tells me they're awarding Cosima their highest honor for the great work she did here on this case. She's in Rome still being debriefed and filing her reports before she goes back to Milan," said Brunson.

"Any word on Tucson Lou?" I asked.

"Geez, what a tough son of a bitch, huh? Can you imagine purposely fucking jumping in front of a bullet for someone?"

"That's what he's trained to do," I said.

"Well, he did it fucking better than anyone I've ever fucking heard of. He saved Cosima. No doubt. The tough bastard lost a piece of his rib. The surgeon said he was damn lucky, looks like he'll recover almost fully. The Assistant Director of the Secret Service says all Lou asked for was a transfer to Chicago."

"That's what he always wanted," I said.

"Can you imagine if Lou had been in Dallas in '63? Might be a different world today," said Brunson.

Somehow, I thought to myself that U.S. Secret Service Agent "Tucson" Lou Akicita would never ever have a Clint Hill moment in his career.

"Cade, just yesterday I had my eighth meeting with the city manager since everything went down at the fucking Biltmore Hotel. Eight fucking times with that spineless bastard! You know what his little pea brain is fucking concerned with?"

"No, not really."

"The sniveling shit is worried about the city's fucking lily-white pristine image. Coral Gables! The same fucking city that tells you what fucking color to paint your goddamn house, fines you if you park a damn pickup truck overnight in your driveway, and sponsors a goddamn Junior Orange Bowl parade when there isn't even an Orange Bowl parade anymore. That same city!"

"How is this related to us?" I asked him.

"Let's do the math and see." He ticked them off on his fingers. "One Albanian criminal and one dirty Secret Service Agent killed. One Italian politician, one Carabinieri agent and a different Secret Service agent, all shot in one week at the Biltmore. See how it adds up? That's how it's fucking related to us. Apparently, all the gore galore has the city manager's underwear a little crusty."

"Facts are facts. Can't argue with the aftereffect," I said blandly.

"*Aftereffect*? That sounds just like a fucking peachy keen response, Cade. That's just fucking lovely. When you're dealing with members of the Continuous Fainting Society like I do, well you just have to listen to their piss-scared shitweasel rants and pretend that you have as much concern for what trembles their scrotum as they do. Truth is the feeble fucknut City Manager is just trying to act like he has a fucking say in the matter. I have to keep fucking reminding him that there *is* no say in the fucking matter. It fucking happened. It's fucking done. Get the fuck over it."

After all these years and time spent with Major Brunson I still found myself occasionally gobsmacked by his use of profanity.

"So where are we in all this?" he asked me.

"Gary's been in close contact with the forensic accountants and the Criminal Investigation Division of the IRS. They've made some big inroads with regard to Borges' finances. It looks like it started getting odd a few years ago. He was a stickler about reimbursements for parking, tolls, meals on the road, all that stuff. They identified a pattern of him spending a lot of time in Miami and not nearly as much time at his desk in Palm Beach. Lots of trips up and down I-95. They think that's when he may have started seeing Janice Gordon."

"That doesn't say a whole lot. There's no crime in having a snuggle hut hullabaloo with a married woman," Brunson said.

"Well, it's a start. Human nature can be funny," I said.

"How so?"

"After the home invasion at the Gordon residence Borges' miserly ways of constantly seeking reimbursements tapered off quickly and then became nearly nonexistent the past few years."

"Maybe he was staying in Palm Beach and didn't need to get any reimbursements?" asked Brunson.

"Normally I'd be onboard with that idea as well, but he used his Treasury-issued gas credit card almost exclusively in Miami Dade County."

"Meaning?"

"Like I said, human nature can be funny. It seems like he wasn't too interested in chasing dimes and quarters when he was living a much more affluent lifestyle squiring Janice Gordon to black tie affairs, yacht dinners, Miami symphony tickets, club memberships... You get the idea."

"Still doesn't say a whole lot. What else you got?"

"Big disposable income rise in the Gordon household after the home invasion. Doesn't seem like Matthew Gordon was around to be aware of it, but financial records show a big spike in expensive living in Janice's life after Mathew's so-called disappearance."

"Again, I say it's not a crime."

Now I was ticking the numbers off on my fingers. "Her husband disappears. He was the major bread winner. He was the chairman of a tier II bank. Not only does the family not suffer any financial hardship, they actually had an acceleration in affluence. No life insurance policy awarded yet. Money still rolled in. Why? Because she and Borges staged the home invasion together. That's why!"

"Big leap there, Cade," he said.

"Is it? Private schools for the kids, exclusive New Hampshire summer camps, vacations in Vail, St. Moritz, and St. Lucia. Looking at Borges' vacation leave, they coincided with whatever financial records and newspaper stories Gary could find related to Janice Gordon's trips and forays. The arrows are lining up."

"You really think she traumatized her kids with a staged home invasion?" he asked.

"Janice Gordon told us as much at her home. *"The bank didn't want the bad press. The official response was 200,000. But I know it was more like six million."*

"The FBI and the bank low-balled the figure that was stolen. They told the press it was a 200,000 dollar loss. Janice Gordon said it was more like six million dollars. She probably low-balled it too. I'd be willing to bet it was easily nine million dollars. So, you ask me, would she traumatize her kids with a staged home invasion? For nine million dollars I'd say hell yeah, I think she traumatized her kids. I think Borges and her split the money with the Albanians and Janice Gordon and Tom Borges started feathering their life together."

"So why didn't the party keep going?" he asked me.

"Something went south somewhere. Something between her and Borges. My guess is she wanted more and found it in Baldassare Constanino. I think she broke it off with Borges and took up with Constanino."

"So why didn't he take what money he'd gotten from the home invasion and from his ongoing cuts with the Albanians and move on?" asked Brunson.

"Human nature is funny. He loved her. He wanted her back."

"Cade, are you fucking telling me that this whole assassination attempt on Constanino had nothing to do with politics, drugs, or anything other than a loser Secret Service agent pining over a Miami socialite who dumped him?"

"Major, with all due respect I think so." I said before elaborating further "I think he used his criminal connections with the Albanians to carry out his own lovelorn plan to get her back. With Constantino dead, he probably thought he could sweep back in and win her over. Be her protector. Her white knight," I said.

"What about the fucking Albanians?" he asked.

"He probably enlisted them on the promise of a reduced cut going forward. If he was making three percent of everything they were doing, and he dropped his cut to as low as two percent, it would be a considerable savings for the Albanians. Especially over time." I reasoned.

"Human nature can be funny," Major Brunson said

"I said that already. With regard to Agent Verratti—"

"Cosima," he said, cutting me off.

I went on. "Yes. Cosima and I went out on a Saturday morning to interview Janice Gordon. When we knocked on the door she was on the phone with Building and Zoning—"

"Those damn dimbulbs at Building and Zoning don't work on the fucking weekends," he interrupted.

"Exactly. I picked up on that right away. I think she was on the phone with Borges. She was not happy, and she felt he was putting pressure on her."

"How so?" asked Brunson.

"She thought that whoever she was talking to sicced the police on her. I think Borges knew that if we were at her house we must have made a connection from the motorcyclist, Erjon Dren, to the home invasion. He must have realized everything was starting to unravel; the hit on Constantino failed, a Carabinieri agent was viciously wounded, the Carabinieri were flooding Miami with agents from New York, Cosima was here from Milan and now she and I were knocking on the door of his flame's house. In for a pound, in for a penny. I don't think Arica Sweetin was the Albanians' target that night on the Taragona Drive bridge. It was me. Definitely me," I said.

"Cade, if what you're telling me holds water, you're saying that Constanino surviving the hit probably pushed Janice Gordon further from Borges and even deeper into the arms of Constantino. Borges feels you and Cosima getting close to making a connection between the home invasion and the assassination attempt, so he tries to cut off the head of the snake that's about to bite him. Namely you," said Brunson, sans profanity.

"Precisely," I said. "When the attack on me and Arica failed, Borges knew the loose ends had become too much to tie back together. It was time to cut and run. He needed to get rid of the Albanians. He knew about Coldstream Drive all along. He volunteered to put himself on the end of the street that he knew the targeted house was on. He waited for the gang member house sitter to come out and he killed him, making it look like they had struggled over Borges' gun. He never counted on Gary working with the court system to help us locate Luvas Dren and his ankle monitor. That same ankle monitor which us led us to the rest of Albanians. Cosima and I killed them and that solved all of his problems. Or so he thought."

"Cade, right now this has a neat bow on it. Per our earlier discussion do you still want to go down the path you're on?" he asked me.

"Absolutely!" I answered.

"You realize how it can all fucking backfire and blow up in all of our goddamn faces."

"I do."

"Knowing that if you're wrong," he said, pointing at my face, "it'll be all our butts on the line here."

"I do."

"I can't take a fucking loss on this one. *We* can't take a fucking loss on this one. If you're fucking wrong, we are *all* fucked," he said.

"Understood," I said.

Major Brunson glared at me from behind his desk.

"I mean, I understand."

We sat in silence in his office, the clock ticking rhythmically on the credenza behind his desk. There were two hot sauce bottles on his desk. "Charred Chaos" and "Lava Surge."

Charred Chaos couldn't be a better title for what would happen to us if I was incorrect in my belief.

"You can't be wrong," Brunson said huskily with a declaration of finality.

"I'm not wrong," I said.

"Okay then. Be at his office at 8am. I'll have everything staged nearby, waiting to hear from you."

With that I walked out knowing that what I just set in motion could come back on us like a cornered wolverine.

Chapter Thirty-Two

A T EXACTLY EIGHT in the morning, I was at the courthouse waiting in the outer office of the Honorable Robert Lenz. The mercurial magistrate is known for being fastidious about brevity, and razor sharp to get to the point of any conversation. The twenty-four hour news station CNN was playing on an overhead TV above his secretary's desk. Within a few minutes the secretary ushered me into his chambers. Calling the inner office "chambers" was a loosely used term. The room was more reminiscent of a man cave with sports memorabilia on all the walls and every open surface, all paying homage to the Florida Gators and the L.A. Rams. The disparity in the sports programs, both in scope and in geography, couldn't be more obvious.

Judge Lenz sat behind an overbearing oak desk. "Have a seat, Detective," he said to me.

He had my warrant in front of him. He was reading it thoroughly. He glanced up and noticed me taking in all of the sports memorabilia.

"Have you been here before?" he asked.

"In chambers? No, but you have signed for me at your residence before," I answered.

"Oh, right. You're one of those disturb-me-at-home kind of detectives," he said.

"Your Honor, I was just wondering how you developed such a strong affinity for the Florida Gators and the Los Angeles Rams."

"Easy. I was born and raised in Miami," he said matter-of-factly, as if it made complete sense.

We sat in silence as he continued reading the warrant. When he finished, he placed it on his desk. He still hadn't signed it.

"Detective Taylor, on the surface there are a lot of things about me that may not seem to follow a logical pattern. I'm a red-headed Cuban American kid born in Miami with a non-Hispanic last name. I speak fluent Spanish, and my wife is from Massachusetts—who, by the way, makes the best *arroz con pollo* you'll ever find south of Ybor City. I like the Florida Gators because that's my alma mater, and I like the Rams because before the idea of a Miami Dolphins football team ever existed, there were the Los Angeles Rams. I grew up watching players like Jack Snow, Roman Gabriel, Deacon Jones, and Tom Mack. So, things that look like they don't make sense, actually make perfect sense to me."

I wondered what this could possibly lead to. "This warrant, to nearly every other officer of the court, would probably make no sense. At its core, it's a stretch. It's a leap. It's a lunge. Are you getting my drift here, son?"

"Yes, your Honor," I replied.

"Fortunately for you I see through the veneer. I get it. I see the dominoes stacking up," he said as he signed the warrant. "Does it mean I think you're right? I guess we'll find out. Based on the circumstances and the way you articulated yourself, I've signed it. Whether this a CLM for you or not we will also see."

"CLM?" I asked.

"A career limiting move."

He handed me the signed warrant. I thanked him and I left his office.

I called Major Brunson. I informed him the warrant was signed. He had a set crew standing by at Fire Station Three, the city's southern-most firehouse located way down on Old Cutler Road. It took me nearly an hour to get from Judge Lenz's chambers to the firehouse and meet with the crew Brunson had assembled. It was decided that I would go ahead a few minutes and then the crew would join me up the road at 11027 Girasol Avenue.

The Gordon residence.

I parked down the road from the house, allowing the front of the residence to be fully accessible for the crew to park their vehicles. I walked to the front door and rang the bell. Esperanza, the same housekeeper that Cosima and I had seen hosing down the driveway answered the door. I identified myself and gave her a photocopy of the warrant. I held onto the original. She momentarily closed the door as she sought Janice Gordon, and within a few minutes Janice came to the door. She was so livid, she was practically shaking. She had the photocopy of the warrant in one hand and her cellphone in the other.

"You and this damn city have crossed me once and for all. I am going to have your job. I am going to have your badge. I am going to own this city! I'm calling my lawyer right now. Right now!" she shrieked.

"Thank you for informing me of your intentions, Ms. Gordon. Please get whatever essentials you need like prescriptions, reading glasses and the like, because once we start you cannot go back in the residence," I calmly stated.

"You are a complete disgrace. A menace! My attorney will have a field day with you and this damn city," she said, raising her voice even louder.

"I can empathize with your opinion," I said with an even more droll tone.

City backhoes, pumper trucks, pickup trucks with portable generators, and other earth-moving equipment started filing down Girasol Avenue towards us.

"My attorney Kathy Abello is going to shred you. All of you!" she screamed.

"I'm sure your attorney, Ms. Abello, will be more than eager to assist you in this legal dilemma," I said, keeping my affect very low and monotone.

The city workers dismounted from their trucks and equipment and met with the foreman on the lawn. With clearly understood instructions they descended upon the house with purpose. Within forty minutes two large industrial pumps were draining the water out of the swimming pool. Long hoses ran from the back of the house, positioned to deposit the pool water directly into the sewer grate down the street.

Janice Gordon was frantic. She paced about, holding her cellphone, waiting for her attorney to call her back. When her attorney finally called, Janice was panicked, shouting, and near tears.

Now she wanted me to talk to her attorney. I calmly informed her that the warrant had been served, and I did not need to talk with her attorney.

Meanwhile, water from the swimming pool continued to be pumped out and the city workers were removing ornamental plants around the pool to make room for the backhoe to fit in the backyard.

Against my better judgement, I finally spoke with her attorney on the phone. As a courtesy to Ms. Abello, I permitted Janice Gordon to stay in the house while the work continued outside on the sole condition that she could not go upstairs, and I was to be inside with her. It may seem magnanimous on my part, but it was part of my plan along. I didn't want to be outside all day and much preferred being in the comfort of her air-conditioned home while the work unfolded. By "giving in on this concession" it painted me as a reasonable affiant. Most of the warrant was centered on the outside of the house anyway.

Janice Gordon and I sat in the same living room that Cosima and I had interviewed her in, only this time there was a solid hour of silence between us. The workers continued to drain the pool and position equipment. Finally, she spoke.

"My attorney should be here any minute. I'll be happy to see that shit-eating grin swiped off your face," she said to me.

"I'm not grinning, Ms. Gordon. I don't see anything funny about this."

"Oh, no? Then why the dramatics? Thank God the children are at school and away. Haven't they suffered enough? They get terrorized in their home, their father up and leaves, and now you and this goddamn city are terrorizing us again," she said.

"Sounds as though they've been through a lot. Realistically though, think about it Ms. Gordon. How much of this is on you?"

She acted as if I had just insulted every cell in her body. She shot up off the couch and stood in front of me her fists clenched at her side.

"What are you getting at, you tin badge piece of shit?" she snapped angrily

"Ms. Gordon, Tom Borges told us everything before he died," I said.

"Tom! Tom? This is all because of something Tom Borges said? I don't believe you." she said waving her arms about her.

I just watched her. Lips closed. Waiting.

A full minute went by before she sat down across from me, arms folded across her chest looking off to her side with a deep scowl on her face.

"What did he say? What did he *say*?" she implored of me.

I stayed quiet sitting on the couch. It didn't take long before she started talking more.

"You can't believe anything a crooked agent like Tom Borges says. I hear he was up to his eyeballs in all kinds of things. I should have never gotten involved with him, but I was vulnerable. Matthew was gone and Tom was there. It was a mistake on my part, allowing him into our lives. I rue the day I ever met Tom Borges."

"Apparently," I said, "that day was long before Matthew disappeared."

"What are you saying?"

"I'm saying Tom Borges told us everything before he died," I bluffed again.

Outside the pumps draining the pool had stopped. It became noticeably quieter. The workers started assembling their tools for the next phase of serving the warrant. Two uniformed Coral Gables officers had arrived, as did three detectives, one of them being Johan Williamson. I could see Johan outside through the decorative windows. Aside from the turmoil that Janice Gordon was going through and the noises of the workers and police outside this midafternoon was almost identical to the last time I was here at Janice Gordon's house.

"Ms. Gordon last time I was here with the Italian agent. I remember how peaceful this house felt." I said. "The custom swimming pool, the jets plumbed through the plaster koi. I remember the gurgling of the one fish with the water streaming out of his mouth, and sinking into this sumptuous leather sofa, I was just mesmerized by the scenery."

Janice Gordon just glared at me.

"It was serenely peaceful sitting here on this leather couch looking out at the pool. I recall now what you said then about your husband, Matthew."

"What was that?" she said with an iciness.

"You see, I was sitting here talking to you, looking at this beautiful swimming pool and yet when Matthew was here, there wasn't a pool. You said he was 'desolate, just staring out at the yard and the bushes.' The pool was put in after Matthew was gone. Isn't that right?"

At this point the backhoe claw was smashing into the bottom of the pool and breaking up the pool's concrete surface. The noise was horrific, and it caused vibrations in the house that rattled a crystal figurine on a sofa table behind me.

Janice cleared her throat. "The swimming pool was installed on the advice of our family therapist. She thought that redefining the family home as an oasis from the outside world would help the children to adapt and cope better. It would help them to know that even though the home was once violated and that their father was gone...the family home...this home would always be a place for them. The family unit could be a safe haven once again," she said.

I nodded, seeing the logic in that explanation. And another forty minutes of silence ensued. Until she broke it.

"You asshole."

Workers had descended into the drained pool, using pickaxes and shovels to remove the chipped and broken pieces of concrete. The three detectives stood on the edge of the empty pool, watching the workers remove the concrete.

"You've been having an ongoing battle with Building and Zoning here at the city," I said. "You said it was a constant battle with Immoral Gables. Funny."

"Right now, I hate you more than I hate them," she said.

She'd started perspiring. Her eyes kept looking past me at the workers outside. She continually checked her phone. Nervousness seeped out of every pore in her body. The pounding, shoveling, scraping, and hauling of concrete had to be a swelling cacophony in her ears. Each exclamation, raised voice, shout, or loud comment from the workers outside caused her to flinch and stir.

"I pulled the records from Building and Zoning. You were supposed to a have a rebar and concrete inspection on April nineteenth, 1995. Coincidentally, that's the last day you saw Matthew. You delayed the inspection until later in the afternoon. When inspectors finally got here the concrete was nearly set and you blamed the swimming pool contractor for the mix-up. Inspectors demanded the entire pool surface be taken up and done again but you pleaded that the concrete was wet enough that the inspectors could reach in and feel the rebar. They reluctantly did so...in the shallow end."

She swallowed once.

"Not the deep end of the pool. The concrete had already cured in the deep end. The now-fired inspector signed off on your pool anyway and ever since you've been fighting Building and Zoning about everything and anything you do to your house. They want to see everything done exactly to code because they don't trust you or the contractors you hire. The police department had a deposition with your swimming pool contractor last week. His records show he was working on a faulty valve at a house in the north end of the city on April nineteenth. He didn't pour the concrete for your pool that day. Someone else did."

Over her shoulder I saw that the activity around the pool had stopped. One of the detectives was excitedly waving the workers out of the pool. The uniformed police officers had gathered on the edge and with startled faces were looking down into the pool's void. Also crouched at the pool's edge, Johan Williamson peered intently down into the hole. It had become very quiet outside.

Very quiet.

Janice Gordon had gone almost catatonic. With her back to the activity outside she was somewhere deep inside of herself.

"I asked you about Matthew. Do you remember what you told me?" I asked her. She sat rigid, not answering.

"Ms. Gordon do you remember what you said?" I asked again, but again she didn't respond or even blink. "I remember your words. *'To me he's down under and I hope he's found his peace.'* You said he was like a submarine running silent under the surface. Do you remember saying that to me?"

Two streams of tears rolled down each cheek from her unblinking, glassy eyes.

Johan Williamson was now at the threshold of the room with a pensive look on his face. He looked at me. I looked at him. He didn't say anything. His eyes roamed over to Janice Gordon. She just sat silently staring ahead. Williamson walked into the room and stood between me and Janice Gordon.

"We got him, Cade. We got him. He was in the deep end," he said quietly. He gently clasped Janice Gordon by her arm and lifted her up to her feet.

"Janice Gordon. You are under arrest for the murder of your husband, Matthew Gordon," he said as he placed handcuffs on her.

The clicking of the handcuffs sounded exactly like a wonderful life ending.

"How'd you know, Cade?" Williamson asked me.

I simply said the first thing that came to mind.

"I'm here to work and I'm in Miami. I shouldn't have to explain."

THE END